a PATHWAY *to* GOODBYE

PALMETTO
PUBLISHING
Charleston, SC
www.PalmettoPublishing.com

Copyright © 2024 by Laura Ritter

All rights reserved
No portion of this book may be reproduced, stored in a retrieval system, or transmitted in any form by any means–electronic, mechanical, photocopy, recording, or other–except for brief quotations in printed reviews, without prior permission of the author.

Paperback ISBN: 9798822967687
eBook ISBN: 9798822967694

a PATHWAY *to* GOODBYE

LAURA RITTER

For my grandpa, Wayne.

A Pathway to Goodbye

CHAPTER 1

Life as I know it is gone. Into the wind goes my hopes, my dreams, and all of my plans. There's no need for them anymore. That true soul crushing feeling of disappointment that comes around only a handful of times in a person's life, threatens to overwhelm. I'm so angry that all I want to do is cry and I know that if I let this anger fester it could get beyond anyone's control.

    I hate this feeling. The one where you're helpless, hopeless and a whisper away from falling off the cliff into a pit of despair. In the back of my mind, I always knew where this would be headed, but I admit that hearing the words from my doctor is a heavy blow. I wonder how people can handle such news with grace.

    I have a decision to make and it's the kind of decision that has the big life altering consequences that come attached with it. I sit in my hospital bed like a good little patient mulling over my predicament. Blankly staring at the eggshell-colored walls, I show no emotion on my face. My mask is up. Inside, however, I am enraged.

I sense the rising pain in my stomach but thinking about my current crisis brings on the feeling of complete numbness. I try to revel in it, wanting to feel anything but that damn pain. This new sensation shifts me into some kind of twilight zone where every word is tunneled and the clock on the wall stands still. I drift into the air of nothingness. I certainly don't hear, or even want to hear anything further from my surgeon, Dr Jenkins. He's trying, and failing, to explain my unfathomable situation with something that resembles sympathy.

The love of my life sits silently next to me. He continues to hold my hand in hopes that it will bring me some sort of comfort. I don't have the heart to tell him that nothing can give me the relief I need right now. Wayne grips my hand tighter as tears well up in his beautiful blue eyes. It's hard to speak and know he must feel the same way. The phrase 'frog in your throat' comes to mind at the moment.

This past year has been difficult for him as well as our whole family. Even though I'm the one who was diagnosed with cancer and went through months of chemotherapy, Wayne has been my haven. He is my rock and someone I could lean on during tough times. At this moment, I don't know how I can ask him to be my place of solace when I know he needs one himself.

Our vows 'in sickness and in health' seemed to have taken on a new meaning. More than that, it seems to have aged him ten years in that span. A total cliche, but no other words fit for the new wrinkles seen around his eyes and the gray that now consumes his once brown hair. His face fills with worry and despair.

My husband is everything to me. He knows all there is to know about me as I do him. That's what happens when you have been best friends since high school. Our relationship started ever so slowly in science class dissecting a frog. I couldn't stand the thought of torturing the poor animal, even though it was already dead, but Wayne jumped right in. The only reason I happened to pass that class was because of him and what I like to call his 'nature skills.'

We grew up very differently. He lived in a rundown house across the tracks with a few acres to grow vegetables and chickens that peck the ground. I lived in a quiet suburban area and had never even seen a chicken. Fate, or God, placed us together. He was, and still is, very handsome. He's a manly man of sorts; tall at about six foot three to my five foot seven. Living by the lay of the land he grew muscles in all the right places, however, my cooking and joy for baking over the years gave him just a bit of a belly.

Wayne told me after we got married that he knew that he was going to marry me the moment he walked into science class and laid eyes on me. He even made another student get up from the chair next to me so that he could be my lab partner for the semester. Some people might call his love for me Hollywood love. Unfortunately, I needed five more years of convincing before I would even entertain the idea of a date. Five years wasted that I could have spent with him.

I've seen and done so much throughout my lifetime and there are so many things that I could've done differently. If I had to choose my biggest regret, the one thing I would have done differently, it would be him. I wouldn't have waited so long to know that I had a good man. Luck, or maybe it was his stubbornness, was definitely on my side that he stayed single until I got my head out of my ass.

My heart aches knowing he is just as worried about me as I am about him. I stare at him in wonder of what he sees in me, of what he saw in me, and how in the world have we made it through when so many others called it quits over the years.

My thoughts are interrupted by the pesky voice of my surgeon. I want to stay in my cozy bubble of thinking about my incredible life with Wayne, but I guess reality is calling my name and his name is Dr Norman Jenkins.

"Mrs. Graham, are you still with us?" Dr Jenkins asks.

I blink a few times, "I'm sorry, what?"

"I was just explaining to Mr. Graham that the surgery was unsuccessful. The tumor is more aggressive than we originally thought and unfortunately, we were unable to remove it."

I sigh in frustration. I heard him the first time, but hearing it again causes my anger to start boiling over.

"I don't understand, the chemo was supposed to shrink it enough so you could go in and remove it. The scans showed decreased markers or whatever it's called," I say with distaste clear in my tone. I'm not sure if I'm more upset that he wasn't able to do his job or that I suffered through all those months of chemo for nothing.

He rushes in an attempt to reassure me, "the chemo was able to shrink some of the metastasis. Unfortunately, there were new mets and one is wrapped around a major artery. We couldn't remove it safely. Your cancer is growing more tumors faster than the chemo can stop it."

I lay back in bed in stunned silence. I don't know what to say, or even do, so I turn my attention to Wayne for some sort of hope. He looks at me with the same longing of hope. Not knowing what to say, he turns his focus to the doctor wanting him to come up with a new course of action.

"So, what can we do?" Wayne asks, his voice a little shaky while his hand remains in mine.

Hesitantly Dr Jenkins says, "Well we could try a different chemotherapy. It would be more aggressive than the last one. That said, it will only buy you a little more time. We are not going to be able to beat this cancer."

"What would happen if I chose not to do another round of chemo?" I ask. The question leaves my lips without me being able to stop them. I think, perhaps, my subconscious is trying to tell me something that I have not fully accepted yet.

"If you choose not to go through another round of chemo then I would recommend starting hospice. If you want to do more chemotherapy, then we will get that started tonight while you're here in the hospital."

Wanting all the information Wayne asks, "How long would she have if she did the chemo versus not doing the chemo?"

Dr Jenkins looks to the ceiling and places a finger on his chin. It would be comical that he looks just like the thinking emoji if the situation wasn't completely depressing.

After taking a moment, he answers, "If Ellie did the chemotherapy, then she is looking at about six months. Without the chemo she's looking at about three. I do have to warn you though, this other chemotherapy comes with harsher side effects. More nausea, more dizziness and fatigue. She is also looking at low platelet counts so she'll be at risk for bleeding."

He pauses, giving a traumatic effect. I want to laugh. All of this is some kind of sick joke, right? I've been desperately waiting since my diagnosis for someone to tell me that they got my results mixed up somewhere and I don't in fact have cancer. Cancer is something you see in the movies or hear about when a friend of a friend got diagnosed with the dreaded 'C' word. I never thought it would happen to me even with the knowledge that my grandaddy passed away from the same cancer that is now going to take me.

I have no idea how to begin to make this decision. Do I want to suffer more in hopes that I will get a few more months? Or do I cut it short and start hospice?

I look to Wayne for an answer, but he just shakes his head at me, "I can't answer this one for you Ellie. This is your decision."

I love him more for that. I love that he is giving me the support I need to make this choice. A decision that will no doubt affect his life as well. This is all so overwhelming.

My eyes fill with tears. The pain rises in my stomach. An itching pain can be felt at my abdominal incision, but the all too familiar ache rises in the pit of my stomach. I don't think I can do this anymore. I don't think I can handle another round of an even harsher chemo drug. I don't want to spend my days with a puke bucket by my bed. I can't stand the thought of having 'chemo brain' and staying in a fog. It takes so much energy and effort to remember things and stay present in conversations with my family.

I blink a few times in disbelief. I think I have my answer. Hospice. My brain tries to absorb this new decision along with the feelings that accompany it. Thinking it over for a moment I begin to feel the emotions of relief and contentment. Does this mean no more pain or nausea? No more waking up almost every day wishing it were already over.

Here lately, I feel disgusted with myself for taking multiple pain pills to keep my pain level tolerable. I hate it. The decision is a clear one to make. I am ready for this and if I'm being honest with myself, I have been for months.

In the split second of feeling that relief, the tension starts to build again. How do I tell the love of my life? The man that has stood by my side for the last thirty-seven years. He has done everything this last year to make it bearable for not only me, but our entire family. How do I tell him?

Wayne sits patiently waiting for my decision. He tries to speak, probably trying to reassure me in some way. I can tell that he is having trouble finding words again. I take the opportunity to get my thoughts out in the open.

I clear my throat to choke back the tears that are trying to burst forth again, "I'm so sorry. I want more time with you. I want another thirty-seven years with you, but I don't think we get to have that luxury. I know what I can handle and what I can't, and I can't do a harsher chemo. I don't want to fill my days with being sick over a puke bucket. I want to spend my time with you and the kids."

There, finally it's out. As the words left my mouth, I felt a weight being lifted off my shoulders. I think they are words I have been wanting to say for months and I finally have the chance to.

I take a deep breath and continue, "I can't keep doing this. Our days are filled with doctor's appointments and infusion treatments. The topic of my treatment always seems to be brought up at our Sunday dinners and not on the joys of life. This is not a way to live, and you know it." I place my hand on his cheek to offer whatever comfort I can give him. I'm not sure how much it is worth. How do you spend over half your life with someone only to get pulled apart by cancer?

"Ellie, please," is all he can muster, his voice quiet and tortured.

I don't think my decision is the one he thought I would make. For a fraction of a second, I think about changing my mind and telling the doctor to get the damn chemo. As soon as the thought pops into my head the pain rears its ugly head, increasing to a solid eight out of ten. Knowing I'll need to call the nurse soon for another pain pill I try to forge ahead and get this conversation over with. I stand, or rather sit, firm on my decision.

"I'd like to spend what time I have left with you and our kids, surrounded by love and family," I repeat to him. My voice is giving that 'my decision is final' tone.

I feel my eyes water with sadness. I want to cry, to scream and shout, and throw a temper tantrum while destroying this room. Even though I really want to, I know expressing those feelings will destroy my husband. I force the tears back. I swallow it down so that I can stay strong for him as well as my family. I do allow one more small tear to fall. That one tear is for me and the memories I know I will miss in the future. I must shed it so I can move forward to this next chapter.

I turn my focus to Dr Jenkins. He stands at the foot of my bed with his arms across his chest waiting to hear my decision. The arrogance of this man. He doesn't even have the decency to sit in a chair to tell a woman that she is dying. He must be numb to it.

"So how does this work? Hospice?" I ask.

"Well, if this is the route that you choose to go then I will write an order for hospice, and someone will be in to talk to you about it. They will answer any questions that you have and get the ball rolling."

I want to roll my eyes at him. My emotions of wanting to cry quickly turn into hot anger once again.

"Get the ball rolling?"

I look at him once again. Yup, perfect hair done exactly right, with just the right amount of gel. Black slacks, white collared shirt with a perfectly straight tie and a white coat that was probably washed in starch to give him that all around clean look. To put the final cherry on top, he is sporting a flashy watch that would have cost me three months' salary to afford.

I wish I could tell him off for the arrogant nerve he has. Dr Jenkins is making me feel like I am just another task to check off his list. No one should have to subject themselves to that feeling. I swallow my desire to pop him upside the head and just ask him, "When will hospice be in to see me?"

"I'll write the order, and they will be in to see you sometime tomorrow." His response is matter-of-factly and almost nonchalant. He has this look of judgment and defeat in his eyes, like he is disappointed that I'm not going to continue to fight. Does he not realize that I have no more fight left to give? The only fight I have left is for my family and the time I plan to spend with them.

I want to scream at him to have some sympathy for a dying woman, that it is not his life or his decision. He doesn't have to live with the symptoms of liquid poison being pumped into his veins. I know bringing any of this up will only fall on deaf ears.

Not all doctors are like this. I have met some of the most personable physicians throughout my time with cancer, so I don't understand how his bedside manner has become so uncaring and almost cruel. I want to tell him to go back to school and learn some bedside manners, but I don't think that will do any good.

"Ok, thank you." I don't want this man in my room anymore and I'm hoping the way I said it would help prompt him to leave. Thankfully, he takes the hint and walks out of my room shutting the door behind him.

Silence and tension fill the room as I turn to face my husband. It's difficult to look at him. He sits with his face in his hands, and I can see him visibly trembling from the decision that will change the course of our lives.

Suddenly he stands up and moves to join me in my hospital bed. I scooch over to a side to allow him enough room. He lies down on his back, and I place my head on his chest to listen to his heartbeat. The sound is soothing. He crosses his feet at the ankles as he rests his arms around me. He appears as comfortable as he is going to get. I place my arm across his belly and soak in the solace that I still have him to help me get through this. Whatever this is.

I lay there for a long moment listening to his heart and his breathing. I don't know what to say to him to give him any sort of comfort, so we just lay there holding each other in the uncomfortable silence.

I long to escape this hospital room. It isn't much to look at anyway with a considerably basic look and not too much thought put into it. A TV hangs in the corner, a small uncomfortable couch sits by the window that looks out to a busy parking lot which is next to a bustling highway. Everyone seems busy in their own little world, while mine is falling apart. A chair sits next to my bed, now empty. A computer projects out from the opposite wall for the nurses to use for charting. No glamor, no fuss, just plain. They really need an interior designer to spruce up the depressing room.

    My eyes move to stare out the window. I hope that if I look hard enough, I can be transported anywhere, anywhere else that isn't this room. It is the end of October, and the gray skies and bare trees show the promise of an early winter. The weeks and time to Christmas have never changed, yet each year it seems Christmas creeps up faster. That is all right with me as the holiday traditions were always my favorite.

    I can almost see it as my mind drifts to thoughts of Christmas. My green Christmas tree would be lit up with all the ornaments twinkling. The fire from the fireplace lighting up the room that my loving husband was so proud to have made. The scent coming from the freshly chopped wood permeates the space. Our two lovable chocolate labs are always nearby in hopes they'll get an extra scratch on the head or a piece of scrap food. I could see Carmel enjoying her new bone with a plaid bandana around her neck and Moose jumping around Carmel trying to get at her bone that she refuses to share. I could see myself resting in my favorite chair with a cozy soft blanket and a smile on my face. It wouldn't be complete without a book in one hand and a glass of wine in the other. The picture-perfect Hallmark scene.

    Of course, in true holiday fashion, my book would be interrupted by the sound of the kids and grandkids piling in through the door with their gifts wrapped in pretty ribbons of all different colors. Everyone would be eagerly trying to shrug off their coats as they greeted each other with excitement and anticipation of present time. It could be seen on all their faces, not just the grandkids. I could just hear the timer going off to let me know that the fresh baked cookies were done, and the aroma would soon be filling the air. I could almost see it. Almost.

In the midst of my daydreaming Wayne pulls me out of my thoughts with a shift in his body. He looks down at me with questions swarming in his mind. I lift my head to meet his gaze, he breaks the silence and asks, "Are you sure this is what you want?"

I give him the respect he deserves and think hard before giving him an answer. Is this what I want? Heck no, I want twenty more years. I want to be at my grandkids' graduations and weddings. I want more adventures with my husband and dogs. I want to be able to go to Hawaii and swim with the sea turtles. I want more of what life has to offer. Unfortunately, at the moment life is giving me the crap end of the stick full of pain, exhaustion, nausea, and doctor's visits. I would love nothing more than to cut that part of the stick off and throw it into a fire.

My instinct is to give him my 'go-to' answer of putting everything in God's hands. I've experienced some troubled times in my life. Come to think of it, right now it is pretty horrible, but I've never let my faith be shaken before, so why start now? I secretly detest the phrase "everything happens for a reason". While I really believe that everything occurs because it's God's will, it doesn't mean I have to agree with it or like it. Even though I don't understand it, I will keep putting my faith in Him. I hope that maybe one day He may give me an explanation for why I am experiencing what I am. Maybe I will have the opportunity to ask Him some other time.

Through the wave of emotions that I have experienced this morning; anger, tearfulness, relief, and then back to anger again, it feels like I just went through the worst rollercoaster of my life. Like I am Will Ferrel in that movie about an anchorman and he's in a telephone booth calling his friend hysterical because his dog just got kicked off a bridge. I am in 'a glass case of emotion' and I don't see a way out.

   Nothing I think of seems like the best answer to give. They say that honesty is the best medicine, or whatever, and I guess that is what I will have to go with. I look at Wayne with all the confidence I can gather and simply reply "yes."

   He nods and then turns his head to quietly stare out the same window that I tried to use as my escape earlier. I hope like hell that it works better for him than it did for me.

   I get up slowly out of my hospital bed and shuffle to the bathroom not caring that my hospital gown opened, and my butt is showing off to Wayne. My back begins to ache from laying down as much as I have recently. You'd think that the hospital would give their patients a decent mattress to sleep on, but I guess that's too much to ask. It feels like the old plastic mattresses used at summer camp when I was growing up. It's so worn out that you can feel the metal bar on the bottom of the bed.

   I make it to the bathroom and shut the door behind me, grateful to have the time alone even though Wayne is just a yell away. After using the toilet and washing my hands, I stand silently at the sink. I look in the mirror and see a different person. My face is pale with distinguished features. The cancer has taken all my weight and put it right to my belly. My hair is depressing with little peach fuzz that now grows in the place of my once beautiful chestnut colored hair.

   I despise my current hair. I grab my head scarf from the towel rack and work quickly tying it on. The last two weeks in the hospital have been all consuming trying to get my electrolytes and blood count levels perfect for surgery. It feels better seeing all my stuff strewn across the bathroom like at home.

   I place my hands on either side of the sink and take a deep breath. I stare back at the woman in the mirror that I don't recognize. This isn't me. I'm not this weak and fragile person. I hate what the cancer has made me become. I question why have I let it happen? I am strong and confident. I love to make people smile and laugh, although there hasn't been much to smile or laugh at in this last year though. Each treatment and new pain seem to have chipped a little away from me as time passed. Sometimes it seems so subtle that I didn't even notice.

Now I stand in a hospital bathroom, my butt showing off all its glory, and the decision of starting hospice. A thought comes to mind of my next actions. I could let this new decision deplete me, give in, and be done. However, that feels like letting the cancer win. The other option would be to give the cancer a big middle finger and live the rest of my life on my own time. I can be me again and not what the cancer has made me. The decision, once again, seems like a simple and easy one to make.

I stand tall and take another deep breath. No more. The weight of the cancer is now off my shoulders. I refuse to play its victim. I will be me and live my life now on my own terms, not the cancer's. I look back in the mirror before leaving the bathroom, now I see the woman I used to recognize. Yes, I still have the pain, the cancer seems to be giving me the middle finger right back, but I am not going to let it control my life anymore. I leave the bathroom feeling more like the woman Wayne married. I am ready for whatever lies ahead for me knowing that I have my loving husband by my side supporting me and loving me through it.

CHAPTER 2

About a half hour goes by when we hear a soft knock. Wayne and I continue to lay in my hospital bed holding each other. Remaining silent and turning our attention to the door, we wait to see who is visiting. It's probably against hospital policy for Wayne to be in my bed with me, however knowing that I'm now a dying woman, I don't quite care anymore.

The door slowly opens to our nurse walking in the room. Over the last two weeks Kelly has grown to be one of my favorite nurses at the hospital. She appears to be unique among the group. As the days passed it became clear that she didn't just work for the money—rather, she loves her job for the sake of the patient and helping them feel better. Kelly made sure to spend time with us each shift she worked and seeing her smiling face gave a little glimmer of happiness to a dreary situation.

She provides us with quality time, and if I am forced to spend my days in this hospital, I am happy it is with a compassionate nurse like her. She does the simple things, like remembering that I really appreciated the ice chips or that I liked the red Jello but loathed the orange, worth the needle sticks and scans. Her presence has been a true blessing to our stay here.

When she gets closer to my bed, I can see that her eyes are red, and her face is blotchy like she has been crying. She is making the effort to seem casual and professional, yet her face and caring demeanor gives her away. I have a feeling Dr Jenkins broke the news to her that I decided to meet with a hospice consultant.

"I brought your scheduled medication along with your pain pill. I didn't want you to get behind and go into a pain crisis," she says with just a small sniffle. She places a fresh cup of ice chips and another cup of ice water on my bedside table. She reaches for the scanner by the computer and scans each medication before placing them in the pill cup. After handing me the small cup full of pills she slides into the rolling chair and moves to my bedside.

I swallow the pills easily and hand her the empty cup. She takes it and throws it away before sanitizing her hands and coming to sit by me once more. All of her focus is now on Wayne and me.

"I'm so sorry," Kelly says as she grabs my hand, "what can I do for you?"

Her gaze reflects a caring and desire to know. I love that she didn't even mention the fact that Wayne is laying down in bed with me. I need his comfort right now and can't bear the thought of him getting up.

I look at Kelly and see her genuine smile. Her blonde hair is pulled away in a loose ponytail. Many stray hairs have fallen out probably due to her running around helping her patients. Kelly always seemed to be busy trying to complete one task or another. It became clear after a few shifts of being with her that she made sure to carve out the time to sit down and talk with her patients and families. The small gesture did not go unnoticed, at least by Wayne and me. Her contagious laugh was also a nice reprieve and never ceased to put a smile on my own face.

This is what Dr Jenkins lacks, compassion and empathy needed in a healthcare provider. Wayne and I have known this beautiful nurse for only a brief time, but Dr Jenkins has been following my case for a while. He may be a doctor, but he could learn a thing or two from this beautiful nurse.

"Nothing dear. I don't think there's anything anyone can do. Although now that there is a decision, I want to make plans to go home."

She nods her head in understanding that I prefer to be surrounded by familiar things and the comfort of my home versus the sterile hospital room and antiseptic stench.

I never understood why hospitals have that certain smell. That smell of staggered old people, cleaning supplies and the occasional putrid odor of urine from down the hall. Do they not know that there are aroma diffusers now? Another thing to add to the list for their interior designer.

"I completely understand that I would want to be home myself if I was in your shoes. However, it's Friday afternoon so the hospice consultant won't be in to talk to you until tomorrow morning at the earliest. They will set up whatever equipment you might need and have it delivered. Then they can work on a plan for discharge. You're probably looking at Sunday afternoon though," Kelly replies.

"What do you know about hospice and how it works?" Wayne asks from beside me. "Dr Jenkins really didn't give us any clue and we've haven't really experienced anything like this before."

"Well, I'm not surprised there. Most doctors don't like to talk about hospice because they feel like it's giving up. Honestly, hospice has been shown to give families more time together than if treatment would continue. Being the surgical oncology unit, we do end up working with hospice pretty closely. They have some amazing nurses and doctors. They will be able to help manage Eleanor's pain and anxiety much better than we ever could."

"So, are they just going to throw pain medicine at her?" Wayne asks almost defensively. I know he is asking out of concern for my well being, but it still sounds a little harsh. I am curious to hear Kelly's answer though.

"Oh no, she can stay on her current pain medications as long as they are effective. However, if they stop working or her pain increases then they have stronger stuff to help. The number one rule in medicine is always to start low and go slow and that remains true even in hospice. So, if she needs morphine, they start at a low dose before increasing anything. I'm sure the hospice nurse will explain it better than I can," Kelly states.

Her words give me a sense of hope and I can feel Wayne relax at her response.

"Thank you so much Kelly. That eases my mind a little," I say, patting her hand. I like knowing that the drugs aren't going to be started right away. For some reason I had it in my mind that I would take some pills, drift off to sleep and never wake up again. That thought feels like someone is squeezing my heart. I still want time. As much time as I can get in order to say my goodbyes. If that is even possible at all.

Kelly sits with us for a few moments checking my incision and talking about nothing in particular before needing to leave to check on her other patients. The wave of emotions that we have experienced over the last few hours has been overwhelming and I am exhausted from it all.

I look at Wayne and see that he is just as tired as I am although he continues to scroll through the TV channels hoping to find something decent to watch. He settles on a football game, and I immediately lose interest.

I start to reminisce once again about our lifetime together. Wayne and I had a beautiful marriage. Oh of course we had our ups and downs, but what relationship didn't? I continue to feel that ping of regret that I didn't open my eyes sooner to what was right in front of me. The five years that I took waiting, for what I didn't know, seems like wasted time.

Through all our trials, we built the foundation of friendship. He was and still is my best friend. Knowing that I am leaving my best friend behind just sucks. That pain is worse than the cancer.

My heart starts to have those moments of regret, the what ifs, when Wayne clears his throat. Thankful that he saved me from going down that dark rabbit hole, I turn my attention to him to see that he is no longer engrossed in the game playing on the television.

"I'm just going to ask one more time and then I will get on board and stand behind you. Are you sure that this is what you want?" he asks, both hope and anguish clear in his tone.

I think he is going down his own dark rabbit hole of worries and regrets. I know my answer is not going to be what he wants to hear, but the reality seems pretty clear to me, and I need to somehow make it clear to him.

I look at him, truly look at him with so much love and devotion. Knowing that he will go through his own pain makes this even more difficult. The last thing I'd ever want to do is to be the cause of his pain or my family's.

I clear my throat. "I'm so sorry. I'm sorry that I am leaving you first. I'm sorry that I didn't see what was in front of me in high school so that we could have had five more years together. I'm sorry that I am going to put you through this," I take a deep breath, "but yes, this is what I want and need."

"Ellie, you do not need to be sorry about a damn thing. You didn't ask to get cancer, and you have been so strong throughout all of this," he replies with tears now steadily flowing down his face. "And those five years were some of my favorite memories as I tried to find a new way of wooing you.

Who knew all it would take was a slow dance and a kiss at the end to seal the deal?"

I think back to that moment that changed everything. It was a beautiful November day with the sun shining brightly making the few fall leaves burst with color. We went to a wedding together for his good friend's brother. I didn't really know the couple, but I was happy to get out to be around some friends.

I shopped all day the weekend before trying to find the perfect dress. I'm not sure why I cared so much back then. Wayne and I were just friends, and I really didn't know anyone aside from our small group. So why did I feel the need to dress up?

Deep down I think I knew that I wanted our friendship status to change. Wayne had always been there for me, even during the few horrible relationships that I had. He stuck by my side and showed me what a true relationship could look like. He helped me see that I deserved so much more than the crap that I settled for with guys who really didn't care about me. When I finally found the perfect blue dress with shoes to match, I became even more anxious for the wedding to arrive.

Wayne picked me up, obviously having just cleaned his truck. He gave me a hug like he always did, but something felt different. More intimate somehow. His cologne was enough to swoon any girl. I smiled seeing his gray collared shirt and blue tie that matched my dress perfectly. I found out later that he called my friend to ask what color dress I was going to be wearing.

Wayne stayed by my side throughout the day and evening. He never crowded me, but I didn't miss the subtle ways he would guide me by touching my lower back wherever we walked. When he asked me to dance it was a surprise. Wayne hated dancing and would often tell me when school dances were getting close.

After my initial shock I agreed, and he led me onto the dance floor. A slow song came on and he held me close. I knew now why Wayne hated dancing, he was, and still is, a terrible dancer. However, the way he looked into my eyes made the world disappear. My heart raced because I knew he was thinking about kissing me.

So many questions formulated in my mind. Did I want this? What happens if things don't work out? Would I lose my best friend forever? I was so lost in my head that I didn't realize that the song was ending, and he was leaning in closer to me.

That first kiss blew all the questions I had out of my mind. His lips landed on mine, and I wanted nothing more than to continue the kiss until we needed to break for air. He thankfully knew we were in a public place and kept the kiss short, but oh so sweet.

I looked up at him and realized he was everything I could have ever asked for in a man. He was my best friend, my confidant, my protector when I needed one, and so much more.

As I reflect on everything and despite what the doctor told us earlier, I have the biggest grin on my face thinking about that day.

"Yeah, you took a big risk with that kiss. I could have slapped you and said that I never wanted to see you again," I reply with a small chuckle.

Wayne smiles back at me and wipes the tears from his eyes with the back of his hand.

"I knew by the way you were looking at me that something changed. That risk was the best thing I have ever done in my life. I wouldn't change anything about our life together, Ellie. This last year you have fought so hard, and I feel like you have done that more for us than for yourself. I want to do what's right for you and not what you think the rest of us want. So," he pauses before getting the courage to ask, "is starting hospice what you really want?"

I want to leave behind the world of cancer and hospitals. The weeks and months of liquid poison pumped into my chest port in attempts to kill the cancer cells. The nights were filled with nausea and mornings of pain. The perfectly baked meals that went untouched on my plate. I want to leave it all behind and forget the past eight months. I yearn to move forward to a new life and better memories. I nod my head, but I can't bring myself to say the words again.

"Ok, then let's do it together," is all he says. He holds my hand and kisses the back of it. I can see in his eyes the determination of being strong for me and love him more.

CHAPTER 3

The next morning, I'm awakened to the smell of delicious hazelnut coffee and Wayne bringing in breakfast for two from my favorite bakery. One of the perks of coming into the city to get my chemo was to stop by the Little Heaven Scent bakery around the corner to get a sweet treat or a coffee. Wayne continues to spoil me with the little things and it's these moments that put a smile on my face.

I sit up in bed with renewed enthusiasm for the day and enjoy my coffee and breakfast sandwich. Wayne takes his usual spot in the chair next to my bed and we use the bedside table together to savor our meal. I can't help the small moan from coming out as my taste buds envelop around my sandwich. Sausage, egg, and cheese croissant, my favorite. I know I will only be able to enjoy a few bites, but those few bites are heavenly.

"I spoke with the kids last night and told them that you are being placed on hospice," he says, finishing the last bite of his own sandwich.

He wipes the crumbs from his face with a napkin and sits back in his chair. My mind starts to race, and I feel the guilt move through me. I should have been the one to call them. I should have been the one to tell them that I am starting hospice, and that the surgery had been a failure. After everything that happened yesterday, the exhaustion overwhelmed me, and I fell right to sleep after Wayne, and I had talked. I should have called Katie and Michael first to speak with them about everything.

Wayne can clearly see the worry and guilt on my face and says, "It's ok Ellie. I told them that you were still exhausted from the surgery, and you fell asleep. They understood why I was calling."

"Are they upset?" I ask, almost dreading the answer.

"Katie of course was tearful, and Michael is being stubborn and showing no emotion as per usual. I'm sure they will need to come to terms with it in their own way, as we all are. How about we wait to get more information today on hospice and then take it from there, huh?"

I nod my head in agreement. He's right, there's no use in starting to worry about anything when I don't have the full picture of what to expect. That doesn't stop my mind from racing ahead with all sorts of different questions though.

What's going to happen with my medications? When will I be discharged? Is this all covered through insurance? If it isn't, then how is my family going to afford this? Are Michael and Katie okay with this decision? And of course, the unending question of how much time will I have left. That one hangs at the forefront of my brain. Before I can go into full panic mode we hear a knock on the door.

"Come in," Wayne calls out. He starts gathering the trash from our breakfast to throw away.

A small petite blonde walks in wearing a white polka dot shirt and business skirt with pantyhose and sensible black high heeled shoes. She has with her a small black briefcase in one hand and a coffee mug in the other. She looks like she belongs in a courtroom not a hospital.

"Hi Mr. and Mrs. Graham. My name is Amy and I'm from hospice. I was told by Dr Jenkins that you were looking into hospice care and would like some information," she says in a quiet calming voice.

I take a deep breath in, glad that the good Lord heard my prayers of needing answers, "yes, surgery didn't work, and I have run out of options. I'm hoping that you can make me a little more comfortable so I can be home with my family."

"Ok, yeah. I'm so sorry that the surgery wasn't successful. I'm sure it must be difficult being at this point, but I hope I can put your mind at ease a little bit and answer any questions that you have."

Amy places her bag on the small table in the corner and pulls up the same rolling chair that Kelly sat in yesterday. Having someone sit eye level with me makes me feel more relaxed. I have come to appreciate the small gesture.

"Thank you. I never thought I would be here. I thought I could beat the cancer and go on living my life like nothing had happened. Apparently, that's not in the cards for us," I admit more to myself than her.

"Have either of you experienced hospice before?" she asks, looking at Wayne and me.

"My grandmother was on hospice, back when hospice first became a thing. And honestly, it's a little hazy. She was only on hospice for like three days before she died and she didn't seem all that comfortable," Wayne states.

"Same, my grandaddy passed away from the same cancer that is going to take me, and we had the same experience," I say.

I'd be lying if I said I wasn't nervous thinking about the pain grandaddy went through in his final moments. I hope like hell that wasn't going to be how my story finishes.

"My mama passed away in her sleep from a stroke when I was about twenty and our middle child passed away tragically, so they didn't have hospice," I continued.

I'm not sure what compelled me to share the latter information. Maybe it was the constant thought of death and dying and wondering if I would get the chance to see my mama and baby boy again.

"I see. Well, the good news is that hospice has come a long way. Back then many people went on hospice, and it only lasted about two weeks, but that was because doctors waited too long before placing a person on hospice. Now we have patients who are in hospice for six months, sometimes longer. We have improved medications to help with pain and anxiety, but we still have a long way to go before hospice is thought of as something more than what it is. Almost every single hospice worker genuinely believes that the end of life should be just as beautiful as the start of life," Amy states.

Her words resonate with me, and I feel better about my decision, stronger even. A small smile sweeps across my face, and I look at Wayne who now has tears in his eyes. I swear this man has been more tearful in the last few days than in all the years I have known him.

"Sorry, now it sounds like I'm trying to sell you something. I'm not, I promise. I just want to tell you what hospice has to offer and then you can make your decision from there," Amy says with a small chuckle.

For the next hour we sat in my hospital room discussing hospice and its benefits. It is a relief to know that it is one hundred percent covered by insurance and even the equipment that might be needed would not be billed to us. It almost seems too good to be true, but I am grateful for this blessing knowing that my family won't be stuck with a bill after I am gone.

"Before we move forward, I just want to ask, are you ready to start hospice and sign consent forms?" Amy asks hesitantly.

Wayne and I look at each other briefly before I turn my attention to her and nod in agreement. Although Wayne and I had discussed beginning hospice care last night, being here and completing consent forms releases some pressure that I wasn't aware I was carrying.

Amy walks us through each one as she places the sheet in front of me to sign. I think about how crazy it is that these documents might be the last official documents I ever sign. I push that thought out of my head trying not to think of such depressing moments.

"And this form is signing whether or not you want to be resuscitated if your heart should stop beating," Amy says as she places the next form in front of me.

Wayne and I look at her in confusion. Was signing this document just a formality? Why is she asking me to sign a Do Not Resuscitate paper? I thought that is what hospice was.

"I don't think we understand what you're asking. I thought that's what hospice is," Wayne says perplexed.

"Some people wish to still be a full code even though they are signing up for hospice. They are ready to start hospice and be made comfortable, but they are not quite ready to sign the paper that says they are a DNR or Do Not Resuscitate. If that's your choice then you can sign at the bottom of the page and you can remain a full code," Amy replies, pointing to the last line of the paper.

"What would it look like if I stayed a full code," I ask.

"I get this question a lot and I had to have one of my nurses explain it to me. If you choose to remain a full code, which again is completely your choice, then when your heart stops a few things will happen. The hospice nurse will call 911 and begin CPR. This will likely break some of your ribs in the process. When 911 arrives, they will transport you to the hospital while continuing CPR. If they can resuscitate you, you would be placed on a ventilator to help you breathe and then moved to the ICU. From there it would be up to your family what happens next," Amy says with compassion, but also matter of fact.

I think it over for a moment. The scene plays over me like a nightmare. My family surrounding my bedside as my heart stops. The faceless hospice nurse starting CPR and calling 911. The blue and red flashing lights coming in from windows as I am placed on a stretcher. The feel of a tube being placed in my throat to help me breathe as I gag at the taste of plastic. The thought of seeing the scared faces of my beautiful grand babies, McKenna and Nathan, sends a shiver down my spine and haunts me. I grab the sheet of paper immediately and sign on the DNR spot.

"I can't do that to our family. I will not traumatize our kids or grandkids with the scene that just played out in my head," I look at Wayne, willing him to understand my decision.

"Ellie, this is your choice. Your life. I'm just along for the ride and will do whatever I can to make this easier for you."

How did I get to be so lucky as to have a man like this one? Who is taking our vows as seriously as the day we said them? In sickness and in health until death parts us. I'm not sure what I did to deserve him, I am just thankful to call him mine.

I sign the rest of the documents, and we begin to go over the equipment that I might need to be able to discharge home. I already had many items that I acquired over the months of treatments like a walker, wheelchair, and shower chair.

"It's standard that our patients have oxygen set up in the home just in case of shortness of breath and I'd also recommend a bedside table, unless you have a nightstand that you'd like to use," Amy suggests.

"I think I'd like a bedside table. I've gotten kind of comfortable with the thing and it'll make eating my meals in my recliner easier," I joke.

"Hey now. I thought you said no eating meals in the living room?" Wayne quips back at me.

"I'm dying, let an old woman eat while watching her favorite shows," I jest back at him. He lets out a small chuckle and I am thankful that the mood is lightening up a bit. I have missed hearing his laughter, but there hasn't been much to laugh at recently.

"What about a hospital bed?" Amy asks innocently.

"No, I'm not ready for that yet," I reply.

Thinking about a hospital bed sitting in the corner of my house and knowing that that is where I am going to end up makes me nauseous. I don't want it sitting around as a reminder, calling my name like death itself. I plan on enjoying my days with my family, not dwelling on the inevitable and having that bed there will dwindle my joy.

"Ok, that's not a problem. The nurse visiting can always revisit this if it is needed and have it ordered and delivered within twenty-four hours," Amy states.

"So, when can Ellie be discharged?" Wayne inquires. I love that he knows I am eager to get back home. I have missed my grand babies over the last several days. I asked my daughter not to bring them up for fear that they might pick up a virus and get sick. Of course, I also miss my daughter and son and their spouses as well, but there's nothing like grandkids to make your day better.

"I can have the equipment delivered to your house by this evening, but that is going to be too late to set up an ambulance transport. So probably tomorrow," Amy reports as she starts looking over the paperwork, I signed ensuring that it's completed correctly.

"Oh, we don't need an ambulance dear. I am perfectly capable of sitting in a car. No need to fuss and take an ambulance away from someone else that needs it," I say and look over at Wayne.

He nods his head in agreement and looks to Amy with hopes that that might speed up my timeline for discharge.

"Okay, no ambulance, but it still is going to be tomorrow morning before I can get everything in place for discharge. I'm not sure if I am going to have a nurse be able to see you when you get home tomorrow though. Typically, we like to have a nurse come out and do what we call a 'tuck-in' visit to make sure you're settled before your regular nurse comes out to see you."

I look at Wayne, place my hand on his and sigh, "one more night then." I look over to Amy, "and that's okay, I think we will manage one night without a nurse coming out to see us."

"Alright, I can have your regular nurse come see you first thing Monday morning, probably about nine a.m. Is that okay?" Amy asks.

"Nine a.m. would be just fine," I say.

Amy packs up the consent forms I signed and places them in her briefcase. She walks back to Wayne and I and holds out her hand. I take it with gratitude that she was able to answer some of the questions I had rustling around my brain. My head is reeling with all the new information given to me today and I feel like I only consumed half of it.

"I know your head is probably spinning with everything that has happened over the last twenty-four hours. If you need the same questions answered fifteen times, then please ask it. We are here for you, for whatever your needs might be. Call our twenty-four-hour number and someone will be able to answer your question or send a nurse who can assist you. On Monday morning expect your nurse to come with a binder full of information. She'll explain everything as well as a bag of medications. These are emergency medications and it's easier to have them in your home in case you have a pain crisis in the middle of the night. She will explain everything to you," Amy states.

Wayne and I nod our heads. My mind feels as if it is about to go into a panic mode once again with the new information about medications. I take a deep breath and reel myself back in before I could go into a full panic attack. These are worries for another day and like Amy said the nurse would explain everything.

I send up a prayer for strength remembering my favorite quote from Matthew 6:26, Look at the birds of the air; they do not sow or reap or store away in barns, and yet your heavenly Father feeds them. Are you not much more valuable than they? Can any one of you by worrying add a single hour to your life?

I take another deep breath using God, Wayne, and my faith as strength. I will get through this. The alternative would be turning into that person that I didn't recognize, and I refuse to become that person again.

"It was a pleasure meeting you both," Amy says. We say our goodbyes to her as she walks out the door,

Wayne and I breathe another sigh of relief once the door closes. Well, if one thing this experience has taught me, it's breathing. I don't think I have taken this many deep breaths in all my life. I want to laugh at the small gesture that I continue to make.

"What's so funny?" Wayne asks.

"I was just thinking about how many deep breaths I've taken recently. If someone didn't know me well, they'd think I practiced yoga or something," I say in amusement.

Wayne chuckles, "there she is. I missed my wife cracking jokes at every little thing."

He stands and kisses my forehead before pulling out his cell phone from his back pocket. "I'll call Katie and then Michael to let them know the plan. I'm sure they will want to have our traditional Sunday night dinner tomorrow night to welcome you home."

"I know, we've missed the last two," I frown, feeling guilty for missing our weekly tradition.

"Ellie, I think you've had a good reason to miss the last couple of weekly dinners. It's been tough trying to get your blood work perfect before they could try surgery. We can make up for the missed ones with extra dinners if that's what you would like."

I beam at that idea, "yes, please. But please tell them not to come up here. Katie and Jason would bring the kids and then one of them would likely get sick. And Michael and Josie have enough stress on their plate that we don't need to send Josie into early labor."

"Yes dear." Wayne takes that moment to walk out of the room to make his phone calls.

The next twenty-four hours are long, and it seems like each minute that goes by stretches out even longer. All I want to do is leave this sterile, ugly room and never return. After eating my lunch and making sure that everything is packed for the hundredth time, I am finally being discharged home.

It is bittersweet saying goodbye to Kelly and some of the other staff at the hospital. They are beautiful souls, and I wish nothing but the best for them. However, the thought came to mind that this is just scratching the surface of saying my goodbyes. I shudder to think about the other goodbyes that I will need to make, but that will have to be a battle for a different day.

The drive back to the house is long and I guess that's what we get for living out in the country. Good treatment for cancer doesn't happen in "the sticks," but following a chemotherapy session, the serenity of our home was quite helpful.

Wayne always said that he wanted to live far away from people because he hates being around crowds. I think it is karma and slightly hilarious how he seems to have the personality that everyone wants to gravitate towards. Another piece of irony for the books.

We built our forever home about thirty years ago. It sits back behind some trees off the main road in a little town with one stop light. It takes about twenty minutes to get to a Walmart or decent restaurant, however the stars shining brightly at night and the sounds of nature make it all worth it.

Our ranch style home has always been my oasis. The large front porch was perfect for those cooled off evenings and sitting in a rocking chair watching the sunset. I was thankful Wayne let me pick the colors and help 'design' our house. I would think about something, and he would be able to build it exactly like I imagined. We made the perfect team.

We are luckier than most I suppose. We have five acres, a small pond with fish, and a little vegetable garden that has given us a plethora of vegetables this year. My husband's work shed sits off to the corner with all his tools and unfinished projects. He likes to work on those when I start to annoy him with my antics, giving him my 'honey-do' lists.

I feel a sense of relief as we pull down the long rock driveway. There is some guilt forming for not making it to church this morning, but I make a mental note to say some extra prayers later tonight.

Wayne helps me out of the car, and we are immediately greeted by Carmel and Moose. I make sure to pat each of them on the head and give them a little scratch behind the ears. They both trot off, most likely to jump in the pond again. Even with the cooler air and much colder water they still prefer to swim at least once a day. True water dogs to be sure.

We walk to our front door, and I enter the home that Wayne so beautifully built for us. As I step inside, I take a deep breath in, the smell of something delicious baking in the kitchen hits my nose and my stomach growls thinking about a nice home cooked meal. I can hear my daughter Katie talking with her husband, Jason, in the kitchen as I take my coat off in the foyer.

I look into the living room and see my grand babies playing and fighting over a new toy car. McKenna and Nathan pull a car back and forth until it slips out of their hands and almost hits their uncle in the face. Michael catches the car in mid-air before it knocks anything over or breaks the toy.

"Sorry Uncle Michael," McKenna and Nathan say at the same time in sing-song voices. Michael places the car on the floor next to him and wraps an arm around his very pregnant wife.

"Hey Michael, are you and Josie getting some practice in before she pops?" Wayne asks my youngest son with a laugh.

"Wayne, that's not nice to say when a woman is eight and half months pregnant." I scolded him and smacked him in the chest. He places a hand over his heart like I just wounded him.

Both Michael and Josie chuckle at our banter. Josie smiles, "Mom, it's fine. And yes, it gives us some good practice, but I don't think a three- and five-year-old will help us to know what to do for a newborn."

I love how Josie and I have always been able to have a close relationship. She has called me mom since the day she married my son. The fact that she never had a close relationship with her own mother broke my heart. I've always made a conscious effort to not be 'that mother-in-law' and include her and love her as I would any other family member.

It really is a joy to walk in our home to laughter, especially after Michael has been gone for so long. I wouldn't hold his military job against him, but ten years of flying around the world can leave a mother lonely. It was hard to let go of my incredible son after raising him for eighteen years. I knew deep down, however, that I couldn't stop him. It wouldn't be fair of me to hold him back from everything he wanted to do in life.

Growing up in a small town puts limits on one's employment options. In addition, we lacked the funds to send him to college—not that Michael was really focused on education anyhow. Joining the Navy was the best option for him. He was able to be everything he wanted to be and more. His love of airplanes helped him secure a job working on the F-18's. This eventually led to his current job back at home working at the airline. Sure, he must drive about an hour to work one-way, but he says he is happy to do it to have some peace on the days he is off.

He met Josie during his time in the service. Unfortunately, since they worked together, they had to keep their relationship private. I was thankful that he didn't keep it private from me. I loved the phone calls I would get on the weekends about the elaborate dates he would set up. She's such a lovely girl and the way she looks at Michael reminds me of the way Wayne still looks at me.

When it came time to reenlist, they both decided to get out. Michael proposed the day after. They got pregnant quickly after getting married and thankfully decided to raise their family here. The world seemed to align perfectly. They were able to find a house quickly and close to ours after Michael secured a job with the airline. Not too long after they got settled into their new home I was diagnosed with my cancer. Funny how life happens like that.

I shake my head trying to bring me back to the present. I find myself still standing in the foyer watching my family.

"Everything alright?" Wayne whispers in my ear. He places a hand on my shoulder.

I grab his hand in reassurance. "Yes, just reminiscing," I say quietly.

"Hey mom, just in time. Jason was just about to run out and grab dessert. The meatloaf will be done in about an hour. What are you in the mood for?" Katie asks, coming out of the kitchen wiping her hands on a towel. She strides over to me for a hug, and I embrace her warmly. There is much to be said in this hug. I want to grab hold of her and cry, but I push the urge down not wanting to make a scene in my foyer.

"I don't care. Whatever everyone else would like is fine." I eventually say, letting go of Katie. Both McKenna and Nathan take the opportunity to jump up and say "cake!" We all laugh.

"If grandma is okay with that then we'll do cake," Jason says coming out from around Katie.

I lean over putting my face closer to my grand babies and say, "I think cake would be the bestest."

Both McKenna and Nathan give a resounding "yay" before focusing back on their toys. I start walking over to my recliner, moving past the toys on the floor and Michael and Josie sitting on the couch. I can see Michael remove his arm from around Josie and stand to also envelop me in a hug. Once again, I feel as if the dam is about to break. It takes every willpower I have to hold him in a hug without breaking down. I feel words being said in our embrace without actually speaking. I feel as if I could hold on forever, but at some point, I must let go.

With tears now choked down I continued the short walk to my welcoming recliner. Before I can get comfortable McKenna runs to sit in my lap.

"Kenna, why don't you give grandma some time to relax before jumping on her," Katie says out of concern.

"Katie she's fine," I say, helping McKenna onto my lap trying to be careful not to pull on my stitches from the unsuccessful surgery. I sigh and kiss the top of her head as she stares at the TV. I am content holding the beautiful little girl that made me a grandma and I feel so much more at ease since heading to the hospital two weeks ago.

Wayne settles into his recliner next to mine and we watch as Nathan continues to play with his cars on the floor. McKenna relaxes further into my arms and stares at the T.V. as the latest episode of Spidey and His Amazing Friends pops on the screen.

I smile happily at Wayne as I look at him over the top of McKenna's head. The knowing gleam in his eyes and the smile that returned to his face gave me the impression that he knew all I needed to do was be at home with my loved ones.

"What time is the hospice nurse coming?" Michael asks, returning from the kitchen with a handful of nuts. He sits down on the couch putting an arm around his wife and popping a few nuts in his mouth. He rests his foot up against his thigh. Despite his appearance of ease, I know he is anything but.

"I asked her to come tomorrow. I just wanted a night with my family before getting into the hospice world. She'll be here at nine," I tell Michael.

"Well, are they starting medication? How often are they coming?" He starts almost impatiently.

"I don't know Michael; we'll find out tomorrow morning. And stop talking with food in your mouth," I say.

"What did they say?"

"That they will be here tomorrow morning at nine and give us more information then. You know everything that I know. We'll find out tomorrow," I say, rolling my eyes. I start to get annoyed with his questions, yet I feel like that is unfair of me. He is going to be affected by this change just like everyone. I am thankful that Wayne steps in for me before I say anything out of annoyance.

"Stop stressing your mother out Michael," Wayne snaps.

"I have to make a phone call to cancel a meeting," he huffs out a reply and stands up. He takes his cell phone out and punches in some numbers before getting to the front door. Josie looks at me as if to say, 'I'm sorry.'

I wish I could tell him that he didn't need to be here for the meeting, that Wayne and I have it covered, but I know he won't listen. In reality I know that my family would drop everything to be with me, even if I didn't ask. I know that they are just as curious about what to expect as well as the timeline of everything. That was the most daunting question of them all. How much time do I have left?

After about thirty minutes of hearing Michael's muffled voice on the front porch he walks in with Jason closely behind him. Jason is holding a freshly baked cake from the local bakery. Cherry chip, my favorite. Of course, no bakery could hold a candle to one of my cakes, but it's not like I'm in any condition to bake one right now.

I should've opened my own bakery. I think that would have brought more meaning to my life than being a simple receptionist at a dentist's office. However, that's just asking to open another can of regrets. I'm sure I will have my fill of them as time goes on.

Dinner is just as I hoped it would be. Love and laughter fill the room as we joke and tease each other about memories made. The few bites I can eat before I get full are delicious. It seems like my appetite just keeps declining.

A few more hours go by before everyone finally says their goodbyes. Michael walks his wife to the car, helping her get settled in the passenger seat. A sleepy McKenna and Nathan cling to Katie and Jason as they walk out the door. I shut the door behind them all with a loud sigh.

"Are you alright?" Wayne asks, rubbing my shoulders. I keep my hand on the door while my head hangs low.

"Yeah, I'm just tired I guess," my exhaustion threatens to overwhelm me. I don't want to let Wayne know just how tired I am for fear that the weekly Sunday night dinners may cease because I'm 'too tired.'

He hesitates at my answer. Thankfully after a moment he lets it go before moving to get himself ready for bed. I complete my nightly routine before laying my head on my pillow. I make sure to say my extra prayers for missing church this morning as I drift off to a troubled sleep, while Wayne holds me secure in his arms.

CHAPTER 4

The next morning, I woke up a lot later than I had planned for my nine am meeting. I was hoping to be up to make breakfast for the uninvited guests. I'm sure they will insert themselves into my business even though I never asked them to. I guess that comes with the life of being a mom with grown adult children. I have just enough time to get myself together before I hear the front door opening and Katie and Jason walking in with their arms full of stuff.

    I walk out of the master bedroom down the hall to see that Michael and Josie are coming in the door as well. I make it to the kitchen and see the kids shrugging off their coats, putting them around the barstools at the large island. My thoughtful Katie is amazing for bringing fresh donuts for everyone to enjoy. I quickly set to work making a fresh pot of coffee for everyone to sip on with their baked goods.

    "Well, it's 8:45, should we take our coffee and donuts into the living room and wait for the nurse?" I ask no one in particular.

Everyone stops what they are doing, Michael in mid-chew. The looks on their faces makes me feel as if I asked them if they saw the alien in our basement.

"What?" I ask incredulously.

"Who are you and what have you done with my mother?" Michael replied sarcastically.

"Yeah mom, you said that we're never allowed to take our food in the living room. The kitchen and dining room are for food, the living room is for relaxing," Katie says in a mock tone.

"Is that voice supposed to be me?" I ask with humor in my voice. "Well, it will be more relaxing if we have our donuts and coffee in the living room instead of this cramped kitchen or stuffy dining room."

"Hey, you love our dining room and kitchen," Wayne squawks, following me into the living room.

I sit down in my recliner and place my donut and coffee on the bedside table. I grab my favorite soft blanket and place it over my lap.

"I do, but for this type of conversation I want to be comfortable in my recliner with my blanket." I acknowledge.

At nine am sharp there is a knock on the door. Wayne gets up to answer it and soon he is walking back with the hospice nurse in tow. Wayne thankfully grabs a chair for her and places it next to my recliner. I can feel the air shift from relaxed and happy to tense with anticipation.

"Hey everyone, I'm Elisha. I'm the nurse who will be helping out and getting stuff set up," Elisha says to the group with an awkward wave. Her hands are full of a bag of medicine, a binder and what looked like a very heavy backpack on her shoulder.

Everyone quickly introduces themselves as Elisha gets settled into the chair next to me. The donuts and coffee are quickly forgotten. I look around the room to see Katie fidgeting nervously at her nails, Jason leaning against the doorway into the kitchen, Michael sitting on the edge of the couch while Josie rubs her belly anxiously. Wayne is by my side, as always, continuing to be my rock in my time of need.

"Oh my, I hope there's not a quiz on everyone's names at the end," chuckles Elisha. That seems to lighten up the mood slightly to everyone but Michael. I am thankful that I got a nurse with a possible sense of humor, the jury is still out, but the small joke went a long way.

Elisha is a beautiful middle-aged woman. Blonde hair tied back in a pony, beautiful brown eyes, round face and not a speck of makeup. She is wearing teal scrubs and a pink stethoscope around her neck. She has an air of confidence with a very calming presence. She conveys that sense of being knowledgeable as well. Like she knows a thing or two because she's seen a thing or two. It is comforting to know that she will be helping guide us through this process.

Elisha quickly gets to work taking vitals and completing an assessment all the while typing the information on her laptop. My family remains quiet and watchful as she completes each of her tasks. When she finishes, she sets the bag of medications and binder on my bedside table to review with us.

"Okay, so Amy talked with you at the hospital?" Elisha asks and I nod my head quickly. "Do you have any questions about what she already explained?"

"No, she was pretty thorough in her explanation of what hospice does. She explained that I have a nurse, assuming that will be you," she nodded, and I continued, "and an aide to come out and help me with a bath, but I don't think I really need that right now. A chaplain will be by to see me, but I also have my own pastor that will come out too. However, I am not quite sure why we would need a social worker."

"Don't worry, she's not going to try to take your children or anything." Elisha starts. I'm taken back by the comment she makes.

"I'm sorry, that is Gina's, our social worker, trying to make a bad joke about other social workers," Elisha stumbles to say to make sure I knew she was making a joke.

"Well damn. Our kids are grown, but you're welcome to take them if you want," Wayne laughs.

I smile when I hear Michael say "hey" and Katie shout "dad!" Now I know I'm going to like this nurse.

"Gina, our social worker will be by at some point to be another resource for you. She will call you before she makes a visit. She is there to be a listening ear if you need one. If FMLA paperwork is needed she can help with that. She can coordinate to set up placement if someone needs a nursing home or find private duty caregivers if that is a better option. You can see her as much as once a week or not at all after her first visit. The same with our chaplain," Elisha explains.

I look to Wayne, "Please don't stick me in a nursing home."

"Oh, honey the confusion is already starting to take place. This is your nursing home. Now you be a good girl and eat your pudding, okay?" Wayne teases with a wink in his eye.

"Watch it old man or you'll get a face full of pudding," I tease back. Our enjoyable banter is back, but my smile doesn't stay long as I see Michael's jaw clenching.

"You guys are going to be a fun couple to work with, I can tell," the hospice nurse giggles. She bends over to pick up the binder from the floor and the bag of medications.

"This binder is going to be very important to you. It has some basic things in there like the hospice numbers and when to call. Basically, if you have any questions, call us. If you feel like you need to call 911, call us first. I recommend programming our number into your phones so it's a quick dial and you don't have to look up the number. This is your purple DNR

41

form signed by our doctor. Hang this on your refrigerator. If for some reason 911 is called they are trained to look for this purple form and they will know what to do," Elisha says handing me the form that I signed a few days ago. Out of the corner of my eye I can see Michael's hands clenching into fists. Katie sits stock still with a faraway look in her eyes. I didn't get the chance to tell my kids that I signed a Do Not Resuscitate.

Elisha continues to explain the binder, "also I will be writing in this binder after each of our visits so if an emergency visit needs to be made by a different nurse, then they can read this and basically know what happened during our last visit."

I nod my head in acknowledgment. I can feel my head swimming and I am starting to get overwhelmed by all the information being thrown at me. I know I was frustrated about the kids being here, but now I am grateful. Hopefully, they understand everything and will help me later with the stuff I will undoubtedly forget. I feel Wayne rubbing my back in comfort.

"Ellie are you okay?" he asks.

"Yeah, this is just a lot to take in."

"You're doing great," Elisha says reassuringly, "all that's left to talk about is the medications. And I want to take the time to make sure you understand each one."

Michael's knee is now bouncing up and down while Katie's outward appearance has not changed. If anything, she is more lost in thought.

"So, all these medications you can just stick somewhere out of the way until it's time to use them. Some of these are basic. Tylenol is for fevers and the Dulcolax suppository is in case you get severely constipated. Some of these meds have a side effect of constipation so this one may come in handy. Zofran will help with the nausea," Elisha explains. "The Ativan tablet can also help with nausea but is mainly used for anxiety. Now morphine will obviously help with pain, but it can also help if you feel short of breath. The dosage is labeled on the bottle. I will warn you that the liquid morphine doesn't taste good so you may want to chase it with something that tastes sweet."

"Well, I guess that helps to keep people from drinking the whole bottle," I joke. Elisha chuckles. My small joke and her laughter must have been too much for Michael. He stands up abruptly, raising alarm in all of us.

"You think this is funny? Making jokes?" He says through clenched teeth looking at me. He turns his ire to Elisha "and you just want to drug her up, is that it?"

To Elisha's credit she remains very calm only sitting up a little straighter in her chair, "not by any means. Your mom is currently on pain pills and she's needing them pretty regularly. It's not if, it's when the pain pills no longer work that she will need something stronger and that's where the morphine comes into the picture. Nothing we do is meant to sedate or speed up the process. Its only purpose is to make your mother as comfortable as possible while she goes through the natural process."

"Yeah and make her a drug addict while she's at it. And there doesn't seem to be anything natural about dying of cancer. Natural would be to pass peacefully in her sleep when she's ninety and has more time," Michael says now pacing the floor.

"Michael Jerome, that is not what she is saying, and you are out of line!" I snap at him, but I can see the pain clear in his face.

With a furious expression, he lets out a sigh and turns to go out the back door. Wayne sits back in his chair with a huff and the rest of the family just look at each other in shock at Michael's tantrum.

"I'm so sorry. I didn't mean to upset anyone. I'd be happy to talk to him to explain more about the medicine and how we manage," Elisha says. "I hope you don't think that's what hospice is about. We don't drug people up for the sake of drugging them up."

"No dear," I say, patting her hand. "He's just having a tough time with this. I know that's not what you do."

"We know. I did some research last night on my phone about hospice. This definitely sounds like the best way to go for Ellie. I'm sorry for our son's rudeness. That is not how he was raised," Wayne says from beside me.

I turn my head and stare at him in disbelief. "You researched about hospice?" I ask.

"Well yeah. I couldn't sleep last night and the more I thought about it the more I got anxious, so I decided to look it up. It gave me peace of mind," he answers me.

I can't believe he did that, especially knowing how much he hates being on a phone. 'All these apps will just make us mindless drones'; I've heard him say one too many times. We may have smartphones, but we don't need all the gadgets that come with them.

My heart fills with love, knowing that he is starting to fully accept my decision. Right now, though, there is one person in particular that needs to see things from my point of view.

Josie tries to stand to go after Michael, her pregnant belly making it difficult. I remove my blanket from my lap and push the bedside table out of the way. Walking over to her I placed my hand on her leg to stop her from getting up.

"Sweetie, you sit, let me deal with my son. Wayne, can you figure out a schedule with Elisha? I don't think we need the aid just yet though."

"Yes dear," Wayne replies. I love that after all these years he has finally learned to just say 'yes dear' at the right moment instead of arguing. It just makes life easier.

As I pass Katie sitting in the lone chair, I notice she is staring out the front window looking into the yard. The distance in her eyes is daunting. I want to stop and desperately ask her what she is thinking about so hard, although I feel like I need to deal with her brother first.

I walk out the back door and turn to the direction of the shed. The fall air seems to be crisper today and I'm thankful that I remembered my sweater and cap before walking outside. It is a gloomy day, gray skies that look like rain is on the way. The wind seems stronger with the trees now bare of their leaves with the last major rainstorm stripping them naked. In the distance I see Carmel and Moose wrestling playfully. The sight would have brought a smile to my face if I wasn't so concerned about my son's outburst.

As I walk to the shed, the crunching leaves under my feet, my mind drifts to Thanksgiving in a few short weeks. I make a mental note of all the things I need to get ready and gather for the big dinner. It makes me exhausted just thinking about it. Or is it the walk that is doing that?

I pull my sweater tighter around my body, careful not to touch my abdominal incision. This is probably the most active I've been in recent weeks. The pain starts to creep up again despite taking my pain pill this morning. I reach the door of the shed hearing a bang and something being thrown across the room. I open the door to find Michael standing in the middle of the room. He is out of breath and his head is hanging low in defeat.

My husband's beloved shed and most of the tools are thrown about, everything in disarray. The room is dark. The partial sun peeking through the murky clouds is the only source of light visible through the windows. Clearly shattered in the heat of his rage, the lightbulb lays in broken pieces at his feet.

I stand in the doorway with my arms across my chest. For the moment he doesn't notice me standing there. I know better than to startle him during one of his fits, so I clear my throat to get his attention. He takes a step back in surprise. He gets his bearings and stares at me with a look that I can't interpret.

"Go on then. Get it out," I say calmly. I guess I need to be the one to break the silence.

"No mom! Just no! We aren't doing this." Michael waves me off and turns his back to me. He walks over to a counter and rests his hands on it, dropping his head once again with anguish. I hear him sigh loudly from the doorway.

I'm not sure what he means by 'we aren't doing this.' Not doing hospice? Not doing this talk? Whichever one he meant doesn't matter. It isn't his choice. It's not his life, not his pain.

The pain he's suffering is something completely different, but I need him to get it out. I wait patiently as he keeps his back turned to me. I finally walk over to a stool to sit down when he finally breaks the silence.

He pushes up from the table and turns to me. "You can't do this mom! Please don't do this!" He begs. "They missed something, a scan or or or another treatment. Something! Tear up the damn consent forms for hospice and let's go back to the doctors and figure this out." Michael is back to pacing the room and running a hand through his dark hair.

I knew the second I made the decision for hospice that Michael was going to have the most trouble with it. Wayne of course had a hard time, but I knew he would support and respect my decision once he knew I was set on it. Katie has always been my laid-back girl, ready and willing to help wherever she could. Very much like her father, she would respect my wishes to start hospice.

After his older brother Samuel had died in a tragic accident when he was very young, Michael has never been quite the same. He has needed a little bit more of a push when it came to big decisions and commitment. Perhaps that's why he waited so long to marry Josie.

"Mikey," I hope using the nickname I have for him will snap him out of his anger, "they didn't miss anything. The surgeon was very clear that the cancer had progressed. Chemo is not working and all it does is make me feel worse. I have no energy, I can't eat anything because of the nausea, and I get dizzy walking short distances, so your father has to cart me around in a damn wheelchair. There's no other tests or medication to try that will fix it Mikey. All that's left is this, where we are now."

Michael turns to look at me with tears filling his eyes. "No, please no. We need more time." He inhales sharply and walks over to me. His voice cracks as he continues. "I've been away from home for ten years. I finally got back here with Josie to be a family with you and dad and sis. She's about to have your grandchild, mom. You're supposed to be here to show me how to be a good husband and father. You're supposed to help me. I can't do this without you. Please mommy don't leave me."

Michael goes to his knees and places his head in my lap, arms wrapped around my waist. At that moment I wasn't holding my thirty-one-year-old son in my arms. No, at that moment it felt like he was six again and all of this was just a bad dream. I wish with all my heart that I could rub his head like I used to and slay all his dragons. Unfortunately, that is not the reality we live in.

I feel the anger rise inside me. The anger that I felt back at the hospital when Dr. Jenkins told me he had failed. The hurt that this is causing my family is almost unbearable. I know that my own anger will not change the course of the path that I am on so there is nothing left to do but join my son in his tears.

I don't hold back my tears anymore as I rub his back like I did when he was a small boy. The tears fall as I say, "I'm so sorry Mikey. I'm sorry that it has to be this way. Please know that I would never choose to leave you. Or your father. Or your sister. I would love nothing more than to watch you raise your child and make so many memories with every one of my grand babies." I place my hands on either side of his cheeks and raise his head so that he looks at me. "But it's not in the cards for us my sweet boy. There is no other treatment or option. This is it. And… I'm scared. I'm scared of what the future holds. I'm scared of the pain I know will come. I'm scared of how you and your father and your sister will react once I'm gone."

I hadn't meant to admit that I'm scared, but the truth of the matter was that I am. I'm terrified. Of everything. I have my faith, but it still doesn't take away from my fear. It only helps alleviate it some.

I gently pushed a lock of hair out of his face. His brown eyes are red from crying. I continue, needing to get through this, "but I need you. I need your strength, your quick wit, and your lovable laugh. I need you to help me get through this next part."

"I can't," he cries.

"You can because I need you to. It's ok to be sad, for a while, even angry. But don't let it consume you. You have a wife and a baby on the way. They will need you too," I smiled down at my son through my tears.

"I know mama. I know. This is just so much harder than I ever imagined it would be. The thought of losing you makes me want to throw up."

"Well baby I'm not gone yet. I'm still here and still able to spend time with you. And that's what I want. To be able to spend as much time with my family as I can."

"If that's what you want then I can do that." He takes a breath and looks back at the mess he made in his fit of rage. "I'm sorry I acted like that. The thought of you taking those drugs made me lose it. I've seen too many people get addicted and their lives thrown away because of it."

It all makes sense now. Michael isn't just scared of losing me to cancer, well it isn't just that, but he is afraid that he will lose me as me. That my personality will change due to the drugs. He has seen it one too many times for my liking working in the Navy.

"If it comes time to take the stronger medication, promise me that you will listen to the nurse before making assumptions about addiction and all that."

He nods his head in agreement and then he places his head back in my lap as I stroke his hair. For a long moment neither of us moved. We relish in our embrace before gathering up the courage to go back into the house. I stand to leave and turn to him, "you better clean up your mess before your father sees this. As he always says, a clean tool is a happy tool. And they don't look too happy right now."

"Yes ma'am," Michael says with a small chuckle, wiping a stray tear from his eyes.

I close the door to the shed leaving him to his business and his thoughts. I only make it a few feet towards the house before I have to stop and catch my breath. I look to my left and see the tree that we had to cut down a few years ago. Nothing but the stump is left.

I close my eyes remembering the sound of Samuel giggling as Michael pushed his older brother in the tire swing. The laughter filled the air on a warm spring day, and I could almost hear Samuel say, "hey mommy watch this." I miss those moments, especially since nine short months later Samuel would be taken from us.

I miss hearing the giggles and laughter. The boys played cowboys and Indians while Katie read a book on the back porch, and I tended to my rose bushes. The thought brings a small smile to my face. I wonder what Samuel would think about all of this.

I take one more deep breath and walk back to the house feeling a little lighter. There's that yoga breathing again. I think back at all the regrets I have. What I could have done, should have done. Maybe the yoga thing would have come in handy throughout all of this.

I look up to the house and see a figure of someone looking out the back window. Probably Wayne or Jason making sure everything is okay.

I knew that Michael and I would need to have some sort of a conversation about this, but I didn't think it would be at the expense of poor Elisha.

With the tough talks out of the way I now know that one more conversation needs to be had with my daughter. Being the strong independent woman that I raised I know I will have to wait for her to come to me with it. I enter through the back door and walk into the living room to finish the meeting. Everyone is sitting relatively on edge waiting for the verdict of what happened.

"Everything okay?" Josie asks in an almost frantic voice. I think Michael has only shown that side of him a few times to her, which is a good thing. His temper tantrums really increased after Samuel's death, and it was difficult trying to teach him to control his anger.

"Yeah, everything is all good. He is just cleaning up his mess," I say and then turn to Wayne, "Don't go in your shed for a little bit."

Wayne's eyes get big as if he can imagine the horror of his beloved shed in shambles. Thankfully, he doesn't say anything with Elisha still at the house. I can see his breath quicken as he is thinking about all the things Michael could have destroyed in his anger. I sent him a silent thank you for not immediately getting up and walking out the door. I still need him at my side while the hospice nurse is present.

"Anything interesting happen while I was gone?" I ask, sitting back in my chair and pulling my blanket back onto my lap.

"No ma'am. We were talking about the football game that was on last night," Elisha says nonchalantly.

"Yeah, the woman knows her stuff. Although she's a cowboy fan, we're not going to hold that against her," Wayne adds.

The rest of Elisha's visit is uneventful and wraps up quickly. We plan the schedule for Mondays and Thursdays for her visits. Before she leaves to see her next patient Elisha encourages Wayne and me to call for any concerns. Josie stays for a while longer waiting for her husband to finish cleaning up the mess he made. Katie and Jason follow quickly behind Michael and Josie's departure.

For the first time since I woke up, I feel like I can breathe a sigh of relief. I take another pain pill and sit back in my recliner. My loving husband sits beside me in his chair and watches me as my eyelids drift close for an overdue nap.

CHAPTER 5

We settled into a routine over the next few weeks. The kids come over every Sunday like normal for dinner as well as some extra nights during the week. That is something new, although not necessarily unwanted. I enjoy the time I get to see my family and grandkids. This is what I was imagining when I signed the consent forms for hospice.

A few friends have also stopped by to see how I am doing. I am now at the center of prayers in the prayer group that I have been a part of for so many years. The prayers are comforting, but I shudder to think that I am now the focus in every group meeting. I have never been one to be the center of attention. I would rather someone else take the limelight and I could fade into the background. I'm just happy to be a part of someone's journey and help them along.

It's a weird concept if you think about it. You're always given the position in other people's lives to give them grace and prayers and whatever it is that they need. At the same time, when it is your turn for help and grace, you're embarrassed by it. You hide everything inside, storing up your anxieties, fears, self-deprivation like a squirrel stores nuts for winter. It's difficult to let anyone in.

Thankfully, God knows. He sees it all.

As many friends and acquaintances visit, I welcome the many casserole dishes knowing it will help Wayne to not concern himself about cooking dinner. The casserole dishes are soon filling the freezer, and I have to send some home with Michael and Katie. Is it too much to ask for a fruit basket or something small I can nibble on?

I think it's interesting how people want to spend more time with loved ones when the clock starts counting down. I know I should be grateful, and I shouldn't look a gift horse in the mouth. So many others pass away unexpectedly that getting these moments of reminiscing about old memories should be a welcoming time.

Thankfully, Wayne saw my decreased energy in trying to entertain our many guests that he let them down gently, telling them that this time is just for family. With my family I know that I can fall asleep while they are visiting, and they'll forgive me for it. With friends, I feel as if I must keep up a facade and entertain them until they feel as if they did their due diligence.

During this time, I found Wayne to be more accommodating than usual. He is fussing over my every need. I learned quickly to try and not moan if I have an ache while changing positions. The second I do he goes to attention so fast asking what I need. He is almost worse than a new expecting father.

Michael has come around to my decision of starting hospice. I knew it was going to be difficult for him, but he has become almost as bad as Wayne attending to me on his visits. Thank goodness Josie kind of knows how I am feeling and told him to stop it one evening. He must be doing the same to her.

Josie's belly has dropped the last few days, and it seems like she could go into labor at any moment. She has two more weeks to go, but that baby seems to be trying to wiggle its way out. I'm excited to see if it will be a boy or girl.

Michael said he wanted it to be a surprise when his wife first got pregnant. This also helped to make sure that they got what they needed for the baby and not just a bunch of cute baby clothes that the baby will only be able to wear once.

Katie and Jason bring the kids over whenever they can. I enjoy seeing the smiling faces of McKenna and Nathan. They make sure to run to me with their arms wide open as soon as they step foot into the house. I love these moments, and a smile never leaves my face whenever they are around. The only thing distressing me now is Katie.

I know my daughter, sometimes better than herself. With each visit that passes she grows increasingly distant. I don't even think she realizes that she's doing it. She is present, yet she is not here.

Katie has always been my quiet one. She's not an introvert by any means. You can't have a successful clothing boutique by not having a personality that people gravitate towards. She thinks about everything in fine detail and then prays on it before making any decisions.

She met Jason in high school, and they were the true high school sweethearts. She told him in no uncertain terms that she needed to go to college, get her business degree, and open her own store before they could even talk about marriage. Like the wonderful man he is, Jason just smiled and said, "yes dear." He proposed to her the day she cut the ribbon on her store. Jason is also remarkably successful as an electrician working for his dad's company. He is set to take over when his dad retires.

McKenna and Nathan just put that little cherry on top for our family. I was especially grateful that I could cut back to part time at the dentist's office when McKenna was born. Being a part time receptionist and a full-time grandma had brought me so much joy. I looked forward to finding different crafts I could make with my grandkids or going out to the pond to do some fishing.

Unfortunately, when I started treatments, I had no energy to keep up with the kids and Katie had to put them in daycare. I lost my job due to so many days of calling out sick, not that I blamed them for finding someone else. I didn't have much to look forward to except our Sunday dinners and even that was centered around how I was feeling and what my next treatment would be.

I fell into a depression and became someone that I didn't recognize. Now, I get to live for myself, and I get to do whatever I want because that's what I want. I am free. Who could have imagined that dying would be so liberating, but in a way it kind of is.

Today is Thanksgiving and it is also a good day. I find myself having good days and bad, some have more pain and less energy than others. When I woke up this morning, I just knew that today was going to be one of my good days. I just hope that I will have the appetite to try a little bit of everything.

As thankful and grateful as I am, I know that I must get to the bottom of Katie's distance before it taints any more memories. I can't bear the thought of her slipping into a depression like I did during my treatments.

Wayne really outdid himself this year. He hired a cleaning lady to come out and clean yesterday knowing that I stress more with a dirty house. My grandmother always had floors so clean that you could literally eat off them. You didn't need a five second rule at her house. I inherited some of her cleaning habits, but not all of them.

Wayne had me make a list of all the things we'd need for dinner and then braved the grocery store to gather the items. For the first time in our marriage, I found him sitting with me in the kitchen preparing a thanksgiving feast. He is taking directions nicely, only groaning and rolling his eyes once when

I told him he wasn't mashing the potatoes right. There actually is no wrong way of mashing potatoes, but what's Thanksgiving without a little family squabble.

Dinner is perfect. Everyone sits around after eating with their bellies full. No one seems to be in a big hurry to go anywhere as laughter fills the air. Even Katie seems to be a little bit more relaxed today and letting her hair down, so to speak.

I can eat about half of my plate before the nausea creeps in. The items I was able to eat were delicious and mouthwatering. Why is it that the food on Thanksgiving is so much better than literally the same food not on Thanksgiving?

I look around and feel at peace. Contentment and happiness surround me. I feel blessed to have another moment, another memory of being around my family and knowing they will look back and smile. Making memories that will continue to live on in all of our hearts means more to me than words can honestly say.

My eyes move to meet Katie's. The color seems to slowly drain from her face and the easygoing smile once shown on her face is now gone. The distance is back in her eyes, and she starts to shut down once again. It is subtle, but even Jason picks up on it.

I watch him lean over and whisper in her ear, "everything okay?" She nods but keeps quiet. He doesn't seem satisfied with her answer, yet he doesn't push her forward. I guess he decides not to press the issue in front of everyone.

"So, mom, when is Elisha coming back?" Michael asks, putting another helping of sweet potatoes on his plate.

I clear my throat and shake my head, "tomorrow," I reply. "I figured she needed a Thursday with her family, you know since it's Thanksgiving."

Everyone chuckles except Katie. "Oh, I can't be here for the visit tomorrow. It's Black Friday and I have to be at the store," Katie says sadly.

Michael and Katie have been taking turns being at the house when Elisha makes her visits. It helps having another person there to hear the information, although we've only made a few changes to my medication.

"Don't worry sis, I'm off tomorrow. I can be here for it." Michael replies nonchalantly in between bites of more food.

"Is this that pregnancy support eating thing? Where you try to gain more weight than your pregnant wife?" Wayne asks in amusement of Michael's eating.

"Tsk. Wayne! That's a horrible thing to say!" I say playfully smacking his hand. Everyone is back to laughing except Katie.

Josie rubs her belly and smiles down at her soon to be bundle of joy. Michael, Wayne, and Jason start talking about sports while McKenna and Nathan play on the floor with a movie on in the background. When Katie stands to start clearing plates, I join her.

After a few short trips we have the table cleared off and a mess on the counter. We both start dividing the leftovers into containers for each family to take home. Usually at this point we would sit back down and start on the desserts, but Katie seems to have other ideas on starting with the dishes.

She turns on the water and adds the soap. The voices in the other room seem to fade and sound as if they are off in the distance. I let her start on a few dishes, grabbing them from her as she finishes cleaning them. I dry them carefully and set them on the other counter.

I always loved having my window overlooking the backyard above my sink. I loved to wash dishes and get lost in thought looking outside at the world passing by. Katie must have had the same thought as she stares out absentmindedly. We wash a few more dishes before I break the silence.

"Amazing how the water can help wash all your worries away. You think that washing dishes is all it is, but it also helps organize your thoughts," I say to her.

Katie blinks a few times and takes a large breath. She places her hands on the corner of the sink and turns to me, "what are you talking about mama?"

"You don't think I can see it in your eyes baby girl? You're a million miles away. So lost in thought that I might have to send a search party to find you." I tucked a stray strand of hair behind her ear.

"Yeah, maybe so," Katie says with a smile that doesn't reach her eyes.

"Penny for your thoughts?"

"I don't even know what to say mama, or how to say it."

"Usually with words to form sentences."

She chuckles slightly and looks down. "Are you upset with me?" I finally asked her.

She rolls her eyes so big that if she were an animated cartoon she would probably see behind her. "God, no mama. Why would you think that?"

"I don't know. I'm trying to figure out why you've been so distant lately. Each time you come over it seems like it's getting worse. Your father had some issues at first, but he became okay with it. And we all saw Michael's outburst."

She nods her head at that. I clear my throat. "I just want to help you through this too."

My words seem to have opened the floodgates. The tears flow through my beautiful baby girl, and it is breaking my heart. She hugs me tightly, startling me.

I should have talked with her sooner than this. I should have seen the signs that she was not handling this well. I feel like I have failed my daughter at this moment and tears burst forth from my eyes.

It is a long time before we can gather ourselves. Out of the corner of my eye I see Wayne coming into the room, most likely looking for the desserts, and walks right back out. I love him for knowing we need this moment. I think I see someone behind him, although I can't make out who it is.

Katie wipes the tears from her eyes and says, "I'm scared mama. Every time I come over here, I fear that it will be the last time. Or the last time I talk to you. Or the last time I hear your voice. And then today I realized that this is our last Thanksgiving. We don't get anymore and that's killing me."

It feels like someone stuck a knife in my stomach at her words. And yet, that doesn't make them any less true. How do I make this okay? I woke up this morning feeling great, but something inside me knows that next year I won't be here to witness my newest grand baby's first thanksgiving. Or fight over the wishbone with Michael. Or enjoy the board games that have become a tradition at the end of the meal. How do I make something so profound all right?

I release my hold on her and look up to God for an answer. Please God help me make this better.

I begin to speak hoping my words will calm both her and me, "I'm sorry baby. I'm sorry you're struggling with this and that we haven't had this talk sooner." I take a deep breath, "At some point there will come that last time. I'm scared for that day too, but if we only dwell on the what if's or when then we miss out on the enjoyment of the here and now. I don't want you to miss everything that is going on in front of you because you're so lost in thought, and you lose focus on the important things. I said this to Michael and now it's your turn. It's okay to be sad for a while, but don't let it consume you. Live your life and share these moments with me. You don't want to look back one day and wish that you had been just a little more present."

"I'm sorry mama," Katie says, wiping her eyes. "I'm sorry for being distant. I didn't realize I was doing it until you just said something. I know I can't be selfish with you. You are the one person that I cannot be selfish with."

"I'm not sure I know what you mean there," I reply in confusion.

"Mama, you have been the most giving person I have ever met. You have sacrificed literally everything for your family. Growing up I saw the sacrifices you made. You sewed your old clothes that had holes in them so that Michael and I could have a new outfit for school. You didn't go on girl's weekend trips because I had a recital. You took a second job so that I had enough money to focus on my studies in college instead of working myself. Even this last round of chemo. I could see that you wanted to stop, but you kept going for us. You gifted us more time at the expense of feeling like crap. You kept going even though you wanted to stop. I cannot be more grateful for that. I know I need to make the sacrifice now and let you have this time. I'm just struggling with it."

"There is nothing that I wouldn't do for you, Michael, or your dad. Even Samuel, if I could have prevented it. My family is everything to me and I'm sure you know that in your own way from being a mama." I smile and continue, "I'm not going to start spewing out that the Lord doesn't give us more than what we can handle or anything. 'Cause even though He doesn't, and it still applies here, those words won't help. I think people have said it so many times that it's become a cliche and not helpful, but maybe lean a little bit more on Him and a little bit more on me. 'Cause I'm still your mama and I will be here for you always, even when I'm not."

Katie starts tearing up again and pulls me back into a hug.

"I didn't mean to make you start crying again baby girl. Promise me that you'll stop getting lost in thought. Enjoy the moments with me, please?" I begged her.

She sniffles and nods her head yes. "I just keep praying that God will give us a miracle. That He will heal you and all of this will be over soon."

"Baby girl, God gives us miracles every day. People think that He just sprinkles out the big ones like when Jesus walked among us. More often than not it is not the miracle that we pray for. Sometimes they are so small that we don't even realize what happened, but that's why we have to remain in the present. It's so that we can recognize the miracles when they come."

"You're right. I didn't think about it like that."

"I know I'm right. That's why I'm the mom," I say. A small smile forms on her face. I wipe a stray tear from her cheek with my thumb. "Better?"

She nods again.

"Good now let's get some fresh water in this sink because I think it got cold while we were standing around."

Katie drains the sink and starts to fill it again when Jason pops his head in. "Hey babe do you think we'll be starting dessert soon? The kids are getting antsy."

"Oh, the kids are huh?" Katie asks knowingly.

"Well, the kids and me and your dad and…. Look, are we doing dessert or not?" Jason quips.

Katie and I turned to look at each other and burst into laughter. A nice reprieve from the hard conversation we had just finished.

"The rest of the dishes can wait. Let's feed these starving hoodlums," I say to Katie, hitting her with a towel. We all chuckled and got the desserts out to serve.

Dessert is devoured although I only had a few small bites. The tradition of board games starts and is in full swing. Michael pouts as I dominate in our short version of monopoly.

The day finally ends at about nine pm when the mess is cleaned up and dishes are put away. There are a few I didn't get to, but I plan to take care of them tomorrow. I lock the front door and look back in the living room to find Carmel snoring on the couch with her paws in the air. Moose lay in my recliner making small barking noises in his sleep. I smile and shake my head as I head to the bathroom to get ready for bed.

    Today was a success. I had a wonderful day with my family. I was able to talk with Katie and it seems like everyone in my family is now on board with my decision. It was a good day. A great day. As I walk to my bedroom, I begin to struggle with the thought of at what cost?

CHAPTER 6

The next morning, I wake up with no energy to get out of bed. While I still feel my usual pain, I'm not used to wanting to stay in bed. I always made a slight judgment of others who would sleep past 8:30 in the morning. Knowing it was around that time is definitely out of character for me.

With my eyes closed I become aware of my surroundings. I can hear Wayne piddling around in the kitchen. I know he's trying to clean up the few dishes that I didn't get to last night. I wish I could be grateful for his assistance around the house, in reality I just want to scream at him to keep it down. It's unfair of me to feel that way especially after everything he has done for me so I keep my eyes shut in hopes that I can fall back asleep.

I feel the warmth of the sun on my face as it shows through the window. I consider rolling over to get back to sleep more quickly, but then I remember that the weather outside is anything but warm, so I start to feel grateful for this small blessing. As I lay in bed with absolutely no desire to get up, I finally drift back to sleep. The hopes of a beautiful dream are shattered as I relive the frightful day of getting my diagnosis.

I sat in the office of my primary care doctor. Dr McIntosh was a humble man. Tall and skinny with longer legs than the average person. I always imagined him playing basketball in school until he corrected me one day and said that tennis was his passion, aside from his family and little dog of course. I had profound respect for this man. He was always up front and to the point, but with empathy behind his words.

I came to him with complaints of nausea and losing weight. He ordered multiple tests, bloodwork of every letter and then a scope down my throat. At the time I thought it was a little over the top for just some pesky nausea. Well, and some stomach pain if I'm being completely honest. Once he had gotten all of the information, he asked us to come into the office to go over the results.

Wayne and I drove to my appointment and even got to Dr McIntosh's office early. Both of us seemed anxious as the good doctor would typically just give us a call to discuss a diagnosis and treatment. That wasn't the case this time. As soon as we entered the room, I knew something was horribly wrong. The look on his face had sympathy and regret written all over it. This wasn't going to go well.

We exchanged pleasantries with Dr McIntosh before he dove into talking about each test and blood work done. It felt like he was beating around the bush, and I just wanted to scream at him to tell me what was wrong with me. With a deep breath he said the dreaded 'C' word. The word that gets tossed around but is feared by everyone. For me, though, this wasn't just cancer, no, it was stage four cancer. It spread to multiple places in my body.

I sat in the gray chair of his office clenching the arm rests as if holding it tighter would make the diagnosis go away. My heart sank knowing that this was the same cancer that took my grandfather. I looked next to me to find Wayne's face pale, as if every drop of blood was gone from his face. I went into a twilight zone and felt mostly numb. My gut twisted into knots praying that the doctor was playing some sort of cruel joke, and he'd say "gotcha" with a wink and finger pistols.

Oh, if one could only be so lucky.

Dr McIntosh spoke with such tenderness and sadness in his eyes as he delivered the news. He went through several scenarios and options, one being the need to see a medical oncologist. He seemed fairly confident that chemotherapy was my best option. After a few rounds of chemotherapy, surgery would be set up to remove the rest of the tumors. So other doctors would be added to the mix, a surgeon as well as an oncologist. The thought made me nauseated. Previous experiences showed me that most surgeons were jerks with the worst bedside manner. Thinking about it though, if it helped cure my cancer then I would put up with the possibility of having a rude surgeon.

I thought further about doing chemotherapy and the side effects that came with it. I know medicine has come a long way, but I hated the idea of losing my chestnut-colored hair. It fell a little bit past my shoulders, and it took me forever to figure out how to style it. My go-to was to throw it up in a ponytail or a bun and move on with my day. I worked so hard to finally find an easy flattering way to style it. I felt vulgar for thinking of something so mundane as I played with a lock absentmindedly.

Wayne covered my hand with his and said, "it'll grow back Ellie. I don't care about your hair. I care about you."

I smiled through my tears and nodded. I would never get over how this wonderful man was able to read my mind as I was coming to terms with the idea of losing my hair.

"I guess I'll try some new hairstyles when it grows back," I say, trying to make light of the situation.

We talked more with Dr McIntosh and got the referral for an oncologist and a surgeon. The next steps were to make an appointment for the oncologist and set up chemotherapy as soon as possible.

The drive home was done in silence, even the radio was turned off. Both Wayne and I were stuck in our heads about the recent news. I wasn't sure what to say to him to give him any comfort as I'm sure he didn't know what to say to me. Anything said could be taken the wrong way. Do I make light of the situation and make a joke? That was my go-to, but that could possibly make him upset. Do I reassure him that everything is going to be all right? That seemed like a load of crap. Nothing that popped into my head to say seemed like the right thing, so I stayed silent as he did.

We pulled into the driveway, and I got out of the car not waiting for him to come around and open my door like he usually does. I always loved the small gesture, however, today I am so in my head that I didn't even think to stop and allow him to be a gentleman. The cancer already seems to be changing me.

I watched Wayne head to his beloved workshop with the dogs trailing after him. He needed some alone time, I guess. I sent up a prayer for strength to get through whatever was to come our way.

Before I knew it, I found myself in the kitchen, not sure how I even got there. I needed to bake something or do something. I just needed to focus on something other than the fact that I am now living full of cancer. I set the oven to 350 degrees and started pulling out the ingredients to bake a cake.

I turned to the refrigerator to pull out the eggs, milk, and butter and froze with my hand still on the handle.

Stuck to the refrigerator door with a magnet was an ultrasound picture of Michael's new baby. Michael and Josie broke the news last Sunday that they were expecting a sweet bundle of joy. She wasn't far along yet, only seven or so weeks, but the excitement carried through that night at dinner.

I walked in a daze to my bathroom and quickly shut the door. I could feel myself about to break and could not risk Wayne walking in on that. I needed to stay strong for him and our family.

As soon as the door shut, I locked it. My knees gave out. I sat on the floor with my breath caught in my chest. It was several moments before I could even take a breath. What came out of me next was choking sobs. I scrambled to the counter on my hands and knees to grab the towels sitting on the edge. In a swift and quick motion, I folded the towel to bury my face in it. And I screamed.

I screamed for the loss of the life that I had envisioned. I screamed for the frustration of knowing there was a possibility that I might not meet my new grandchild. I screamed so that the terror of knowing what I will go through does not eat me alive.

The thought of losing time with my family put a pain in my heart. It felt like thousands of tiny shards of glass were cutting me open and my heart was about to burst. I laid down on the floor of the bathroom. The cold from the tile was a welcoming numbness. Then I cried. I cried until there were no more tears that could be spilled out and then I cried some more.

The pain from my belly jolts me awake and out of my nightmare. I sit straight up in bed. The pain from the movement shoots through me causing me to cry out. Within seconds Wayne is throwing the door open and by my side. Michael follows quickly behind him. He stops short in the doorway, never fully entering the bedroom.

Wayne sits on the bed next to me and holds his hands out. His hands aren't touching me, it's as if he is afraid to touch me and make the pain worse.

"What's the matter? Where's the pain?" he asks frantically.

All I can do is hold my belly and rock back and forth in the bed to try to get the pain to stop.

"Everywhere," I cry.

Wayne looks at Michael in a panic. "Go get her meds," he says in a stern voice.

Michael leaves in a rush and is back within thirty seconds with my pain pill bottles and something to drink. I quickly take them from his hand and swallow the pills. I know taking them on an empty stomach will probably make me nauseous. I try not to think of that discomfort at the moment and focus on trying to get the pain to stop. Another problem for another time.

"What happened baby?" Wayne asks after a few minutes. My cries are now soft moans, and I am finally able to stop rocking. The pain changes from a sharp stabbing sensation to a dull ache. It feels like the knife is still in my stomach, but my body has gotten used to it.

I take a deep breath, trying to ignore the fact that even that causes me discomfort. "Just a bad dream. I think over sleeping made me miss my time to take the medicine."

Why? Why did I have to relive that fateful day? Why did those memories have to fill my mind with despair? Couldn't I have dreamt of something else? Something happy?

I have enough to worry and concern myself with, knowing that I will be leaving my family soon. The cancer will win and consume my body. I feel the pain be replaced with dread as it fills my soul.

Where are you God? Do you even see me? Do you even care?

I sit up in bed with my legs crossed, my back against the headboard. This position is starting to get uncomfortable. I began thinking about where I should move and how to make it to my recliner, anything to take my mind off of my nightmare. The more I think about it the more I don't think I can make it. There is no way that I'm going to be able to make it all the way to the living room.

How? After all this sleep, how am I still so exhausted?

"Ellie," Wayne says gently, interrupting my thoughts, "you haven't missed your medication time. You still had another forty-five minutes before it was available to take another pill."

I stared at him in shock. Another forty-five minutes? My mind races with the meaning of all of this. Increased pain, no energy or appetite and wanting to sleep. The signs are obvious. The cancer is progressing further since the treatment has stopped. Once again it is giving me a bigger middle finger. I close my eyes and send up a silent prayer for the strength I need to get through this day. Prayers for the pain to go away. Prayers that seem to go unanswered.

God, where are you?

No answer.

I nod my head at Wayne. Michael continues to stand leaning against the doorway with his arms crossed. I open my mouth to speak, but what comes out is a choked cry. I cover my face with my hands, and I begin to cry. I let the dam break with my tears. Knowing that my pain medication is no longer working is the straw that finally breaks the camel's back. I can't stay strong any longer. I want to be done. All of it.

"I can't do this. I can't do this. I can't do this," I repeat, more to myself than to anyone else. Wayne tries to rub my back like he always does to comfort me. I shrug him off. I don't want comfort at this moment. I want the pain to end. I'm done.

"I'm tired. I'm so freaking exhausted and tired of doing this. I'm tired of the pain. I'm tired of taking the medication. I'm tired of feeling sorry for myself. I can't do this anymore. I can't be strong anymore. I want this to end," I wail out. I look up to my husband who now looks at me with pity in his eyes. "Please help me make this stop."

Since the moment of my diagnosis my husband has never looked at me with pity. He has never once felt sorry for me or made me feel anything less than a strong woman.

"Please," I say again.

At this point I am begging. I have stayed strong for so long, but reliving the moment of my diagnosis did me in. I don't want to be constantly reminded that I'm not going to be here for much longer. I have never been one to even think about suicide, but if ending my life would end the pain, both emotional and physical, then end it I would.

Wayne sits looking at me dumbfounded, unsure of what to say. His eyes are glossy from tears welling up. Michael remains unmoving in the doorway. And then I see something shift in Wayne's face, he is no longer on the verge of tears. He looks as if months of built-up anger are about to burst forth. And it does.

"I don't know what you want me to do here, Eleanor!" His voice is stern, boisterous, and almost alarming. He doesn't call me Eleanor unless we are fighting, and I have not heard him talk like this in a very long time. I know that I am in trouble. Like the nuns scolding me as a little girl in the classroom for talking.

"I have been by your side for the last thirty-seven years. We have gone through some difficult times together and this is no different. You have been strong and have fought so hard. Now keep fighting!"

"Keep fighting? Are you kidding me? You want me to keep fighting with cancer pushing on all my nerves and causing excruciating pain?" I feel like my nerves are rattling and I am shaking. I have never felt like this before. Is it pain related?

Michael speaks up for the first time since entering the room. "Come on mom, are you really going to play…"

"The cancer card? You're damn right I am because I'm the one living with the damn cancer," I snapped at him, effectively cutting him off from his question. I am acting like a child at this point. I can't seem to help myself.

Behind Michael is a figure of a man. I can't make out who it is. Jason maybe? Why is he here? Did Katie ask him to come? Wayne squeezes my hand pulling my attention to him.

"You are my wife. My everything. I have loved you with more than I ever thought possible in a man's life. I have seen you in your brightest moments and now in your darkest of times. And I love you more still. You are asking the impossible of me. You are asking me to sever our ties together. The day you leave me is the day I walk around with a knife in my heart for the rest of my time here on this earth. I said yes to hospice. I said yes to getting you the medicine you need to be comfortable, but here and now Ellie, I am telling you no to dying. It is not time. And I am not ready to let you go. So, yes, fight. Fight with whatever strength you need to find because dammit I am not ready to lose my wife. I am not ready to watch them put you six feet in the ground and see dirt poured over your casket. I need you to hold on because I'm not ready."

Wayne and I continued to stare at each other. He is a little blurry from the tears in my eyes that refuse to spill over. He doesn't know what he is asking of me. I understand why he is, and I will of course do as he asks for his sake, but he doesn't understand the continual pain that I have. That I will continue to suffer knowing that it is only going to increase.

I hear someone clear their voice from the hallway. Michael moves aside to reveal Elisha behind him. Josie must have let her in during our heated conversation. I am embarrassed that she overheard what we were talking about. My breathing picks up and I feel like I am on the verge of uncontrollably crying again.

"Hi Ellie," she says in a sweet voice. "What's been going on this morning?"

I can't talk. I don't even think coherent words will come out of my mouth if I try. I just sit there breathing quickly.

"She had a great day yesterday, but today she woke up late, screaming in pain, and she's spouting off nonsense about wanting everything to end." Wayne says with anger and a hint of fear in his voice.

"Elisha, I have never seen my mom like this. What's going on?" Michael asks.

"You know what, how about we start by getting new scenery and we will take it from there. Do you think you could walk to your recliner if I helped you?" Elisha asks gently, turning from Michael's direction to mine.

Wayne stands from our bed and leaves the room without a word. Michael watches me intently from the doorway.

I think about my pain and realize that it has improved somewhat. My nerves are still shaky, and I don't think I can make it without her help. I nod my head fervently. She helps me to the side of the bed. I sit there for a moment before standing up. Elisha is right in front of me making sure I don't fall.

"Just get your bearings about you and then we'll take a step forward," she says. She holds my hands as I take a few steps forward and she takes the same amount backwards. She has become my makeshift walker.

We walk to the living room slowly and toward my recliner. I am taking some deep and shaky breaths. It continues to feel like I am not getting enough air throughout our short walk to my chair. I turn and sit down as Josie brings over my favorite blanket to place on my lap.

Elisha grabs her bag from the front foyer area and turns to Wayne and Michael. "Could you give us a few moments? I'm going to do my assessment and take some vitals."

Wayne walks out the back door towards his shed once again without uttering a single word. Michael ushers Josie into the kitchen to give Elisha and I some privacy.

"Wait," I say, "where's Jason?"

Michael stops just before entering the kitchen and looks at me with confusion. "What do you mean? Jason is at home with the kids. Daycare is closed today because of Thanksgiving."

"I thought I saw him in the hallway earlier," I say perplexed.

"That may have been Josie you saw," he replies. He leaves without saying another word.

That couldn't have been Josie, I think to myself. There is no mistaking that giant pregnant belly. This was a figure of a man that I saw. The same figure that was peeking out the window the first day that Elisha visited and was in the hallway yesterday when I was talking to Katie.

I have already made a fool of myself this morning, I don't want everyone to know that I'm possibly seeing a person that is not there. They will lock me up and throw away the key for sure.

Elisha settles into the chair that has now become hers on the day of her visits. She gets her computer out to chart and all of the necessary items to take my vitals and listen to my heart.

"Tell me what happened this morning," she says as she begins her assessment.

I go through the events of the morning starting with the dream I had and up to the point when she walked in the room.

"What medicine have you taken this morning?"

"Just my pain pill. And Wayne said it was about forty-five minutes before I should have taken it," I confess.

"Have you taken any anxiety medication?" Elisha asks.

"No, all of it is still in the bag on the counter, unopened. We haven't touched it."

"Okay, I think it would be best if you took some of the Ativan. You are having high anxiety right now and it is probably from both the dream you had and the pain you are in. That's possibly why you are acting so out of character and shaky," Elisha explains.

It all makes sense now. I was having my emotions rush over me, and I started crying and spurting things out before I could stop them. It was as if there was no filter on my mouth.

"Would you be okay trying it?" she asks. "It's a low dose, but it will help take the edge off."

I nod my head, hating the feelings that I'm having at this moment. Elisha leaves my side to go grab the medicine. She returns with Michael following closely behind. Josie comes too. She stops just before entering the room completely. She has one hand on her belly and one on the wall.

Michael sees the concern in my eyes as I look at her. "It's Braxton-Hicks again. She's been having this off and on all morning."

Elisha gives him a questioning look then turns her attention back to me. "Okay so you're taking just one tablet of the Ativan. That's only 0.5 milligrams. It will help you relax a little bit."

"Is anxiety medication really necessary? My mom has never had anxiety in her life." Michael asks, now crouching down beside my chair. I take the pill willingly, hoping anything will help me feel better at this point.

"Yes, we use it in all of our patients regardless if they have a history of anxiety or not. Even though Ms. Ellie has never had anxiety before, what she is going through is incredibly stressful for both her mind and her body. Anxiety and pain go hand in hand. When one increases so will the other and if you don't get it under control then the pain can become severe and then we're playing catch up. It is possible that Ativan will need to start being utilized with her pain medication in order to have effective management. Also, since her current medication is no longer effective, I'd like to call my doctor and see what else we can try. It could be something as simple as increasing her current pain pills or doing something different like adding a fentanyl patch."

Michael shakes his head in an exaggerated manner. "No absolutely not, there has to be something else."

"I can call my nurse practitioner and ask her to come by for a visit and consultation if that would make you feel more comfortable," Elisha suggests.

Michael is about to answer when we hear a strange noise coming from the entryway of the living room and kitchen. Josie continues to hold her belly with one hand and the wall with the other. She is looking down at the floor and slowly brings her head up to look at us in the living room.

"I think my water just broke," she says.

Sure enough, a large puddle of fluid is at her feet. Silly of me, but all I can think about is how thankful I am that it is at least on the hardwood floors and not the carpet. That would never come out.

Everyone springs into action, except me who is stuck in my recliner. I am no good physically. At least I can still bark some orders at people. Michael goes to his wife who starts screaming at the first hard contraction.

"Elisha, there's towels in the hallway closet. Go get them and put them on the couch folded up," I ordered.

Elisha does as she is told and places a couple of towels on the couch. Michael and Elisha help get Josie to the couch and into a somewhat comfortable position. As comfortable as a laboring mom can be in.

"Michael, go get your father. He's probably in his work shed," I state. He leaves in an instant, running out the back door. I look over at Josie who is holding onto Elisha's hand for dear life. Both Elisha and Josie look terrified.

"Josie just breathe, okay? You're doing great," I say in a calm voice. I feel myself snap out of the funk I was in earlier and become more comfortable and like myself. Though I don't think the Ativan works that quickly.

"How far apart are your contractions?" I ask.

"About every seven or eight minutes. I swear I thought these were Braxton-Hicks," she replies, continuing to breathe through pursed lips.

"Honey, if they are consistent like that then that means you're in labor," I tell her. "Elisha, are you okay?" I ask, looking at the frightened nurse.

"Yeah," she says, also through pursed lips. "There's a reason I am a hospice nurse. I got nauseated during my labor and delivery rotation in nursing school. I knew that laboring moms were not going to be my thing. No offense," Elisha says to Josie.

"None taken," Josie tells her.

Michael and Wayne enter the room in a panic. My son moves to the side of Josie that is unoccupied and grabs her hand.

"What do we do? Should we call 911?" he asks, frantically.

"Did all those Lamaze classes you both took go out the window?" I joke. "You have time. She's only having contractions every seven to eight minutes. It's only forty-five minutes to your hospital and this is your first baby, you have time. Take the towels and lay them down on the passenger seat and drive carefully to the hospital."

"Glad to see you're more like yourself," Wayne says.

"Are your bags packed?" I asked Michael, ignoring Wayne's comment.

"Yes, I made Michael pack the car and install the car seat when I hit thirty-six weeks," Josie answers, amping up for another contraction to start.

"Michael, after this next contraction help Josie to the car and then drive her to the hospital. Use the hands-free connection to call the hospital to let them know you're on your way," I instruct.

This contraction must have been worse than previous ones because she is squeezing Elisha and Michael's hands until they are white. All three are yelling from pain. It is almost comical, like out of a Hollywood movie. After about a minute Josie can relax enough to stand up and walk to the car. They leave with a promise to call later.

Elisha turns her attention back to Wayne and me. The room is now eerily quiet after all the commotion from this morning. Wayne moves to sit in his recliner. I can tell he is still angry from earlier by his demeanor towards me. I don't blame him. It was not right of me to ask for his help in ending my life. Although now I know that was a feeling of anxiety and I can get a better handle on it. I make a mental note to take the medications before it gets too far.

Elisha sits down next to me and updates Wayne on my condition and that I had an anxiety attack this morning brought on by the pain and the dream I had. Once the realization sets in of what prompted my uncharacteristic behavior Wayne seems to relax a little more.

"I'd like to discuss different pain medications that may be suited for Ms. Ellie's symptoms, but Michael definitely seemed skeptical about starting something else. I'd like to have my nurse practitioner come by for a visit, if that's okay, to help give some perspective on the medicine," Elisha reports.

"Yeah, I think that would be okay," Wayne says.

"Great, let me step out and I'll give her a call. I'll let you know when she can come out."

Elisha stands and makes her way to the front door. I look over at Wayne as she closes the door behind her. He is in his stoic mood, unbending and unwavering in being the first to break the silence. He stares out into nothingness, lost in thought as he rocks his chair back and forth. I know that I have to be the one to speak up first. I also know that I am in the wrong here. I embarrassed myself, but it's still hard to admit that I'm sorry because at the same time I am desperately wanting this pain to end. How much more am I going to have to endure before I break for good, and I become a shell of the woman I once was?

I think back to that moment in the hospital, my butt showing off all its glory to the world and looking in the mirror at the sad little cancer patient. The woman who was not me but is me at the same time. I remember making the decision of being strong, of giving the cancer a big middle finger and powering through this part of my journey as a proud and confident woman. The woman that Wayne married.

However, the cancer continues to beat me down, berate me, and tell me that I am nothing more than an empty vessel for it to consume. I send up another prayer for calmness in my current storm and for hope that this will end soon. Although I think I will keep that prayer between me and God.

I look over to Wayne who still seems to be lost in thought. I can hear mumblings from Elisha on the front porch and know that I need to clear the air with Wayne before she walks back inside. I clear my throat a little and Wayne looks at me hesitantly.

"I'm sorry," I say, struggling, "I don't know what else to say but sorry. I'm ashamed of what I said, and it was unfair of me to talk to you like that."

The expression on his face is one of relief and love as he says, "It's okay, Ellie. I understand now that you're going to have anxiety, and we can start to work through that together. Maybe taking this Ativan will help. I'm still not ready to lose you. I don't think I'll ever be ready."

"You're right. And hopefully we will know the signs of anxiety and take the medication before it gets too bad," I reply.

Wayne lets out a huff, "wait a minute, did you just say that I was right about something? Can I get that in writing?"

I smiled knowing that the small joke meant the end to our argument. After a few more minutes Elisha walks back into our house. "So, my nurse practitioner Jeane has a full day today, but she will be able to see you on Monday to discuss the medications. Until then I recommend that you take the Ativan every two hours as you need it. You can take it with your pain meds and that will hopefully give the relief you need. I'm on call this weekend so if you need anything, the medicine is not working or whatever, I want you to call me."

"We will. I promise," I assure. I can feel the Ativan kicking in now and the nerves that were still rattling calming down. I watch Elisha pack up her things after sanitizing them. She gives us one more stern reminder to call her before heading out the front door.

I look at Wayne with sorrow knowing that I put him through hell this morning. He looks back at me with the same look he always did after a fight. The 'it's okay and I'm sorry too' look. I sit back in my recliner feeling marginally better than when I woke up and now have the anticipation of wondering if I will have a new grandson or a granddaughter.

CHAPTER 7

Monday morning could not have come quick enough. The weekend was full of pain, anxiety, and general feelings of being uncomfortable. I continued with my regular medication with the exception of adding the Ativan to help with the pain. It was making the pain at the very least tolerable. Unfortunately, I could feel the moment when the medication started to wear off and the pain would increase again. It was a vicious cycle that I was unable to break. God forbid I turned a certain way or even coughed; that sent my pain shooting like a lightning bolt.

    I wait with anticipation for the nurse practitioner to make her visit as I sit in my once very comfortable recliner. It holds no enjoyment for me now. My favorite holiday blanket drapes across my lap as I look out the window. I watch as the birds play in the bird feeders that Wayne refilled yesterday. I sit back thinking about how this once gave me immense joy, to watch the birds and see new ones arrive. Today, I don't take any solace in my recliner or my bird feeders. It feels like this has become my prison with an open door.

That unanswered question remains, God where are you? I need you.

I find it interesting how my mood has shifted from a happy go-lucky attitude with starting hospice to a now very dull and depressed one. My once enjoyable moments turn sour because I know that I won't be able to take part like I once did due to my pain. The words I used to encourage Katie have fallen deaf to my own ears. I am trapped in my head and in my body. Right now, it is not a good place to be.

The weekend after Thanksgiving usually begins all of my holiday traditions. It starts by putting out all of the Christmas decorations while listening to Christmas music. Katie, Jason, and the kids were able to come over to help with the Christmas tree and the rest of the decor. I was stuck in my chair due to my pain. I attempted to help by keeping up conversations from my chair, but it lacked the appeal of actually being a part of the decorating.

Michael had called several times to see how the festivities were going. He was unwilling to leave his wife and new daughter in the hospital by themselves, not that I blamed him.

Josie labored for another twelve hours before needing an emergency C-section because the baby's heart rate had dropped. I can still hear Michael's panicked voice on the phone as he told us the doctors were rushing Josie back to the operating room. I wish I could have been there to give him some sort of support.

It didn't take long for the doctors to get in and get their baby out safely. A baby girl was placed in their arms. A picture of the new parents in scrub caps and a crying baby now occupies the screensaver on my phone. Michael seems to be very infatuated with his new baby girl as he has flooded my phone with pictures. I viewed those multiple times over the weekend. Her chubby cheeks remind me so much of Michael when he was a baby. The beautiful blue in her eyes is mesmerizing. She will definitely have Michael wrapped around her little finger.

They are keeping her name a secret. They want it to be a surprise and plan to bring her by later today so that I can meet her in person. I feel as if this is the only thing I have to look forward to, the only hope of giving me some joy at least.

While the others put the tree together McKenna and Nathan kept me company. We went through the story behind each ornament before putting it on the tree. My mom started making a habit of buying a Christmas ornament that represented what happened each year. It's a tradition that I carried along to my kids.

The pre-lit Christmas tree went up without too much effort right next to the fireplace. A hallmark Christmas movie played on the screen before me as my family continued going through each box with care and talking about memories. This made me both happy and sad as I know I won't be a part of this next year.

As the indoor decorations were wrapping up, Wayne and Jason set out to put up the yard decorations. We really didn't have anyone driving by to see them, but that never stopped me from buying new ones over the years. I used to love driving up my driveway and seeing all the twinkling lights.

This year Katie had surprised me with a light up cow for the front yard in hopes of cheering me up. The smile lasted for about twenty minutes until I realized that I wasn't going to be able to walk outside to see it without extreme pain starting. Furthermore, it's not like I really had anywhere to be to drive home and see it shining through the darkness.

Like I said, my recliner has become my prison with an open door. I watched as everyone set up this thing or that. I wooed and awed at right times, but I really wanted to be a part of it, and I couldn't. It was one of the most frustrating things I have had to deal with yet.

I continue watching the birds play around the bird feeders when I notice a blue sedan pulling down our driveway. A feeling of hope swims through me as I know the only expecting visitor this early in the day is the nurse practitioner. I take a sip of my peppermint mocha iced coffee sitting on my bedside table. I had hoped that the holiday creamer for my coffee would put me in a better mood for the provider, but so far, I've had no such luck.

I turn towards Wayne to let him know that someone has arrived. He didn't need me to tell him. He was already getting up from his chair to meet her at the door. I guess he was looking out the window like I was.

If Elisha hadn't informed me that she was a nurse practitioner I would have believed this was a doctor making a home visit. In my mind I pictured a young arrogant nurse, fresh out of graduate school. That couldn't be further from the truth. She appears to be a middle-aged woman, average height and is wearing what seems like comfortable shoes and black slacks. A blue blouse is hidden behind her white coat and instead of being drenched in starch, like Dr Jenkins', it seems worn and well loved. She walks with confidence, not at all like the arrogant 'I know better than you' walk that other physicians seem to have.

Wayne walks out onto the front porch to meet our guest. I can hear words being spoken; however, it is more than just exchanging simple pleasantries. Feelings of agitation and annoyance start to creep in. What conversation needed to be had without me? She's here to see me, isn't she?

A few moments later Wayne welcomes her into our home. I give both the nurse practitioner and my husband a questioning look as she enters the living room. Wayne takes her coat and gently places it on the armchair. She strides over to me and holds out her hand for me to shake. I take it willingly as she introduces herself.

"Good morning. My name is Jeane, did Elisha tell you I would be stopping by today?" she asks.

"Yes, she did," I reply, as I stare at her beautiful auburn hair and green eyes. The light freckles on her face remind me a little of Katie's when she was a young girl. Unfortunately, Katie's freckles seem to have faded over the years where Jeane's seemed to have stayed. I start to wonder if her freckles came out more during the warmer months.

"I hear that we are having some issues with pain and that our medication is no longer working. Is that correct?" she asks as she gets herself situated on the chair that is usually occupied by Elisha.

Wayne answers before I have a chance to say anything, and my annoyance comes crawling back. The weekend was stifling while the Christmas decorations were being put up. I could feel the lingering tension from our argument Friday morning throughout Saturday and Sunday. He never said anything more about it, but I could tell it weighed on his mind. I'm guessing he is anxious at the moment hoping this nurse practitioner will give me a magic pill that will make everything better.

"Yes, she has been taking the medication around the clock when it becomes available again. We're currently taking oxycodone every four hours as needed with her oxycontin twice a day as scheduled. And Friday we had to start adding the Ativan to her as needed pills," Wayne answers her.

To Jeane's credit she continues to look at me as Wayne speaks. It makes me feel good knowing that she is wanting to hear my response and have it come straight from the source. Her presence begins to feel more calming to me now.

"Ok, well let's talk about that. What medicine you have tried, what's working and what isn't," she says.

"Oh, my son wants to be a part of this conversation. Are you okay if I call him? He's still stuck at the hospital," Wayne asks before we could get started.

"Absolutely. Is everything okay?" Jeane asks with concern, turning her gaze to look at my husband who is now fumbling with his phone to call Michael.

I answer for Wayne, "yes. Our son, Michael, and daughter-in-law just had a beautiful baby girl. They're supposed to be discharged later today."

Jeane responds with that all too familiar 'awe' that people say after hearing about the birth of a child. She bends over in the chair to grab some papers out of her bag sitting on the floor. I can see my name written across one of the folders she has pulled out. She gestures to the bedside table as if to ask if she can use it. I nod and she pulls it closer to her.

"What did they name the baby?" she asks as she gets herself settled again.

"Not sure. They are bringing her by after they leave the hospital. They said her name is a surprise and I'll find out when I get to hold her for the first time," I replied. My voice has little emotion to it and I'm not sure if it is because of being uncomfortable or the anticipation of starting a new drug and not knowing how it's going to affect me. I know I should be happy and excited. I have a new granddaughter for goodness' sake, but I just don't have the energy at the moment.

Wayne finally gets Michael out on speaker phone and places the phone on the bedside table so that he will be able to hear Jeane clearly.

"Hello?" Michael calls out.

"Hi, good morning, Michael. This is Jeane, I'm the nurse practitioner. I hear congratulations are in order on your baby girl," Jeane says with a smile even though Michael isn't able to see her.

"Yeah, thank you," Michael answers hesitantly. I guess he wasn't expecting pleasantries from her.

"We're just getting started so you haven't missed anything" she reports to Michael.

He sighs in relief, "thank you. I was starting to get worried that mom was going to just say yes to any drug without asking some questions first."

"I'm right here and I know better than that," I say in an irritated tone. I know I'm not making a great first impression on Jeane and I hope that she will forgive my rudeness.

"I'm sorry mom. You've just been in a lot of pain lately and I've seen people just say yes to anything to make the pain stop."

Jeane has a look of confusion on her face when Wayne explains that Michael was in the Navy, and he'd seen many sailors get hurt. The one that always sticks out in my mind was an accident with his buddy, Jack, who had been working on the wing of an F-18. Somehow a three-hundred-pound piece of metal came off the hinges and fell. Jack instinctively held out his arms to prevent it from falling while the other crew members stepped away. Jack's arm was pinned under it crushing the bone.

He was unfortunately medically discharged from the Navy. He went through multiple surgeries to correct the bone and in the meantime had gotten addicted to painkillers. Due to his addiction, he was unable to hold any sort of a job and turned to heroin because it was cheaper. About three years after the incident, he overdosed on the drugs and died.

I know Michael is concerned about me and must be thinking about all of those friends he lost due to addiction to drugs. I don't know how to show him that that would not be my story? That I hate taking these drugs and many times feel disgusted with myself? My face remains calm as Jeane starts speaking again, but inside I am screaming, desperate for help.

"So, I looked at the medication that Eleanor has been on and the notes from the nurses. I've also taken a look at the scans and doctor's notes. The first thing I want to know is what is going on with your pain? What does it feel like and then how does the medication help or not help?" she starts.

I clear my throat and begin telling her all there is to know about the familiar torment that has consumed my life.

"I have a general ache all over my body. It is a constant pain that never goes below a three out of ten. By the time my oxycodone becomes available my pain level is a seven or higher. God, forbid I turn a certain way or have a coughing fit; my level will suddenly jump to a ten and it is difficult to get it to come down without the use of medication. If the pain is high enough then nausea begins to creep in and I lose any desire to eat something, if I had the desire at all. Once the nausea is there I won't eat or drink anything and I start getting a headache from not drinking which distracts me from the pain in my body, but it is sometimes worse than my body aches."

"Eleanor how often are you feeling this pain?" she asks while writing down my response. This almost feels like a therapy session and maybe at the moment it is what I need. All that's missing is a leather couch for me to lay down on and a picture of Sigmond Freud hanging in the corner.

"From the time I wake up to the time I close my eyes. I never get the relief I need. Sometimes the pain will get so bad while I'm sleeping that it will wake me up and I have to watch the clock before I can take the pain pill that sits on my nightstand."

"OK. What non-pharmacological interventions have you tried?" she inquires.

"I'm not sure what you mean?"

"Oh, sorry. I mean what have you tried that's not medicine? Like music, warm baths, massage, or distraction."

I think for a moment before responding, "mainly trying to reposition myself until I find a comfortable position and just taking deep breaths, but that doesn't seem to be working effectively anymore." I want to laugh at the thought of using music as a way of relieving my pain.

I look over at Wayne and then down to the phone as if Michael's face would magically appear on the screen. I'm surprised a little at the silence coming from the two most important men in my life. I guess this is the first time that I have ever openly talked about the pain that I endure on a day-to-day basis, and they are soaking in this new information. Wayne's eyes are glistening with fresh tears. He holds them at bay, not allowing them to spill over.

"How much are you eating?" Jeane presses on.

"Not much of anything. I take a few bites of each meal and try to push myself to eat more, but sometimes even the thought of putting something in my mouth makes me want to dry heave. I have tried those Ensure shakes for the calories, but something about them just doesn't sit well with my belly. I'm trying to eat healthy foods, but I keep leaning more towards junk food," I answered her truthfully.

I hear Wayne clear his throat as if choking back a sob trying to come through. I turn my attention to him and hate to see that pity is once again in his eyes. I never wanted his pity. I just want his strength and to also, maybe, give me the benefit of the doubt.

"I'm so sorry Ellie. I had no idea it was this bad," Wayne says. He sees my daily activity and struggles. It is one thing, I guess, to see it and another to *see* it. He gets up out of his recliner and crouches down at my side. He grabs my hand and kisses the back of it. "I have watched you each day and I knew the pain was getting worse, but I never thought it was this bad. Now I understand better what happened Friday morning."

I can hear a small sniffle coming through the phone. I feel good knowing that Wayne and Michael are aware of my pain and what I am going through. I don't think they will ever truly know, but at least this is a start. My mind quickly drifts to the thought of my grandpa. Knowing he passed away from the same cancer that I have makes me question if this is the type of pain he went through. If it is, he never lets on.

I look over at Jeane who is sitting quietly in her chair watching us. She has a very calming demeanor, and her presence continues to be comforting as I talk about my pain. We have only scratched the surface of my physical pain and haven't even touched on the emotional one. I'm not quite sure I am ready to talk about that or for Wayne and Michael to hear about it. Thankfully, Jeane speaks, moving the conversation away from my fears.

"Okay, so I'd like to propose a couple different options. First, I'd like to start you on Mirtazapine or Remeron as it is sometimes called. This is an anti-depression medication, but it is also used to help as an appetite stimulant. Is this something you're open to?" Jeane asks me.

"Yeah, if it will help me be able to eat more then I'm willing to give it a shot," I reported to her.

"Okay, I will get that ordered. So, I want to give you some more education on your decreased appetite before I move on to the pain medications."

I nod my head for her to continue and Wayne and Michael both stay silent.

"One of the first signs that the body is shutting down is a decreased appetite. You don't feel like eating, sometimes the thought of food can make you nauseated and if you do eat it is in small amounts before you get full. Sometimes what tastes good one day may taste gross the next day. Sometimes things can even have a metallic type of taste and that's why many people lean towards eating more sweets. It sounds like you are already experiencing a lot of this."

I nod my head as she goes on, "if you push yourself to eat because you feel like you should or to please your loved ones then you are doing more harm than good. You can have increased pain from eating the food or have projectile vomiting and then you just wasted all the calories you did take in. Your body is not able to properly absorb the nutrition, so when your body is telling you that you are done then you are done. Listen to your body because it will tell you exactly what you need. The Mirtazapine will only go so far to help. It can make people tired, so we recommend taking it at bedtime. Does this all make sense?"

It's almost comical how insightful Jeane is and how much of what she is saying is taking place in my life. It all makes sense now as I think back about my eating habits over the last several weeks. I am relieved to know it's not just from the pain or me going crazy. I nod my head at her in acknowledgment to her question. Michael chimes in over the phone for the first time.

"How long before this medicine starts to work?" He asks.

"Generally, about two weeks. It helps some patients but doesn't help others depending on where they are in the process. It is worth giving it a try in hopes that her quality of eating will improve. Think about your mom as the queen of all beings and you are her mighty peasants. Whatever your mom wants, she gets. So, if she wants ice cream for breakfast then it is calories at this point and have the biggest bowl you would like to enjoy," Jeane says with a small grin on her face.

I gave a little chuckle, "hear that boys? I am the queen of all. I always knew it, but now it is decreed."

Jeane's acknowledgment of my discomfort and plan thus far seems to bring me out of the funk that I'm in. I am glad to know that it is not all in my head and having my discomfort recognized and confirmed gives me a sense of relief. I still have my pain, nothing has changed about that yet, but this is a step in the right direction for me.

Wayne joins in on the playful medieval way of speaking.

"Aye my queen and we, your mighty knights shall serve you faithfully," Wayne chimes with a tilt of his head and a twinkle in his eyes. He places his hand on my cheek, and I relish the feel of it. For a minute I forget that Jeane is sitting next to me and that Michael is on the phone. The rustling of the papers on the bedside table pulls me back into the room.

"Next, let's talk about your pain," she continues trying to get us back on track.

For the briefest of moments all I can hear is the disturbing silence that surrounds us. It is as if Michael, Wayne, and I are holding our breaths to hear what she has to say next.

"The Ativan with the oxycodone was a good solution, but it still does not seem to be as effective as it could be. The long-acting medication, oxycontin, is no longer effective either. You have been on this medicine for the last eight months and I suspect that your body has built up a tolerance to it as well as increasing tumor markers. I would like to recommend increasing the dosage of oxycodone. Continue to take the Ativan with it as it will help the medication work better. I'd like you to start utilizing the Roxanol, or liquid morphine, for when your pain is severe. Think about those moments that you turn a certain way, and your pain jumps to a ten, that is when you should take the Roxanol. When calculated out the morphine and oxycodone it is the same dosage. The difference is that the morphine will act quicker. Does this so far make sense to you?"

"Yes, it does. I haven't tried the Roxanol yet, but it's worth a shot when my pain is up at a ten," I reply.

"Will she be able to take the oxycodone and the morphine? Aren't they both as needed?" Wayne asks. His hand is now laying over top of mine and it feels so good to have this comfort back instead of the tension from the weekend.

"Yes, she can. The oxycodone will take about thirty to forty-five minutes to become effective, but the Roxanol will only take about ten to fifteen minutes. It works quickly to help get the pain under control and then gets out of her system quickly so utilizing both is okay. Now if she is needing the Roxanol like every two hours then that would be when you call the hotline so we can have a nurse come out and assess everything."

I think that gave the reassurance we all needed in order to move forward with ease. That is until she drops a bombshell that is not going to go over well with Michael.

"I would also like to change her long-acting pain medication from oxycontin to a fentanyl patch," Jeane says as calmly as she could. She must have talked with Elisha about Michael's outburst the first day she was here because I could hear the slight hesitation in her voice, and she looked down at the phone anticipating Michael's reaction.

Over the phone I can hear Michael choking on whatever drink he was taking a sip from. Wayne sat back as if her words had the power to knock him flat on his butt. I sit staring at her with no uneasiness in my face. I am ready for this fentanyl patch. I say bring it on, anything to help with this pain, but Jeane is going to have one hell of a time trying to convince my son and husband of that.

Michael never really confided in me about some of the things he saw with sailors and their addictions. He was most likely trying to save me from knowing that horror. I do know that he spoke to Wayne multiple times about it over the years. Wayne kept the discussions he had with Michael confidential. Neither of them could hide what happened to Jack from me. We all went to his funeral. Even though Michael never shared any stories with me and Wayne kept his lips sealed, I could imagine some of the worst.

"No! Absolutely not! We are not starting that shit!" Michael yelled through the phone, the ire in his tone clear to hear.

"Michael Jerome, watch your language!" Wayne exclaims as he looks down at the phone angrily. "We are not going to have another outburst like you did to poor Elisha."

I could hear Michael huffing out a breath. I continue where Wayne left off. I make sure to keep my voice low and motherly as I say, "Michael, you promised me that when the time came to talk about increasing my pain medications that you would listen with an open mind. This is that time, son."

"Mom, I'm worried about you becoming a drug addict like Jack. And Fentanyl? Isn't that what is killing everyone on the streets? So, why are they wanting to give it to you?"

I love my son so much for wanting to protect me. It seems like the tables have turned and he is the one trying to slay all of my dragons. If only it were that easy. I look from the phone to Jeane who continues to sit calmly in her chair as if Michael's outburst and accusations didn't phase her at all. My respect for this woman has grown even higher, and it is already pretty high. She begins explaining the reasons behind starting the Fentanyl patch.

"Yes, Fentanyl is on the streets, and it has a bad reputation because it is being misused and the dosages are much higher than those that are utilized in the patches. A licensed provider also closely monitors the patches. The patch will allow the medication to be absorbed through subcutaneous fat slowly over three days. On the streets people are getting a stronger dose all at once. Many times, those that are addicted to drugs are also misusing them for the simple purpose of wanting to escape the reality they live in. Your mother is safely using these opioids to assist in pain management which is also closely monitored by the providers. If there was concern about any misuse of the medications, then this would be a very different conversation. However, your mom is not going to become an addict by taking these medications. If I were worried about that then I would see her taking much higher doses than what she is currently taking."

"So, there's no chance that my mom is going to become an addict?" Michael asks.

"There's no chance that your mom will become an addict," Jeane replies, once again calm as a cucumber.

I can hear Michael let out a breath he was holding and asks, "Can you go back to the other thing you said about increased tumor markers? How do you know they are increasing?"

"In reality we don't. We aren't doing any scans to show where the tumors are or how they have progressed. Keep in mind though that we have stopped all treatment trying to suppress the tumors from growing. She is having increased pain and weakness. All of this is suspicion at this point, but it is likely that the tumors have grown and will continue to grow making her pain worse," Jeane states.

"That makes sense to me," Wayne says. "I'm so sorry Ellie."

I look over at him to see that his once glistening eyes are now spilling over with tears. I know this is bringing things into perspective for him from this past weekend. I know that I am a 'sissy' when it comes to pain, he made a comment or two when I was pregnant, and I suggested I wanted to try having a natural birth for our kids instead of getting an epidural. This conversation, however, has brought to light that I am not just a wuss, that my pain is real, my struggle is real, and I need more help.

Not wanting to waste anymore of this precious woman's time I ask, "so what happens next?"

Jeane gives me a smile and reports, "I will put in the order for the Mirtazapine, increased Oxycodone dose and the Fentanyl patch now. The pharmacy should deliver the medications to you this evening. Take the Oxycodone as you have been, but with the Ativan for anxiety if you need it. Take the Roxanol for the high pain levels. Take the Mirtazapine at bedtime starting tonight when you get the medication. The Fentanyl patch will go on the fatty part of your arm, and it will start working about twelve hours after you place it on. You'll change arms every three days and rotate the sites. I had everything printed out for you with the anticipation that we would start these medications today."

She hands me some papers with the information about the medications on them. I begin feeling slightly overwhelmed with excitement that my pain is about to be more managed.

Jeane stays a few moments longer and talks with Michael over the phone, making sure to answer all of his questions. I tune them out and look out the window. It didn't give me comfort this morning watching the birds play at the feeders, but their little chirps fill my ears with happy sounds.

I take a deep breath with hope. Hope that maybe tomorrow I can wake up with renewed energy. There is a plan in place, and I feel ten times lighter now than when the day began. As I go through each phase of hospice it seems the cancer wants to pull me down into a crippling depression, but learning from these hospice professionals and relying on them always pulls me back from the edge.

I force myself to shake off the depression trying to creep its way into my mind and heart. There may be things that I am no longer able to do, like decorate my house for Christmas, but why let that taint my memories? I want to leave behind a lasting memory with my family, not the depressing shell of a woman that I have been over the last few days.

I silently pray to God once again to fill my mind and heart with peace so that I can create lasting memories with my family. I beg God to answer this prayer. I have felt lost without Him the last few days. For now, I just have to wait for the medications to arrive.

Michael, Wayne, and I tell our goodbyes to Jeane as she walks out the front door and to her car. God has sent me an angel today. I think it is slightly silly that even though nothing has changed at the present time I am beginning to feel better and more like myself. I have Jeane to thank for that, for giving me the knowledge that my pain is real, but that I am not going to become an addict on drugs. The thought that help is just on the horizon, and it is coming brings on bluer skies and happier days.

Later in the day I sit on the couch holding my beautiful new granddaughter. Michael and Josie were discharged soon after our conversation ended with Jeane. Her words and affirmation to Michael that my situation is nothing like the friends he knew helped him jump on board with the idea of starting stronger medications. I will be forever grateful and in her debt because of that.

Michael and Josie drove straight to our house after leaving the hospital with their baby girl in tow. Josie pulled her out of the car seat and wrapped her in a purple swaddling blanket. She handed her to me with the name Samantha Rose written on the blanket.

My eyes filled with tears as I looked up to Michael and Josie. Samantha, the girl version of Samuel and Rose after my middle name. I'm glad they didn't use Eleanor; Samantha Eleanor just doesn't have the same ring to it like Samantha Rose does. When my eyes met Josie's of course we both started crying, the emotions getting the best of us.

"How did you have a blanket made so fast?" Wayne asks later that evening after Katie and the kids came over for an impromptu dinner.

"We had two blankets made. One for a girl and one for a boy. The names have been picked out since we found out we were pregnant," Josie says smiling at her new bundle of joy sleeping in my arms.

"What was the boy's name?" I ask, looking up from Samantha's cute little face.

"Samuel Wayne," Michael replies with mixed emotions in his voice. It is clear that his older brother has been weighing on his mind lately and in truth he has on mine as well.

McKenna and Nathan were fascinated over their new cousin, but once they learned that Samantha couldn't play with them like they wanted they found other entertainment. Katie piddles in the kitchen cleaning up once again from dinner. She has taken on the task of cleaning up around the house when she knows that I can't. I know she knows how much anxiety I get over a dirty house and I love her for helping. Jason wasn't able to make it over tonight to meet Samantha due to a new construction. The electrical wiring needed to be completed quickly before insulation could begin tomorrow.

"Katie, just leave the dishes. Come and enjoy some family time," I call out to her.

"I'm almost done mama. I just have one more dish to clean and then I'll be in," she hollers back in return.

Out of the corner of my eye I can see the figure of a man with his hands in his pockets. I almost mistook him for Michael, but that couldn't be right. Michael is sitting on the other side of me. I look in the direction of the kitchen entryway and the man is gone. My eyes must be playing tricks on me.

A few hours went by with visiting, and laughter shared. It is complete with the Christmas decorations on full display surrounding us. My heart has not been this full in a long time. When the pharmacy drops my medications off, everyone takes that opportunity as the time to say their goodbyes. I complete my nightly routine and take the new medications while securing the Fentanyl patch to my arm. It has been an eventful day with the nurse practitioner coming by and meeting the newest member of our little family. I lay my head on my pillow and close my eyes with the day complete. Little did I know that it was just getting started.

CHAPTER 8

I find myself walking down a long gravel road with the rays of the sunshine warming my skin. I have on my favorite pair of worn shorts, a comfortable short sleeve T-shirt with a long sleeve shirt tied around my waist. My feet sport a comfortable pair of tennis shoes helping protect my feet from the small rocks as I walk. I have no idea where I am going or where I came from, but the serenity of this place is incredible. It feels like nothing bad can happen and I don't have a care in the world. It's that sensation you get after a long trip, and you finally get home. I feel complete.

That still begs the question of, where am I? How did I get here? And where is my family or anyone for that matter?

I look around to see rows and rows of the most beautiful sunflowers that I have ever seen on either side of the road. I stop to admire one of the sunflowers. The brilliance of the yellow pedals matched that of the sun and the green from the stalk is the most vibrant I have ever seen.

I moved a stalk of a flower to immerse myself into the field. As I grab another stalk, a dove flies past me in a hurry. I place my hand on my chest in fright and then laugh. I watch the dove as it flies higher into the sky and disappears in the sunlight. After marveling at its simple beauty, I take a few moments to enjoy the sun on my face.

A few moments pass as I soak up the rays of light. I take a few steps more into the sunflowers feeling the need to be surrounded by the flowers with such happy faces. It's difficult to look at the perfection of the sunflowers before me and not have a smile on my face.

I feel as if I am being selfish basking in the perfection surrounding me. My husband should be here with me or at least Katie who enjoyed the simple pleasures of nature. My mind begins to drift once again to the thought of where my family is.

A small panic rises in my chest. Before I could go into full freak out mode, I heard a small voice inside me telling me to calm down and that everything would be okay. I take some breaths in and out focusing fully on my breathing. The voice is soothing, like a mother calming her baby after a nightmare.

I turn my attention to a little sunflower attempting to grow out of the ground in the midst of the towering ones. The littlest flower needs to work harder than all the rest whose roots are already firm and strong in the ground. This plant may be smaller, but it is mighty and determined to prove itself.

I spend a moment thinking about how this is one of the little things in life that gets taken for granted every day. From the time we wake up to the time we go to sleep, we hustle from this thing to that. There never seems to be enough time in the day to literally stop and smell the roses. Or maybe there is, but it is the time that we make for other things that get in the way of it.

Working as a receptionist part time and raising a family with Wayne didn't seem to leave room for things like this. Even when we did make the time to fish in our small pond, my mind floated to the other things on my list that I have yet to complete. Then the guilt settles in that I don't have my house cleaned or a home cooked meal made. The vicious cycle never seems to end, but here and now, with nothing on my 'to-do list' I can savor this time.

I inhale deeply and smell an earthy scent. A mixture of dirt, flowers, and something else that I can't quite put my finger on. Smoke maybe? Like a campfire nearby? I make my way out of the sunflower field and back to the gravel road. I look around, but I don't see any sign of another person. The smell of smoke is faint, but there is no mistaking it. Someone has built a fire.

I begin down the road again, curious as to where the path might lead me. I continue to enjoy the sun as it shines brightly. The warmth of it is pleasant, bright, but not uncomfortable. If I had to picture the perfect weather and the perfect day this is what I would have imagined.

Just when I thought the sun was getting too warm a cool breeze hit my face at the ideal moment. When the wind hit me, my chestnut hair blew over my shoulders. I reached up to smooth a strand of hair over my face and froze.

I place both of my hands on top of my head and play with the loose curls. I have hair. I have not had hair in months. I smile in disbelief as I sit down on the gravel road not caring that the dust will most likely leave residue on my shorts.

I have hair!

I carefully examine the locks in my hands. My hair fell past my shoulders just like it had before I lost it to chemo. I even pull on a strand to ensure that it is my hair and not a wig. I find that it is attached. I look down at myself to see that I have gained the weight back that I lost during my treatments with chemotherapy.

What is going on?

I wanted to appreciate the beauty of this place, to not question it completely. I wanted to take this time to appreciate the simple pleasures like the sun on my face or looking at a sunflower, however now I am curious. They say that curiosity killed the cat, yet at this moment I am willing to risk it.

I think back to what I remember before finding myself on a gravel road. It was a Monday; I had just met the nurse practitioner who prescribed new medication. I met my new grand baby, Samantha Rose. After everyone left, I completed my nightly routine and went to bed. I certainly wasn't on any road going somewhere. It was winter and getting close to Christmas, not a warm sunny fall day. I definitely did not have hair.

Did I die? Is that what this is? I don't feel dead, but isn't that what they all say in the movies?

I remain sitting on the side of the gravel road contemplating where I might be and what is happening when I smell the scent of the campfire smoke again. Someone must be nearby and maybe they will have the answers that I seek.

A small twinge of worry comes to mind with how people are nowadays. It wasn't necessarily safe talking with strangers in a strange place. It also didn't bode well that Wayne didn't know where I was, but I am determined to figure out what in the world is going on.

I stand up and dust myself off from the gravel dust and start walking in the direction I was originally heading. At the edge of the sunflower fields appear to be a hill and a wooded tree line. I can hear the birds chirping happy songs in the nearby trees. The tranquility of the scene surrounding me puts me in a calmness that I have not felt in an exceptionally long time.

If this was death, then I would be okay with that. The only pain in my heart was that I did not get to say my final goodbyes to my family.

I come to the small hill in the gravel road and see the wooded area getting larger. The smell of the smoke from a campfire grows stronger in my nose. The hill was simple enough to climb, but I didn't even break a sweat with the sun's rays beating down on me. It has been a long time since I have walked such a distance and don't feel the rising pain in my stomach or the ache in my chest from breathing so hard. Another blessing to count for this place that I am in.

The hill plateaus at the top. The gravel road opens wider like a turnaround area for cars. At the other end of the circle the road continues down a small hill. I walk further to see that the road ends in the water. A river flowing with a steady current stands before me. A small, wooded area lines the edge of the water.

The sounds of nature fill my ears. I turn to my left to see a dragonfly floating past me and land on a cattail at the edge of the water. I watch the beautiful creature as it flies from this thing to that. Its flight changes directions and flies towards me, landing on my hand. I slowly raise my hand to my face so that I don't scare it away and see its grace up close. God must have known what He was doing when He created such fragile creatures.

The dragonfly stays on the back of my hand for a brief time before flying off. I watch it closely when the smoke from a campfire comes into my focus. Oh yeah, I was on a mission to find someone to figure out where I am.

I set out along the bank to the campsite. As I cut through the grass along the bank, I notice that aside from the fragile dragonfly I haven't seen any other bugs. There are no spiders, flies, or mosquitoes. Not even the pesky gnats that always seem to attack my face. Once again, this place feels like perfection, like it took all the amazing things of the outdoors but removed the annoying parts.

To my surprise there is no one at the campsite. I'm not sure I can even call it a campsite when there are no tents or lodgings. The site must be well known as a fishing spot because the grass is worn down compared to the path I just took. A pit in the middle of the site made from rocks has a crackling fire going. A small duffle bag lies safely away from the fire pit. Over top of the small fire is a cast iron rack with a Dutch oven and a coffee pot.

I can smell potatoes and peppers cooking from inside the Dutch oven and the coffee smells strong and heavenly. My mouth waters thinking about drinking a good cup of coffee.

Two well-worn lawn chairs sit off to the side with a cooler in between. On the river is a small John boat full of fishing gear and another small cooler. The boat is pulled up on the rock riverbank. It also has the anchor of a rope tied to a nearby tree just in case the current picks up. This place seems familiar, like I have been here before, yet I am having a hard time recollecting the memory.

There is not much I can do but wait for the person or persons to come back to their campsite. They couldn't be too far away with coffee over the fire and potatoes in the Dutch oven. I walk over to a lawn chair and sit down to wait. I close my eyes to listen to the tranquility of the birds chirping. As I begin to wonder how long it will be until the person I am waiting for arrives, I hear footsteps coming from behind me.

My instinct is to hide and try to see who is coming. I quickly squash that line of thinking though. If I am going to figure out where I am then I need to speak to whoever is walking up to me, plus they are coming from the tree line, and I have nowhere to hide unless I want to take a swim in the river.

I stand from the lawn chair and turn to see a young man wearing jeans, a white t-shirt, and boots. His brown hair is a mess on top of his head, like he rolled out of bed and didn't bother to comb it. His blue eyes are a stark contrast and stood out among his other features.

He looks strong and capable. Capable of hurting a random woman at his campsite. Again, my mind threw the thought out of my head as soon as it entered. He walks closer to the unoccupied lawn chair and a feeling of calmness overwhelms me. I'm not sure where the feeling came from. It feels like the voice inside my head is telling me that he won't hurt me.

When he reaches his chair, I notice he has a small bucket in his hands. His smile widens as he looks at me and stretches out his other hand. I take it with a returned smile. His grip is firm and gentle at the same time. The feel of his touch releases more of my uneasiness and my nerves settle as if I hadn't been about to panic a few moments ago.

"Good morning. I hope you weren't waiting here long. I had to go dig for some more worms," the stranger says. He pulls a small shovel out from his back pocket and sets the small bucket and shovel on the ground before settling himself into the lawn chair.

I sit myself back down in the chair opposite of him and answer, "No, I just got here not too long ago. Although I don't even know where here is."

"Well, you're just in time. The coffee should be perfect. Would you like a cup?"

I should be screaming 'heck no.' I know better than to take anything from strangers, especially an unknown liquid that could be drugged, but something about this man continues to make me relax. Heck, the entire place surrounding me has made me relaxed. I nod my head with just a slight hesitation.

"What's your name?" I ask, watching him get up and walk over to the campfire. He bends over and pulls out two coffee cups from the worn-out duffle bag.

"Bobby," he replies with a smile. He pours coffee into the first cup and strides over to hand it to me. He walks back over to the campfire and pours himself a cup before returning the coffee kettle to the fire and moving back to his lawn chair.

I hold the coffee in both of my hands and inhale that succulent smell. Even on a warm sunny day the heat from the coffee is not overpowering. I take a small sip with concern that the heat from the coffee might burn my tongue, but I shouldn't have worried. Everything about this place seems to be made to perfection. From the beautifully grown sunflowers, the perfect warmth of the sun, the graceful dragonfly and lack of annoying bugs, and now to the tasty coffee that is at just the right temperature to drink. I could not keep the smile from my face. I hear Bobby chuckle from beside me as if he could read my mind.

"Sorry," I smile over my cup of coffee and take another small sip, "this is just so delicious. It's nice to meet you Bobby, I'm Eleanor, but everybody calls me Ellie."

"It's very nice to see you, Ellie." He takes another sip of his coffee and looks out over the river. The color of it reminds me of the muddy Mississippi. The current flowing is strong and powerful pushing the water and anything in its path downstream. The sound is pleasant with the crackle of the fire near my feet.

I know I should be asking him all sorts of questions like where I am and how do I get home, but this place is like a dream come true. My reality sported pain and nausea and taking pills that make me feel funny. Right now, all I want is to feel like myself again. Heck I even have hair in this place. At this time all I genuinely want is a moment to enjoy myself before I go back home to a place of cancer.

As if he can once again hear my thoughts Bobby starts talking, "I know you have a lot of questions, and I promise you that I will answer all of them. However, for right now, right at this moment, let's just enjoy ourselves."

I look over at him and stare in disbelief. Had he really just read my mind? No, that's crazy. I may be in a peaceful place in who knows where, but that's just crazier than a tutu on a opossum. Things like that don't happen. I take a deep breath calming myself. He said that he will answer any and all questions. For now, that will have to be enough and wasn't I just telling myself that I wanted to enjoy this place?

I look from the river to Bobby, "That would be great. I do have a million questions like where am I? Where is my family? How do I get home? But right now, after everything I have been through, I could use this time," I say.

"Good, I'm glad that I get to be the one to give this to you," Bobby replies, putting his coffee cup down on the ground by his feet. "The potatoes won't be ready for another few hours, how about we take this bucket of worms and get into the boat. We can see what kind of fish are biting today."

I smile at him and put my cup of coffee down before standing, "I think that's a wonderful idea. What can I do to help?"

"Well, if you just want to take this bucket and get into the boat. I already have everything else in there that we might need. I'll untie us and give us a push off," he says handing me the small bucket of dirt and worms.

I take a few steps to get to the boat and put one leg in. I hesitate before fully climbing in and sitting on the bench in the back of the boat. What am I doing? Willingly getting into a boat with a stranger? I am acting like one of those teenagers in a horror film who are too stupid to live and do the obvious thing you shouldn't do. Didn't I just tell him that I didn't know where I was or where my family is? He could easily overpower me and dump my body somewhere and no one would be the wiser.

"Ellie," I hear Bobby say in a soothing voice, "you are safe with me. I would never let anything happen to you."

I look up at him to see the heartfelt truth in his eyes. My heart opens up and fills me with more peace. His presence gives me that big brother vibe. The one where you know you are truly safe, and they only have your best interest at heart. I place my other foot inside the boat and make my way back to the bench. I take a deep breath and fully commit to trusting Bobby going forward.

I look in the small boat. There is a small bench in the front of the boat and a larger bench in the back big enough for Bobby to sit and steer the motor while I sit comfortably next to him. In between the two benches are a few fishing poles, a net for catching fish, and a beat-up cooler.

I place the bucket of worms by my feet and watch Bobby outside of the boat. He unties the rope from around the tree before throwing the slack into the boat. He bends over the bow and starts pushing it backwards into the water. He takes a few steps into the water before deciding that the boat is far enough away from the bank before climbing in himself. I can see the wetness on the bottom of his pant legs as he makes his way to the back.

Bobby gets himself settled on the bench and looks out over the river. I wish I could read his mind like he did so easily with me. He looks lost in thought like he doesn't know what to say or maybe it's just that he doesn't have a care in the world.

"It's a beautiful day for fishing don't you think?" Bobby asks me, not looking away from the riverside.

"This place seems just about perfect for anything really," I reply. I look over at the riverside where we just came. The current must be stronger than I thought because I can barely make out the outline of the chairs and campfire in the distance. With each passing second the current is taking us further down its road leading us to an unknown path.

"I know a great spot where we could catch some catfish. And it's not too late in the fall that we may be able to also snag a crappie or two. Either will be good with the potatoes for dinner. I packed some sandwiches and water in the cooler for later if we get hungry."

Getting excited about catching a fish I exclaim, "well what are we waiting for? The fish to jump in the boat? Let's get a move on then. We're burning daylight."

Bobby chuckles before starting up the engine. "Yes ma'am."

He controls the motor with ease as I look out at the scenery passing by. The wind in my face and hair makes me happy, but once I think about the wind in my hair, I think about how in the world am I going to get a comb through it later. It has been so long since I had to worry about tying my hair back and now it's going to be in knots and hurt when I try to detangle it later. I guess I'll worry about that at a different time as well, nothing I can really do about it now.

Only a few more minutes pass by before Bobby reaches a back cove and slows the boat down to an idle. He maneuvers around a down tree before pulling the boat close to a bank on the other side. We sit a few feet off the bank as he grabs an anchor from under the front bench. He throws it in the water feeling the rope as the anchor drags underneath. It must have caught onto something as the rope tightens and Bobby ties it to the front boat cleat so we would be secure in one place as we fish.

"So why didn't you use the anchor at the campsite instead of tying the boat to a tree," I ask with a small chuckle.

Bobby shrugs his shoulders, "Cause sometimes the anchor is more of a pain in the butt to man handle verse just tying the boat to a tree."

"That's fair I guess."

He steps over the smaller bench and sits down pulling up one of the fishing poles. I grab the other and start rigging it to get ready to cast. I pinched off a worm before handing him the bucket. I place the worm on my hook silently telling the worm sorry and thanking it for its sacrifice in order for me to catch a fish. A silly gesture I know, but I have always felt guilty, especially when the fish ate my worm, and I missed catching it.

I place my pole down after getting it ready and lean over the boat to wash my hands from the dirt now under my fingernails. I know fishing can be dirty, particularly when cleaning the fish, but I never could stand the feeling of dirt under my nails.

As I clean my hands in the water, I see my reflection and freeze. The water is calm and still in the back cove. It appears like a sheet of glass or a mirror on the surface. Unconsciously, my hands come up to my face trying to figure out if what I am seeing is real. Under my hands I can feel my nose and mouth. My reflection matches the movement. Bobby, who is only sitting a few feet away, stops what he is doing to watch me.

"Are you ok?" he asks out of concern.

I look at him with shock and amusement, my hands still on my face. I look back into the water to confirm that what I saw in the reflection is really there. I have hair here, is it really such a shock that I no longer have dark circles under my eyes and my cheeks are filled out? I no longer look like the sick cancer patient I am. I am young and youthful at this moment. I feel thirty again, pretty, and full of energy.

"Yes, I'm amazing," I say with more enthusiasm than I planned.

Bobby gives a small nod and picks up his pole to cast. I smile inwardly to myself and pick up my pole as well. I throw on the opposite side from where Bobby casts remembering my fishing etiquette drilled into me from an early age. The close-faced cast was one I have not used in a long time. I much prefer an open-faced one. However, fishing was fishing and it's kind of like riding a bike. I'd never be a champion at fishing. I'm known to my husband and family for getting my lines tangled up more times than I can count, but I still enjoy doing it during the spring and summer months.

After a couple of castings Bobby breaks the silence. "Do you usually enjoy fishing?"

"Oh, good. You're not one of those excessive fishermen that believes talking will scare the fish away," I chuckle, "I enjoy it during the spring and summer months. My husband and

I have a small pond in our backyard that we like to use for fishing. It has been a while since I have been on the river though."

"That's nice that you have your own place to fish. You can go out anytime you'd like and fish until your heart's content. How long have you had your place?"

"About thirty or so years. My husband, Wayne, built us a forever home complete with a pond and vegetable garden. Of course, when we bought the land, it was just a piece of land with overgrown bushes and brush. It was a lot of hard work, but over the years we were able to make it exactly like we wanted it. Wayne had a fit cutting down so many trees around the pond though."

"Why is that?" Bobby asks with amusement.

"Well, he said that it would be perfect for fishing. We had to drain it at one point to clean out all the debris of leaves from previous years. While we were at it, I made him take down half the trees surrounding the pond. I told him that if he wanted me to fish with him then he'd have to get rid of a lot of the trees otherwise he would be spending his time getting me unstuck from being snagged."

Bobby lets out a deep laugh as he reels in his line for another cast. "Or you could learn how to cast properly?"

I shrug my shoulders, "I'm hopeless. I'm better with open areas like this unless someone casts it for me."

"Well, if you get hung up just let me know and I'll see what I can do to help," Bobby states.

"Will do."

I cast a few more times into the open water and watched my bobber float around. My eyes were fixed on my bobber when something caught my attention on my left. I look over to see a small doe walking just past the tree line. It stops a few times sniffing the grass before taking a couple small steps forward. It is surreal to see something so gentle out in the wild. The deer changes direction and starts heading towards the riverbank, towards me. It reaches the edge and bends over to take a drink of water.

"Beautiful, isn't she?" I hear Bobby whisper quietly so as not to spook the deer.

"Yes, she is."

I watch her for a moment longer before she picks her head up and looks at me. This deer wasn't just looking at me, but seeing me, seeing into my soul. All my thoughts and worries are there for the deer to see. My pain, my sufferings are all out in the open. Before I can feel uneasy the deer turns to leave. It reaches the tree line once again and looks back at me as if to say, 'everything will be okay.'

I take a deep breath and reel in my line. Bobby is back to paying attention to his own line and pole. I decided to change directions in my castings and threw the line to the left, in the direction that the deer was just occupying. Only a precious few seconds' tick by before my bobber goes under water and the line pulls tight. I start to reel in my line.

"I got one! I got one!" I exclaim to Bobby.

He reels in his line quickly and grabs the small net sitting in between us. The fish is not big, I can tell from the easy reeling I am able to do, but the adrenaline from catching a fish is still there. It has been over a year since I have been able to catch a fish, since before my treatment started. I haven't had the energy to go out to our pond to throw a line out. The surge of adrenaline and anticipation of seeing how big the fish is makes me miss those moments I got to spend with Wayne and the kids.

The fish reaches the boat and Bobby bends over with the net to scoop it up. A crappie. Not a prize-winning crappie or mount worthy, but big enough to be good eating later on. I take the fish out of the net and hold it up by its mouth. I smile big and hold the fish out for Bobby to look at.

"I did it Bobby! I did it!" I exclaim. I feel like a child in this moment, smiling from ear to ear. Bobby stands beside me with joy and pride on his face as if he had caught the fish himself.

"I always knew you could, my little rose petal."

It suddenly felt as if someone just threw a bucket of ice-cold water down my spine. The excitement on my face falls and shock replaces it. Those words, those four insignificant words which would have had no meaning to anyone else struck a chord with my soul. There's only one person who has ever called me his little rose petal.

CHAPTER 9

"Grandaddy?" I say in complete shock.

"Hi, baby girl," he says with a smile.

Something came over me and I am not able to stop my next movements. My prize fish is now forgotten, I drop it to the bottom of the boat and lunge forward. I wrap my arms around his neck in the biggest hug I could possibly manage. Grandaddy pulls his arms around my back to squeeze me just as tightly. Tears now fill my eyes as I come to the realization that the man that I have been spending all this time with is my grandpa whom I lost as a child.

My grandpa, whose real name is Robert Joseph Grant, Bobby to his friends, was the only positive male role model in my life. He would often call me his little rose petal since my name is Eleanor Rose. I always loved that endearment and wouldn't let anyone else call me that. It was our own special thing.

My mama got pregnant with me about a year after she married my father, but after I was born, he wanted nothing to do with us. He didn't want to have the responsibilities it came with raising a child and left my mom for another woman.

I saw him a few times over the years. He would try to pretend he was a dad for about two seconds, but as sure as the rain made grass grow, he would always flake when something better came up. I learned quickly that he wasn't a man that I wanted in my life and that I deserved so much more than anything he could ever do for me.

My grandpa was an incredible man. He lost the love of his life, my grandma, a few years after my mom and I moved in. I remember bits and pieces about her like keeping the cleanest house in the neighborhood. I also heard many grand tales that grandaddy would tell me at night about their adventures together. Each story was more eccentric than the last.

My favorite stories were the ones where he would act out the scenes. I would be snuggled in my bed with my bunny at my side. Only a lamp would be illuminating the room as grandaddy would be on the floor and jumping over my bed telling a story about how he and grandma battled pirates and dragons and fell in love.

Grandaddy always made sure that my childhood was a happy one despite my father not being in the picture. Even at an early age he taught me everything a boy should know and how a boy should treat a lady. It helped me know what boys can do like how to change a tire so that I never had to rely on a man. At the same time, he also taught me that when I find the right one, I would know how he should treat me. My grandaddy was a rare man and when we found out about his cancer it was too late to even start treatment.

When grandaddy got sick, it was difficult. He had always been a rock for me and mama to lean on. He carried that through for months before he finally sought out a doctor. I know he tried to hide his obvious pain and lack of eating, but it wasn't until he started throwing up blood that mama finally forced him to see a doctor. At that point it was too late. The treatment then was not like what we have now and once they saw how far advanced the cancer was, they immediately said hospice.

Cancer back then was a death sentence. There's no sugar coating it. Grandaddy came home with hospice care and passed shortly after. His death always haunted me because he never appeared comfortable when he died.

I realize that I am still squeezing him with tears rolling down my face when he gives a small cough. I pull back to see him, to look at him not as Bobby, but as my grandaddy. I place my hands on his shoulders. He is still smiling with happy tears in his eyes as well.

"H-how? W-what? I-I don't understand. How is this happening right now? How are you here?" I managed to stamper out.

He gently pushes a lock of my hair out of my face and says, "It's time to answer some of those questions that have been floating around in your head all day."

He picks up the fish from the bottom of the boat and places it on a fishing stringer. He wraps the string around a boat cleat and places the fish in the water. He sits back on the small bench at the front of the boat and gestures for me to sit on the other bench. I, not so gracefully, sit down and wipe the tears from my eyes with the back of my hand.

"I'm not quite sure where to begin," he says, as he clears his throat. "When He asked me if I wanted to come back to help you through this part I didn't even hesitate."

I remember back when I first saw grandaddy at the campsite. He said it was nice to see me and that he was glad that he got to be the one to give this to me. It makes sense now that his words weren't the usual 'it's nice to meet you.' His name Bobby should have been a giveaway, but I never knew him as Bobby, he was just grandaddy to me. He certainly didn't look like the grandaddy I once knew.

"When who asked you, grandaddy?" I asked in confusion.

"God."

The answer is so simple to give and yet I am taken back by the response. God? God asked my grandaddy to come to me? Now I have a million more questions to ask.

The first thing that comes to my mind is of Moses as he speaks to the burning bush when he asks God who is he that he should go to Pharaoh? I ask myself a similar question. Who am I that God should ask my grandaddy to come to visit me? I'm a lowly Christian woman. No one special, but to my family. My thoughts are interrupted.

"Because He sees you, Ellie. He has never left you and He answered your prayers. Sometimes your anxiety gets in the way of hearing them, though. To answer the first obvious question, you're not dead and this is not heaven."

If it was possible I have an even more confused look on my face. I look down at the bottom of the boat willing myself to understand the information given to me. God sees me. He saw me that Friday morning. He saw my anxiety, my pain, my longing for Him.

I breathe a sigh of relief. Knowing that He was there in my darkest moment takes a weight off my shoulders. I'm not doing this alone. Of course, I have Wayne and the kids, but sometimes even in a crowded room I don't feel seen.

I look up to heaven, thank you, God, for being there and for sending grandaddy.

I look back at grandaddy and shift my thoughts to the other things he said. I'm not dead. This is not heaven. Well, if this isn't heaven then boy what must it look like? He chuckles as if to say once again, 'I can read your mind.'

"Let me just get through this part and it will all make sense, I promise," he says.

I nod my head and gesture for him to start.

"You're not dead and this isn't heaven," he repeats, "Right now you are in that place between. You have a foot on earth and a foot in the next life. Your time is coming to a close, but before you can complete your journey there are some things that you need to do and that's why you are here."

He stops to allow me to soak in this information. I sit in silence processing everything he is saying. My time is ending. How much time? What about my family?

"Ellie," he says gently, "take a breath."

I inhale deeply, not realizing that I'm holding my breath. My arms are a little shaky from holding onto the bench. I start bouncing my leg up and down with anxiety, not sure of what else to do.

"I'm close to passing? How much time do I have left?" I question in fear.

"I'm not sure. Everyone's journey is different, but that's really up to you and God," grandaddy replies.

My eyes almost popped out of my head at his answer. "What do you mean it's up to me and God?"

"Well, when God says that you have completed your journey, and you are ready to let go then it will happen."

"What if I am never ready to let go? I just met my newest granddaughter. I don't want to leave her before she even has the chance to know me," I say in exasperation.

"Then God will call you up," grandaddy states.

"So, it's really His choice, not mine," I say firmly.

"God is giving us a choice. He always gives us a choice and He has a plan just like he does for Michael, Katie, and Wayne. We cannot be the selfish ones and mess up His plans. If you come to the end of your journey and you need just a little more time, then ask that of God. However, we cannot be greedy with the time that is given. Once it is up then it is up."

I nod my head not really liking the answer but accepting it. Remembering back to my Sunday school days and learning about the seven deadly sins; pride, greed, lust, envy, gluttony, wrath, and sloth. Well right now greed and envy seem to be my deadly sins. Greed for wanting more time with my family, more than what God can give me. And envy for all those people who got more time, whose cancer mysteriously disappeared. I told Katie that God gives out miracles every day, it's just not the miracles that we would expect or hope for that we get. Deep down, though, I know that I still envy those people who get to move on with their lives and leave cancer behind.

"This is why you're on this journey Ellie," grandaddy says, pulling me out of my thoughts, "To help you move on from the greed and envy and even the anger and sadness you have built up inside of you. There's no room for that where you are going so it is best to get it all out now."

I clear my throat, "so I'm right? You can read my thoughts?"

"In heaven people can communicate without the use of talking. Everything is out in the open for everyone to see and hear. Whatever you have said in the darkness will be heard in the light, and what you have whispered behind closed doors will be shouted from the housetops for all to hear."

"Luke 12:3," I say with a smile that doesn't necessarily meet my eyes.

"It's true. All the hate, anger, and sadness you have built up on your time on earth must be cast aside. There's no room for things like that in the kingdom of heaven."

"You're starting to sound like Jesus, grandaddy."

"Well, I did learn from the best," he smiles and continues, "I am one of four that are coming to help you on your path."

I sit up straighter upon hearing that. I have three more visitors coming? I almost feel as if I'm in a Christmas Carol and the ghosts of Christmas past, present and future are going to haunt me.

"Who? And when?" I ask impatiently.

"When the time is right. They will help you along your journey. You may see them like you do me now, in a dream…"

"So, this is a dream?" I interrupted him.

"My child, would you learn some patience and let me talk," he says with just a small hint of annoyance in his tone.

"Oh, sorry. Please continue, "I say with a small chuckle and a gesture for him to continue.

"Good Lord to the heavens above you have not changed. Once you seek answers you are relentless in your path," he shakes his head and pinches the bridge of his nose with his finger and squints his eyes before continuing, "As I was saying. You may see them in a dream like this or you may see them in the room with you while you are awake. I think you know what I am talking about."

I think for a moment and nod my head. The man. I keep seeing the figure of a man. He was looking out the window when I was speaking with Michael in the shed. He tried to come in from the hallway behind Wayne when I was talking to Katie in the kitchen. I saw him again when I was having my anxiety attack Friday morning and then when I was holding Samantha last night. His presence is subtle, but I'm beginning to notice it more.

"Who is he? I don't recognize him," I ask.

"He will reveal himself to you when that timing is right. Until then don't be afraid if you see him or others. All of them are here to help you on your pathway home."

I once again nod my head in agreement. The tension that I had been holding is gone. I now know where I am and what is happening to me. Although I do not relish the thought of leaving my family behind, I do look forward to the loved ones who will help on my journey to my final destination. Suddenly the thought of hugging my mama as tightly as I did grandaddy gave me hope. I could definitely use my mama at a time like this.

"How about we catch a few more fish to cook with our potatoes before you have to leave me?" grandaddy asks.

"That sounds wonderful," I reply.

Grandaddy and I fish for a while longer, we keep the four biggest fish to enjoy for dinner. We take the short trip back to the campsite and I enjoyed every second of feeling the wind on my face and in my hair. We pulled up to the bank to start making dinner. I am already thinking about going into the woods to gather more firewood for the fire that had to be out by now. To my surprise the fire is going steady just as it had when we left earlier. I shake my head in bewilderment at the site.

"I know. It never ceases to amaze me either," grandaddy says, knowing what I am thinking.

"What can I do to help?"

"Well, I can clean the fish if you want to get the other cast iron skillet out of the bag and put some peanut oil in it. There's a small bag of Andy's seasoning in there as well."

I move the coffee kettle from the cast iron rack and put it on the ground. I place the skillet over the fire and dump some peanut oil in the bottom to heat up. Grandaddy wastes no time in cleaning the fish and placing the meat in the seasoning. While the fish is frying, he grabs out two plates, forks, and two large spoons. He scoops a helping of potatoes onto my plate and then places some fried fish next to it.

"Thank you," I turn to sit on my chair waiting for his meal to be completed. In no time he is sitting in the chair across from me with his own plate of potatoes and fried fish. We say our prayers and quickly dive into the food.

I actually let out a small moan after biting into the first piece of fish. The flavor is nothing like I have ever experienced before. Even the potatoes taste like they came from a five-star restaurant and not cooked over a fire.

"This tastes..." I can't find the words.

"Heavenly," grandaddy finishes.

"Yeah," I say, putting my fork down on my plate. That is the perfect word for it. This entire place, the smells, the scenery, the beautiful sounds, the taste of this food is just so heavenly."

"I'm honestly not sure how heaven can be much better than this," I state.

"Oh, my little rose petal, you have no idea. There aren't even words invented to describe the brilliance of heaven."

Thinking about my grandaddy being in heaven makes me think about his death and how he suffered the last few months of his life. I take a deep breath and look at my grandaddy with both pity and love.

"I'm so sorry grandaddy."

"For what?" he asks, but in knowing my thoughts I know he already knew the answer and just wanted to keep the conversation flowing.

"The last few months you were with us wasn't very comfortable. You suffered and had so much pain. Now I'm going through the same cancer that you had, and you didn't have the pain medicine like I do. It's just horrible to think about."

"Ellie, what I went through was not fun. There's no denying that, but baby I would wager what you went through, and are still going through is worse. I didn't have months of chemo that made me sick for days or have moments of hope that would be dangled in front of me like a carrot before it got ripped away. Yes, I had pain, but it was over quickly. I'm happy and in a good place. I don't remember most of what I went through, just that I had to leave you and your mother. I'll tell ya though, the moment I saw your grandmother I ran into her arms and never looked back. She was waiting with a hug and kiss to greet me."

He falls into silence thinking about the memory. I am relieved to know that grandaddy didn't suffer like I did or rather the suffering that I am still enduring. I wonder whose face I will see on the other side, who will greet me? Whose arms will I be able to run into? I guess it won't be long before I find out the answer. I try to change the topic to a not so heavy subject.

"This place feels so familiar to me. Where exactly are we?"

"This place feels familiar because you have been here before. I took you here when you were a little girl to go fishing. We had a meal just like this one the last time we were here."

I look around me as the memory comes flooding back. I was about seven when he drove me up the rock road in his beat-up Chevy truck. We took the fishing poles from the bed of the truck and walked a way down the riverbank to this campsite. We caught some fish to take home for dinner that night to have with sliced potatoes.

I caught my last fish with grandaddy that day. He was gone the following year before it warmed up enough to go fishing again. I feel a tear falling and I wipe it away with the back of my hand.

"This place will always hold a special place in my heart," he says.

"I love you so much grandaddy."

"I love you too, my little rose petal. Now tell me about your husband and your kids, what are they like?"

I spent the next hour talking about my family. Stories from when the kids were little to trips that Wayne and I would take. Grandaddy listens intently with a smile on his face, his hands clasped behind his head and leaning back in his chair.

He brings his chair forward after telling him another story about Katie and Michael getting in trouble during their teenage years. He lets out a breath and says, "Well, Ellie it's time to get you on your way."

"But I don't want to go yet," I protest.

"Sorry, baby, but my time is up here. I got my time with you and now you must go back. I can't be selfish with you and keep you all to myself. Now do you remember what we talked about?"

"That I have other loved ones coming to help me on my path and that I shouldn't be afraid if I see them." I say as a matter of fact.

"Exactly," he says and then stands up. He walks the few steps it takes to me, bends over, and kisses me on the forehead.

"I will see you again, beautiful girl."

And then he was gone.

CHAPTER 10

I wake up to the stillness of the late morning sun. I look over to the clock radio sitting on my nightstand as it reads 10:32. In all my years I have never slept this late, not even during my early twenties and Wayne and I would be out with our friends all night.

I sit up on the side of the bed and try to get my bearings. What a dream! I'm not sure it can even be called a dream when it feels so real. I can feel the aches and pains start to rise as I stretch and move my muscles from the deep slumber that I was finally able to have. I smile knowing that God allowed my grandaddy to come and see me. I can still feel the lingering kiss on my forehead.

I look over to the giant mirror attached to my dresser and sigh. Here I am, back to having no hair on my head and an old lady staring back at me. I look down to see my protruding belly full of cancer. I guess it's back to reality. I stand to move to the bathroom when my knees give out and I find myself on the floor. Carmel, who has been staying at my side lately gives me a little nudge and lick on my hand. I reach over and pat her head to tell her that I'm okay.

Only a few seconds go by before I hear Wayne opening up the bedroom door, Moose close behind him. He sees me on all fours before coming to my aide.

"What happened Ellie? Are you okay?" He asks with concern. I know he is thinking back to Friday morning and what I like to call my 'freak out moment.' I hurried to reassure him.

"I'm fine. My knees gave out, is all."

He helps me to a standing position. I can feel my knees about to give out again. I'm not sure if I have the strength to make it to the bathroom, much less my recliner. I sit on the edge of the bed before I have the chance to fall back onto the floor again.

"I think I'm going to need some help this morning. I feel a little bit weaker today and I don't think I can get ready for the day on my own," I say quietly. I've always hated asking for help and I don't like to rely on others. Growing up you helped yourself because no one else was going to do the work for you. At least that's what mama and grandaddy instilled in me.

"How's your pain this morning?" Wayne asks, bringing me out of my thoughts.

"It's achy, but tolerable. I think if you can just help me to the toilet and hand me the things that I need then I can get ready for the day."

"Ellie, it's just me here today. And if the kids decide to stop by later, they're not going to care that you're not dressed up. Why don't you just stay in your pajamas and lounge around today. I'll make a fire, and we can even watch one of those romantic comedies that you love so much."

I huff out a breath, "that sounds wonderful. Yes, to lounging, yes to a fire and romantic comedy, but I'm getting dressed for the day. Mama always said 'the better you look the better you feel. It'll suck at the start but be worth it in the end.' And that's what I want to do. I want to continue getting up and getting dressed for the day because it makes me feel better when I have my make-up on, and I look pretty."

"You're always pretty Ellie," Wayne rushes to say as if he is trying to convince me to take the easy road. I roll my eyes at him. Finally, he gives in and helps me stand before walking with me to the bathroom.

My knees continue to try to give out on our short walk. They almost buckled a few times, but Wayne is able to catch me before I can take a tumble.

I complete my morning routine in the bathroom with Wayne's assistance. Now it is time to walk to my recliner and I'm not sure if either of us have the strength for that distance.

"I think it's time to get the walker out of the basement," I spit out. The last time I needed my walker was three years ago when I had a knee replacement. I hated that thing because I felt like an old lady while using it. I shudder at the thought of needing the wheelchair next when I become so weak that I can't even walk. The wheelchair stays in our car due to only using it when we go out places, like doctor's appointments. Unfortunately, we haven't been able to go anywhere fun.

"Are you sure?"

"Yes, no reason for one or both of us to get hurt trying to walk to the living room."

"I'll go grab it and be right back," he says and leaves me sitting on the toilet waiting for his return. He gestures for the dogs to follow him. I hear the back door open as he lets the dogs outside before walking down the steps to the basement.

Although I hate the walker and it makes me feel old, I am able to make it to my recliner with little fuss and without falling. I sit down and pull my favorite blanket over my lap, the movement becoming natural now. The short distance has me out of breath and I focus on taking even breaths in and out to slow it down.

Wayne comes back into the living room with a cup of coffee mixed with my favorite peppermint mocha creamer and my as needed pain pills as well. I am thankful that the patch has been able to help me eliminate at least the long-acting pain pills from my current regimen. The less I have to try to swallow the better in my eyes.

"Would you like me to get you something to eat?" Wayne asks.

I think about what the nurse practitioner said about eating what I want and to not push myself. Typically, I would ask for a full breakfast knowing I only plan to eat a few bites. I didn't want to hear the 'Come on Ellie you need more than that' from my family when all I would ask for is a muffin or croissant. I reply with, "yes, just one piece of toast with some butter and grape jelly please."

"Are you sure that's all you want?"

"Yes, Jeane said to only eat what I am comfortable with," I reminded him. I want to also put in that I am supposed to be his queen, and he is my trusted peasant, but I think that might be taking things a bit too far.

I am able to eat most of my jellied toast and drink my coffee. It feels better knowing that I don't have a huge plate in front of me that I need to try to eat. It's silly, but even a plate full of food can be a little overwhelming.

Wayne starts up a fire and turns the channel to Hallmark. The plots of every Christmas story are predictable and cheesy, yet that doesn't stop me from wanting to watch every new Christmas movie they come out with. Something about the simple experience of snuggling up with a fire on and a Christmas movie just makes my heart happy.

The movie plays for about twenty minutes before I hear Wayne snoring like a freight train beside me. The enjoyment of my movie now doesn't seem so fun when I have to try and drown out that horrible background noise.

"Wayne," I say calmly. He doesn't wake or stir.
"Wayne," I say a little more loudly. Nothing.
"Wayne," I shout.
"What? What? What?" He wakes up in a startle.
"You're snoring."
"Well, it wasn't bothering me," he fusses, pulling the blankets back over his shoulders and closing his eyes.

"Well, it was bothering me and I'm not going to be able to enjoy this movie with you sounding like a train rolling through," I say, semi annoyed.

"What would you like me to do? You want me to go in the other room?" he asks, trying to stand up and walk out.

"No, I want to talk about Christmas," I reply.

Wayne halts his movement and looks at me. We have avoided talking about Christmas. I think for the simple fact that it will be my last one and there's always the question, will I even make it to Christmas?

He sits back looking a little tense. "What would you like to discuss?"

"What do you think we should get for each of the kids and grandkids? We haven't done any shopping yet and I want this year to be a little more special since…" I can't bear to finish that sentence. We both know what I was going to say but putting them out there in the world makes it all too real.

"How about this?" He starts, "Why don't we do most of the shopping on that online stuff? The kids are always talking about how they like the convenience of Amazon. That way you can pick out what you would like for each of the kids, and you don't have to worry about going out. We will have it shipped to the house."

"Thank you." My eyes start filling with tears. Being able to shop online is probably going to be the only way I'll be able to be a part of their gifts. I have been stressing about it for weeks

128

with the realization that I can't go to the store and look like I normally would.

Wayne hands me his smart phone and I start making a mental list of everything I may want to get for the kids and grandkids. I start chipping away a little bit at the list in my head when I realize that I want something more meaningful to this last Christmas. I want something that they can remember me by. It might be selfish of me, but I want to give each of them something that when they see it or hold it, they will remember and think of me.

I look over at Wayne with a mischievous smile.

"What is going on in that head of yours?" he asks with concern.

"I have an idea, and I need you to help me," I say, tilting my head to make him even more nervous.

"Oh boy, what now?"

"I need you to help me up. We need to go to my closet."

"What in the Sam hells is in your closet that you need?" Wayne asks, taken back by my demand.

"I have a ton of spring and summer clothes that I am obviously not going to wear anymore," I start to say.

Wayne cuts me off before I can continue, "Ellie, please let's not think about that." He squints his eyes and pinches the bridge of his nose. "We don't need to pack anything away."

"I don't want to pack them away. I want to use them," I say. I know where his mind is going and honestly my mind went there too. I thought about my clothes and thinking about him going through my side of the closet when I'm gone to pack away my things. It is just too depressing to even comprehend. I figure making some use out of my stuff will help knock out two birds with one stone.

"I'm not following," he says with the look of confusion clear on his face.

"I want to pick out some of my shirts and make them into teddy bears for the grandkids and quilts for Katie and Michael," I explain. "I was thinking they could even put a Scentsy thing that smells like roses in the teddy bears so anytime McKenna, Nathan or Samantha smell the bear they will think of me."

I can see the mixture of sadness and pride sweep across Wayne's face as he ponders my request. He stands abruptly out of his chair and walks over to me. He places my walker in front of my recliner and says, "Well let's go pick out some shirts."

It takes a few days to go through my closet and pick out the perfect shirt for each of the teddy bears and the shirts that would make a good quilt. Each shirt brought back a memory. Wayne and I found ourselves sitting on the floor or on the bed reminiscing about our life together. We had some happy moments and tearful ones as well. I think that's why it took so long to pick out what I wanted.

Wayne is able to find a seamstress that will be able to make exactly what I had envisioned in my head. I decided to have two more bears made for any future grandchildren. I know that Katie and Jason don't plan on having any more kids, but Michael and Josie seem to just be getting started on their family. Michael always expressed wanting three kids, especially after Samuel died. I ask Wayne to keep the extra bears a secret until they have more kids.

Wayne and I drive to the seamstress to drop off the shirts. My loving husband could have done this alone, and it would have been much faster, but I want to be a part of everything that goes into making these bears and quilts.

We walk into the little store as a bell chimes above our heads. A small woman comes up from the back room to greet us. I can see a pin cushion bracelet around her wrist, a tape measurer draped over her shoulder and multiple Band-Aids around her fingers as if she has been pricked by needles multiple times.

"Good morning, how can I help you?" she asks.

"Yeah, I called a few days ago. We're hoping to have some teddy bears, and two quilts made from some shirts," Wayne says as he approaches the counter.

"Ah, yes. I remember. And you are wanting something to smell like roses sewed into the bears?" The petite woman asks as she makes a few clicks on her computer.

"Yes ma'am," Wayne answers her.

"Can I see the shirts?" She gestures to me.

I walk up with my walker and hand over each shirt with the attached name for the grandkids and the two bags of shirts: one with Katie's name and the other with Michael's. I made sure to pick out the more girly colors for Katie and some of my Navy shirts for Michael.

She looks at the shirts for the teddy bears and then shirts for the quilts before saying, "The shirts for the bears should be fine. However, to make a big enough quilt that will be comfortable I will need to add additional fabric. Is that all right with you?"

I look to Wayne for help with an answer. He smiles and nods his head once as if to say, 'that's up to you.'

I look back to the woman and hesitantly ask, "am I able to pick out the fabric?"

"Of course. I have some catalogs with pieces of fabric you can pick out and we'll discuss the details," she says, pulling out a large book with pieces of fabric sticking out from the edges.

We spend several moments discussing fabric and patterns for the quilts until I am certain that I have them exactly right. Wayne listens intently, leaning against the counter. I was certain he would be bored, but he is fully invested in the conversation and decision making.

Before the topic of payment, the patient lady explains to us, "I'm guessing that you are wanting these to be Christmas presents, but I can see on the computer that one of the fabrics for the quilts won't be in until the twenty-third. I can have the bears made, but I'm not going to have the quilts done in time."

Wayne and I both look down and let out a breath of disappointment. I knew this would be cutting it too close to Christmas, but the words still stung.

"If you want, we can see what fabric I have in the back that we could piece together for the quilts," she suggests.

Wayne looks to me for an answer. The thought of changing the quilt from what I have already made in my head seems to be an even bigger disappointment. I want Katie and Michael to have what I made for them even if that means I am not there to share the moment with them.

"No," I say, turning my attention completely to my husband. "I want them to have what I created for them. It will be like one last gift even after I am gone."

"Ellie, are you sure?" Wayne asks, grabbing my hand. "We can try to find something else."

"I'm sure," I answer and take a deep breath in. "I want them all to be able to open them at the same time. I don't want the grandkids to get the teddy bears and Katie and Michael feel left out. So, it's all or nothing and I choose all of it."

I turn to the woman standing behind the counter. She has tears in her eyes as she can clearly understand the importance of these teddy bears and quilts. "Please place the order for the fabric and complete them when you can. Wayne will pick them up whenever they are all ready," I tell her.

We finish the transaction and head for the car. Wayne opens my door and helps me settle in before putting the walker in the back seat and coming around to the driver's side. He shuts the car door, and I know he is going to ask me one more time if I am sure. Sometimes I want to scream at him that

I'm so sure I'm practically deodorant, but I know his concern comes from a good place.

"I have peace with this decision, Wayne," I tell him. "It stinks that I won't be there to see them open these gifts, but it makes me happy that they are all going to have a piece of me after I'm gone. We don't even know if I will make it to Christmas anyway."

He doesn't say anything, doesn't argue, just starts up the car and makes the drive home in silence.

More days come and go, twelve in fact since I had my dream with grandaddy. I am beginning to think that it was just that, a dream. It was a lovely dream, but a dream just the same. I haven't even seen the mysterious man in my house which makes me believe that my eyes were just playing tricks on me. Or perhaps, I was going crazy with my medications.

The Fentanyl patch has helped maintain my pain level to being tolerable. The Mirtazapine has unfortunately done nothing to help with my appetite, but the nurse practitioner said that that was a possibility. My lack of wanting food continues to get worse with each passing day.

Each day is more of the same; I have some pain, I get a little weaker, maybe I'll be able to eat a meal or not. Elisha's visits also come and go as she charts my steady decline. On her most recent visit Wayne excused himself to go to the bathroom while Katie went to the kitchen to make herself another cup of coffee. I used that time to my advantage.

"Elisha, I have a quick question for you, and I don't want my family to hear or know," I start, my heart pounding in my chest from nervousness.

"Okay, what's up?" she asks.

"Do you think I'll make it to Christmas?" I inquire in a whisper afraid that Katie might overhear.

Elisha takes a deep breath before answering me, "Honestly, I don't know. I don't have a crystal ball that will tell me the exact date and time that you will pass. What I can see is that you're not eating much of anything, only a few bites here and there. You're drinking fluids okay, but that's only going to get you so far. We have almost two weeks before Christmas and a lot can happen between now and then."

I nod my head at her response unsure of what else to say. I wanted to know, I asked the question, so why am I disappointed at her response?

"It's possible that you could still be here, but I'm not sure how awake and alert you will be. Hearing is the absolute last thing to go. Studies and experience have shown me that you'll be able to hear what is going on around you, but your body will be too weak to respond to your loved ones," she says trying to reassure me. She places a hand over mine offering support.

I hear Wayne flush the toilet and I quickly thank Elisha for her candor before my family can hear the discussion between us.

I sit at the kitchen table a few days later and reflect on that conversation. I will be able to hear, but not respond. I am supposed to be focusing on the annual gingerbread competition that we have with the kids the second weekend of every December. Katie and McKenna team up together while Jason and Nathan work together decorating their gingerbread house. Wayne is concentrating a little too hard on the candied lights for the roof and Michael seems to be more focused on eating the icing than actually decorating his house. Josie takes a break from helping Michael to feed a crying Samantha.

Unfortunately, my mind keeps slipping away and I feel like a total hypocrite. I begged Katie at Thanksgiving to be present in the moment and here I am thinking about other things instead of enjoying my time with my family.

I stare off into space, 'hear but not respond.' Is it like sleep paralysis? All the research I have done on Wayne's phone has been useless. There's near death experiences, but those are all tragic events and people eventually go back to living their lives normally after experiencing incredible moments in heaven. I am not going to be given that luxury. Once my life ends then I will be gone from this world forever. The internet also talked about what symptoms I am going to show, confirming what Elisha has already told me. Through my research I have yet to find anything about my mind and what I'm going to experience consciously and subconsciously.

I have questions and I want to know the answers. Will it be like when I was with grandaddy? Will it be in a peaceful place, or will I be stuck in my mind, but unable to move or do anything? That thought makes me shudder. Like it's my own prison. I'm trapped in my body.

My thoughts shift to a happier topic of being with grandaddy. He was able to hear me and understand my thoughts without me even talking. 'Whatever you have said in the darkness shall be heard in the light.'

That concept is scarier than I'd like to admit. All my gossip, all my snide comments behind someone's back will be out there in the open for everyone to hear and know. I'm ashamed of the things I have said and the words I have thought. A snap judgment made, or a sarcastic comment said only in my head. Dating back from when I was a little girl in grade school picking on someone who was different from me to a coworker who had a different perspective on things that didn't match my opinion. Every moment, every word and every thought will be judged by my Heavenly Father, and I am ashamed.

Before the tears could begin to fall and my family could become concerned with my tears, I sent up a silent prayer of forgiveness.

Please God forgive my ignorance. Forgive my wrongdoing and spreading of gossip, both knowingly and unknowingly. Help me to be better for you.

"Mama, are you falling asleep there?" I hear Katie ask as she shakes my hand on top of the table.

I open my eyes to see everyone staring at me. I clear my throat, "sorry, just sending up a prayer."

I know my family wouldn't ask questions if I told them that I was praying. I look around to see Katie and McKenna's house almost done and dripping with icing. Jason and Nathan seem to have given up as the gingerbread house lays broken, but with the added flare of a dinosaur next to the fallen house. Michael's house is complete with a little gingerbread family while Wayne has only finished one side of the house. He has it decorated so neatly while the other side remains bare.

In the corner of the room stands a man leaning against the wall. I recognize him now as the same man that I have been seeing, however, this is the first time I am able to see him so clearly. He appears young, in his thirties wearing a pair of jeans, cowboy boots and a green flannel shirt. His captivating blue eyes hold my attention. He is sporting a five o'clock shadow that looks ruggedly handsome on him.

He seems familiar, but I can't for the life of me think of how I know him. His face seems like one that I wouldn't forget.

He doesn't say anything to me, and I don't say anything back. We just stare at each other for a moment when he smiles. I return with my own smile and a warmness fills my heart.

"Mama, are you okay?" Katie asks hesitantly. She looks at me and then at the blank area on the wall. I know she wouldn't be able to see the man that I see, and I wasn't about to scare her or my family with my supposed hallucinations. They may think that they are hallucinations, but to me they are real. He is real and he's here for me.

I cleared my throat once again, "yes, I'm sorry."

"You gotta announce the winner, you're the judge this year," Jason says. "I personally think that this dinosaur destructive home should win. It's creative and authentic."

"Daddy, your house crumpled, and you had no other choice but to add a dinosaur," McKenna states firmly. We all chuckled at her clear observation. "I think mommy and I should win because we used the most sprinkles and so it's the prettiest."

"I wouldn't call that house pretty," Nathan says, scrunching his nose. Both McKenna and Nathan stick their tongues out at each other while Katie tries to end their banter.

"I think grandpa should win because I have the cleanest and nicest house," Wayne says proudly.

"Grandpa you can't win, you only got one side done," Nathan quips.

"Yeah, sorry Wayne, but you're out of the running," I tell my husband. "I think I like Michael and Josie's the best. It's complete with a little gingerbread family."

Michael sits back in his chair with an arm around Josie and a gloating smile, "see the work speaks for itself."

Everyone starts smiling and speaking at once. I look over to the corner to see that man has not left. He's still there and smiling at the enjoyment around our kitchen table.

After about an hour the family festivities continue in full swing with baking cookies. I become too exhausted to keep up. I apologize to everyone and encourage them to continue baking and enjoying themselves. I say my good night to everyone before asking Wayne to help me to bed.

He helps me complete my nightly routine before getting me settled under the blankets. It feels weird going to bed with a house full of people. No matter how tired I am, I am always the last one to go to bed, especially in my own home. However, tonight I just can't do it.

"Do you want me to send everyone home?" Wayne asks as he pulls the blankets up.

"No, let them stay. I like hearing their voices and their laughter," I say with such tenderness.

"Okay love. Get some sleep."

Wayne kisses the top of my forehead and shuts the bedroom door as my eyes flutter closed.

CHAPTER 11

My eyes open to waves crashing in from the ocean on a sandy beach. The sight before me is unbelievable. I see, but I'm having a hard time believing as I was just in my bed a brief moment ago. I guess it shouldn't come as a shock after the experience I had twelve days ago. The perfection of this place is as baffling as being at the river with grandaddy.

The skies above are the clearest blue with not a cloud in sight. I look out to the sea and watch the beautiful changes in the blue. It rushes from a deep royal blue to the lightest blue of the sky as the waves beat against the sand. The moment it hits the shore, the purest white foam appears before settling into a translucent glass exposing the sand once again.

The sound of the crashing waves brings a stillness to my soul. I close my eyes and listen to the calming sounds of the beach. A seagull squawks over my head as it flies around to look for food. The peacefulness I feel is once again serene.

I remember grandaddy laughing when I asked if this was heaven. I am left in wonder and awe at how heaven could possibly be better than the scene set before me. What wondrous works God does!

I stand at the edge of the beach with the waves lapping at my bare feet. I keep my eyes closed for fear that if I opened them, I would be transported back home. I can feel the warm sun on my face and the brightness behind my closed eyes.

I inhale so deeply that even a yoga instructor would be impressed. I smell the saltiness of the air that only living on a beach can bring as a cooling breeze moves in from the ocean. As the wind hits my face, I feel my hair brush over my shoulder and my flowing skirt move.

I bring my hands to my head and feel the silky smoothness of my hair. I open my eyes to look down at the glassy water and see the reflection of a younger version of myself.

Thank you, God. Thank you for giving me this blessing. The small thank you seems insignificant, but it is what I have to offer: my thanks and praise.

I think back to the conversation I had with grandaddy about the three additional people that are supposedly here to help me grow closer to God. I begin to look around to see who might be around me. The only living thing in sight is the seagull flying over my head. Looking to my left I see nothing but waves rushing against the shoreline as far as the eye can see. Behind me sits a rock wall with an empty parking lot. To my right in the distance stands a long pier with a building at the end. I am alone on this beach with not a single person in sight.

I begin to leisurely walk down the sandy beach towards the pier. If I am going to meet the next person on my path, that building at the end seems like a good place to start.

I take a short break from my walk after reaching the top wooden steps on the pier. I shake the sand off my feet and lean against the railing to look out into the vast ocean. The height of the sun suggests that the hour is about midday. The ocean continues to give that relaxing sound as it crashes wave after wave onto the beach.

Looking down the pier, I see that the building sitting on the end is in fact a restaurant. The sign at the top reads Holy Mackerel's Bar and Grill. I straighten after seeing the familiar name.

I know this place. I know that restaurant. I run as fast as my legs will allow towards the hope of finding a person. Not just any person, but my best friend.

I reach the restaurant and swing open the doors in haste. I make my way through the restaurant looking for any signs of life. I don't see anyone in the bar area or in the dining room. The smell from cooking food hits my nose and I stroll to the back where the sign reads employees only. Better to ask for forgiveness than permission. I am on a mission.

Once again, I am met with an empty room, but the scent of shrimp, crab meat, fries, and cornbread wafts into the air. It's intoxicating and makes my mouth water. A tinge of disappointment hits my heart at seeing the empty room. I look around to see that the kitchen is cleaner than a whistle. All of the appliances are shiny, and the cooking utensils appear as if they have never been used.

I'm not sure how it is even possible to smell the food being cooked and not see a soul in sight or even have evidence of a dirty dish. I think about the power of God and not underestimating Him or His ability to do things. There is much I still need to learn.

I feel my stomach growl with hunger the longer I stand in this room. It is incredible how the thought of food typically makes me nauseated, but right now all I can think about is what I wouldn't give to savor the feast that smells so good.

I make my way out to the restaurant and onto the outside sitting area next to the ocean. I might as well sit and enjoy the sounds of the waves and feel the ocean breeze on my face as I wait.

In the middle of the water, I see a fish breaking the surface. It is subtle and could be missed easily if someone wasn't paying attention. Its captivating movements occur as its back curls at the surface of the ocean. I quickly learn that what I'm seeing is a dolphin swimming past the restaurant. The lone dolphin is met with two more as they swim and play to their destination.

The sight before me is interrupted when a plate of delicious seafood is set on the table in front of me. I look up to see a petite blonde woman with a plate of food for herself. She sets her plate of food down in front of the empty seat across from me as she gives me the biggest smile.

I was right! I jump up from the table, not caring that the chair falls backwards hitting the floor. I embrace my best friend in a heartfelt 'I've missed you' hug. Her giggles echo across the empty room and it warms my soul.

"I knew it was going to be you! As soon as I saw the restaurant I knew! Dana, I've missed you so much!" I exclaim, not yet loosening up on my hold from her.

"I've missed you too, Ellie. It's so good to see you," Dana expresses with a hold around me just as strong.

Happy tears trickle down my face as we finally loosen our hold on each other and sit down. I stare at the feast that Dana has placed in front of me. A small bowl of crab meat soup sits on the side of the plate while the main dish of grilled shrimp skewers on a bed of mixed vegetables consumes my focus. The smell makes my mouth water even more now that I see it with my eyes.

Dana's plate sports some sort of fried fish, fries, and a small corn muffin with butter. Before she can settle, Dana stands abruptly.

"Silly me, I forgot the sweet tea. Be right back."

She dashes back to the cooking area and returns a moment later with two glasses full of sweet iced tea. She sets a glass down on my side of the table as well as hers before resuming her original place.

I let out a breath that I didn't know I was holding, "I want to ask how this is happening, but grandaddy already told me that I would get to experience something like this. I just didn't know who my other visitors would be. This is so surreal."

"Tell me about it," Dana chimes in, "Every time I think I have seen it all, God goes and opens another amazing wonder for me to discover. About myself. About my life on Earth and the people around me. I've learned to just bask in the glory of it all. And your grandaddy is a good man. I've enjoyed hearing about stories when you were growing up."

I stare at her in shock with my mouth wide open, "You met my grandaddy?"

"Well yeah. You had such an impact on my life, and I wanted to meet some of the people who had an impact on yours. So, of course I sought him out," she replies.

Dana had become my best friend after I started working as a receptionist at the dentist's office. Wayne and I had just married and grandaddy had been gone for quite a few years already. I can't believe she found grandaddy in heaven.

I look my best friend over and smile. She looks beautiful. She was always pretty, but the beauty of her heart is now shown on the outside as well. Her blonde hair falls into beach waves around her shoulders. Her frame is petite and healthy. Before she died, I remembered her as just on the shy end of skinny, like she never ate enough to keep the meat on her bones. Now she is glowing with radiance and the sight of it makes me so happy.

"You look incredible," I say, taking a bite of my shrimp.

"Thanks, so do you. I mean, like right now, cause woman you have been looking like crap lately."

Leave it to Dana to blurt out the ugly truth.

"Gee, thanks. It's the cancer look. All the rage you know," I joke back with her. I know I wouldn't be able to have this type of humor with Wayne or the kids. There's just something about a best friend that you can turn the dark truth into a joke without anyone's feelings getting hurt.

"So, I hear," she says with a sly smile, "It's so good to finally see you and be able to talk to you."

I smirk, "same. And I'm ecstatic that it is back at the place that holds one of my favorite memories of us."

"Oh, you mean the memory of you getting kicked out of the ocean because you were too drunk, and the lifeguard was worried you'd drown?" She suggests the memory.

"Hey, I wasn't drunk. I was just laughing so hard at the waves spinning me around in the shallow end of shore."

"You got us kicked off the beach."

"No, that was all you because you wanted to be a smart-aleck and mouthed off to the lifeguard," I laugh.

Soon we are both laughing so hard that it takes a while before we can catch our breath. I take another bite of my food to stall, as I try to compose myself.

"I can't believe Josh allowed both of us to take off at the same time for a vacation," Dana recalls.

Josh was our office manager at the dentist's office. I was the receptionist while Dana handled the billing part. Having two members out on vacation at the same time was unheard of in our small building.

Dana and I started working at the dentist office around the same time and instantly became friends. There was just something about her that completed me in a way that only a friend could. After Dana got the courage to finally leave her abusive husband, we begged for a short vacation to take together.

Dana had never seen the beach before but listened to the waves on a CD. Anytime I walked into her office I heard the calming sounds coming through her radio.

"I think after what you had been through, he finally got a heart," I replied.

"Yeah, he was always so grumpy. It didn't help that you constantly played pranks on him," Dana says with a chuckle.

"I don't know what you're talking about."

"Oh, no? What about that time that the Michigan Wolverines beat the Ohio State Buckeyes in a game, and you decorated his office in Wolverine decor?" She makes finger quotes around 'decorated' as she speaks.

"Well, if he didn't voice such distaste for the Wolverines then I wouldn't have to take such drastic measures."

Dana places her hands on the table and leans forward, "you even wrapped his office phone and stapler in Wolverine wrapping paper!"

I laugh remembering how my boss could be heard from the front room cursing as he unwrapped every single office supply.

"He started locking his office after that."

"Can you blame him?" Dana asks.

"No, but it was definitely worth it cause he took the rest of the day off after cleaning up his office," I answered.

"Yeah, he said he felt sick to his stomach after touching Wolverine stuff."

"Best Friday afternoon we had had in a long time," I say. I take another bite of my food enjoying the reminiscing.

"How are Wayne and the kids doing?" Dana asks.

"They're okay, I think. Michael and Josie just had a baby girl, and I got to hold her last night. It was really nice to still be around to meet my granddaughter. Wayne and the kids have each come to terms with me being on hospice, but we're all still struggling with knowing that this is going to be my last Christmas with everyone. It's the big elephant in the room that no one wants to touch with a ten-foot pole," I shrug.

"You know you're going to have to talk to them about it eventually, right?"

I groan at the thought of opening Pandora's box. I know there will come a time when I won't be able to even formulate a word let alone a full conversation. The words 'hear but not respond' come to the forefront of my mind.

"Soon, Ellie."

Her words are straightforward and to the point. There is no denying the meaning.

I look up at her with terror. She knows.

"How soon?" I ask, desperately wanting to know the answer. Will I be here on Christmas? How quick am I declining? How soon is soon?

Dana finishes chewing her bite of fish before wiping her mouth with the napkin sitting on her lap. She shakes her head slowly, "I'm not allowed to answer that. I'm only here to help you on your path, not give you a timeline to the destination."

I slink back in my chair. "You can't give me an idea or a heads up?"

"This is your heads up, Ellie," she blurts out.

I have always loved how Dana has been able to be upfront and candid with me throughout our friendship, even with the hard things that I didn't want to hear. I think it was because she couldn't speak her mind with her husband, at least not when things started to get bad. That doesn't change that her words still sting as they had when she was alive.

The amazing feast no longer holds any appeal to me. The wind whips across the open pier, taking my appetite with it. I turn my attention to my surroundings and realize for the first time that dark clouds have gathered in the distance.

My best friend can now see that I have lost my appetite. She pushes her mostly eaten plate away.

"How about we go for a walk on the beach?" She suggests as she stands up from the table.

"Yeah, that sounds good," I say reluctantly. I pushed my chair back away from the table and joined her to head out of the restaurant.

We make it to the end of the pier where the sand meets the wooden stairs. The soft warm sand feels amazing on my bare feet and the thought hits me that I haven't had shoes on this entire time. I'm getting more and more comfortable in this place as time passes.

We turn our direction to head towards the water. I look out to see the storm moving in on the shoreline. It's not going to be much longer before the clouds open and Dana and I will be completely soaked from the rain.

We make it to the edge of the water as it hits our feet before retracting back to the ocean. I turn my head to see how far Dana and I have walked in silence and marvel at the two sets of footprints in the sand. The waves glide over the marks with ease and erase them as if they have never been there.

"So how are you to help me on my journey?" I ask Dana, turning my attention to her. Better to start whatever conversation that needs to be had.

"I see the years haven't decreased your bluntness," she replies with a smile that doesn't meet her eyes.

"I could say the same to you. I can feel the tension in the air, and I'd rather get that over with so that I can go back to enjoying our time together."

We take a few more steps together before she says, "You're harvesting anger and that's taking up a lot of energy."

I stop in my tracks contemplating what she just said to me. I'm taken back at her words and don't understand. She turns to face me. Her expression is calm while my face shows doubt and bewilderment.

"What do you mean I'm harvesting anger?" I ask with a little more malice in my tone than I intended for. "I'm a happy person, for the most part. Or are you talking about being angry about dying from cancer?"

"Ellie, you are angry about dying from cancer and your plans getting cut short. There's no denying that, but you are also holding onto anger in your heart about the people who have wronged you throughout your life. You're still holding onto the hate and anger about Big Jim."

I take a step back as if her words have the ability to knock me off my feet. The anger she spoke of in my heart feels like it is rearing a head and it's about to explode. The thunder clouds seem to be in sync with my heart and are moving in faster. I can feel the wind pick up around us. The waves crash on the shoreline with more force than they were a few moments ago.

I ball my hands into fists at my side as I spit out through clenched teeth, "I'm sorry for holding onto the anger for the man that murdered my best friend."

CHAPTER 12

Dana and I became instant best friends from the day we started working together at the dentist's office. Something about us just clicked and it was like we had known each other our entire lives. We shared incredible moments and could often be seen giggling at our own inside jokes while others were completely oblivious to them.

Dana was married to James, 'Big Jim' as he liked to be called, prior to starting at the office. When I first met him, he was friendly enough, polite and cordial, but something about him just made my skin crawl. He was a large man, about six foot five and closer to two hundred and fifty pounds of mostly muscle. Hence the name Big Jim. He typically sported a five o'clock shadow and had that air of asserting his male dominance.

He never gave me a reason to think he was anything but a good guy during the first six years of my friendship with Dana. I just couldn't put my finger on it though. Something about him just gave me pause and Wayne felt the same.

When we had BBQs over at the house or a birthday party for one of the kids, Big Jim would fade into the background.

He never really engaged, never smiled, and always seemed to be holding some sort of alcoholic beverage in his hand.

I thank God that Dana and him never had any children. If they did, I think the abuse would have started a lot sooner.

Dana and I grew closer over the years, and I would confide in her about frustrations with Wayne, the kids and the job and she would do the same. The moment things started to change was when Big Jim lost his job as a police officer for drinking.

He started to drink heavily at night, but as time went on, he needed an assist with his hangovers in the morning. That is when he started drinking Vodka while on shift. It was subtle at first, but the more mistakes he made the more it became obvious to his superiors and fellow officers.

One morning in particular I remember seeing Dana come into the office. Something was obviously wrong as she walked past me with her head down. She remained quiet and didn't even utter a greeting. Her face sported a blank stare, much like I had when Dr Jenkins told me about my failed surgery. She walked quickly to her office and closed the door behind her. This too was an obvious sign that something was wrong. Dana usually preferred to leave her door open so that she could hear the laughter or gossip coming from the front desk.

By lunch I was done giving her space. I walked into her office, hearing the familiar waves crashing from her beach CD, with a plate of our favorite Chinese takeout. I placed the plate on her desk and sat in the chair opposite her.

"I've known you too long to know that something is up. Spill it," I demanded of her. I wasn't going to sugarcoat this or tiptoe around and give her the opportunity to tell me some made up excuse for her change in character. We have been friends for too long.

"It's nothing. Just a fight with Big Jim last night. I'll be fine I promise," she responded. Her demeanor suggested anything but. After a few more attempts to get her to say more she became frustrated with me. She thanked me for the food and gave the excuse that she had a lot of work to do, essentially kicking me out of her office.

Dana was anything but fine and I shouldn't have let her drop our short conversation so easily. Over several months, Dana slipped into a depression and became a shell of the person I once knew. Her happy go-lucky demeanor was gone-suffocated by a man who couldn't get a handle on his drinking problem.

He blamed her for not being able to hold down a job due to the stress of 'being her husband.' Dana began taking verbal and emotional abuse from him when he lost his badge. She became a shy and quiet person, only speaking when being spoken to.

One day she walked into work wearing a warm, thick blazer in the middle of summer. I recognized the blazer as part of her winter clothes, and it seemed larger on her now than it did the winter before. I also noted that she had been losing weight during that time and something didn't seem right—the jacket was now two sizes too big on her.

I walked into her office without knocking on the door to see her standing in front of a small mirror looking at a large bruise on her arm. Her eyes went wide as she realized I had seen the unmistakable marks of fingers wrapped around her arm.

She quickly shrugged her blazer back on and said, "it's nothing."

I walked over to where she was standing and pulled on her blazer. She winced at the pain the movement caused. I took the blazer off to see hand shaped bruises on both of her upper arms. I didn't say anything as I inspected her body. I couldn't say anything, I was too mad, too disgusted. Not disgusted at Dana. No, at Big Jim for thinking he had the right to put his hands on his wife.

I gently pulled her shirt up to look at her stomach and back. Dana didn't do anything, she just stood there allowing me to complete my assessment. For once I was thankful that she had the blinds closed on all the windows so that we could have this moment of privacy.

A mixture of yellow, green, blue, and dark purple bruises covered various places over her back and belly. She pushed her shirt down in embarrassment before collapsing on the floor. I quickly joined her.

She hugged her knees to her chest and started to cry. I placed a hand on her arm in an attempt to give her comfort.

After a while, her crying stopped. She turned her face to look at me, her head lying on her bent knees. The bottom parts of her eyes were black from her mascara running.

"When did I get to be like this? How did I become this battered woman?" she asked.

I took a breath and answered, "because it was so subtle and happened so slowly over time that you got used to it."

I shocked even my own self with my insightfulness, though it didn't make the words any less true.

She nodded her head, "you're right. And when he started hitting me it was barely a surprise. Each time he got a new job I thought he'd clean up his act and stop drinking, but it's just a never-ending story with a worse outcome every time."

"Do you want me to help you?" I asked.

Her head shot up. "Help me with what?" she asked, puzzled.

"To pack your things and get somewhere safe?"

"I'm not leaving him, Ellie. That's not what married people do. I can't just leave him when things are tough. I made a vow, in sickness and in health. The drinking is his sickness, and I can't leave just because things are a little tough."

"Honey, I think things are a little more than a little tough. You're not safe there."

"Well, I'm not leaving him so there has to be something else to help," she said firmly.

"Have you tried talking to God about it?" I asked reluctantly, like I was out of any other option. Dana and I have never frankly spoken about God or religion before. I was an avid Sunday morning church goer, and she stated that she believed in something, but didn't know what that something was. I have never been one to evangelize when it comes to God. I love talking to people about Jesus and God, but I was never one to go up to someone and ask if they knew the Lord.

"I don't even know God. So how am I supposed to talk to Him?" She responded with honesty.

I took a deep breath and smiled a little. There was nothing to really smile about in this situation. My best friend was being abused mentally, emotionally, and now physically by her husband. Talking to her about the love of God, though, was something I could do for her and that brought me some joy.

"You talk to Him like an old friend. You talk to Him like you would me. You start by building a relationship with Him because that's all that He wants," I said matter-of-factly.

Dana nodded her head, "I think I can do that. Can you help me get started?"

"Of course. It's settled then, you'll come to church with me, Wayne, and the kids," I stated.

"How am I supposed to get past Big Jim with that? He hates all things religion."

"Just tell him that you're helping me out on Sundays with the kids and then we'll take it from there."

One small nod was all she gave and all I needed.

Weeks led into months of going to church on Sundays. I started seeing the old Dana coming out of her shell by Sunday afternoon. Unfortunately, by Monday morning she would be right back into the shy person she had become. Dana was growing closer to God and that enraged Big Jim. Thankfully, he was still too drunk on Sunday mornings from partying the night before that he didn't even notice her absence most weeks.

The straw that broke the camel's back was when she confessed to Big Jim that she had been going to church. She tried to talk to him about getting him to join her in hopes that it would stop his hatred of the world and the drinking that came along with it. Big Jim became enraged and jealous that she was pulling away from him. He told her that she was trying to change him.

The next morning, she made it into the office only to collapse inside the door. I called 911 and found another large bruise on her left lower back. She ended up in the hospital for a week with a bruised kidney and a few broken ribs.

That hospital stay finally convinced Dana to press charges and he was arrested for domestic violence. She used that time to pack up her things and leave him.

After she was able to heal a bit Dana, and I put in a request for a girl's vacation and headed to the beach. We had an incredible time being lazy while soaking up the sun, finding Holy Mackerel's Bar and Grill and making plans for the future. I felt guilty for leaving Wayne and the kids behind, but this was the time that my best friend needed me.

The weekend after we got back, she got baptized bringing her relationship with God full circle. We celebrated with a small lunch at church, and I gave her a leather-bound bible as a gift. The gleam in her eyes as she held the Bible melted my heart.

After our celebratory lunch she went back to the small apartment that she was renting. She walked up the stairs to the outside of the apartment building to find a drunken Big Jim, out on bail, at her front door.

The day she was saved was also the day her life ended. I'll never forget that horrific phone call from the police saying that he had murdered her. Her bible was still in her hands when the police arrived.

Before that day I had only lost my grandaddy when I was little and my mama before Wayne and I were able to get married. Those deaths hurt, but this one was different. Murder felt like a different kind of sting, one where a hole is placed in your heart and cement fills it.

That hurt was able to help me grieve the loss of my son a few short months later. I knew how to grieve the loss of Samuel without fully losing myself in the process.

Now I stand here on the beach that holds some of the last memories I have of my best friend. A thunderstorm continues to blacken the sky above as she tells me to forgive him. I want to spit on Big Jim. Curse him to hell for taking such a beautiful life. I want him to hurt like I hurt, like he hurt Dana.

Dana stands calmly looking at me for an answer while the increasing wind whips her blonde hair all around. She tucks a strand behind her ear and stays silent.

"I don't know how you of all people can ask me to forgive him," I say. At this point I'm not sure if I should scream at the unfairness or cry at the frustration. I'm on the verge of both.

"Because of where I am now. I would not have been able to get to where I am without you or him," she replies with a small shrug and a smile. Her calmness is a stark contrast to the rage of the storm surrounding us.

"How are you smiling? I don't understand."

"I forgave him, Ellie, because without my death on the day that I got baptized I don't think I would have made it," she takes a deep breath before continuing while I am as confused as ever. "The world is full of sin and temptation. There's always going to be a reason to not go to church, not to open your bible, or say that it's okay to tell the little white lie just this once. Being baptized and then dying so soon, I got a clean slate. It hurt at first, but then I experienced what my eternity will be like. Your grandaddy was right when he said words cannot describe the beauty and its peacefulness of heaven. I am not bitter at Big Jim. He has his own demons to overcome, but he still has some time where you don't. Your time is running out and the hatred you are holding onto is blocking your way. Let it go Ellie."

I'm stunned to silence by what she said as I stand there. I think about the anger that I now know I built up in my heart from him. It's like a security blanket keeping me safe from him hurting me. I've held onto it for so long that I don't know how to let it go.

"I don't know how," I confess with a shrug.

"Come here," she says, grabbing my arm and moving towards the incoming ocean. "Dig your feet as far as you can into the sand."

"What?" I asked, perplexed.

"You heard me."

I did as I was told and began to dig my feet down into the wet sand on the edge of the water rushing in. I wasn't able to dig them far, but it was enough that both of my feet were covered and moving my feet would take some force.

"Digging your feet into the sand is like digging them into your anger. You feel as if you have a good hold on it and nothing can move you. But watch," she says as a rush of the first waves come gliding into the shore. The water starts receding the sand where I dug my feet making the hold not as tight. "The love of God can wash it away. It may take a few waves, but He'll eventually dig you out. Lean on Him. Let Him wash away your anger, your frustrations, your anxiety, and your guilt. That's it, that's all you have to do."

I collapse on the sand not caring that the next wave is coming in and I will get wet. Dana is right. I even remember telling Katie to lean more on God and yet I am not doing the same.

A rush of emotions fills me as I feel Dana crouching down beside me.

"You are strong, but let God take this burden from you."

I nod my head in acceptance. She kisses my cheek and says, "It's time for me to go."

She stands and walks away. I want to call after her, to ask her to stay a while longer, but my voice feels caught in my throat. I watch her take a few steps up the shoreline before her footprints stop in the sand and she is no longer with me.

I look out into the now raging sea. The waves crash into each other with violence as the winds rush from all different directions. Dana's presence was keeping the storm at bay and now that she is gone everything is erupting into chaos. The clouds open and the rain begins to pelt my face as a bolt of lightning strikes in the distance. The rumble from the thunder vibrates in my chest.

How could Dana just leave me like this?

I am scared now. I am out here on this beach with anger in my heart and a terrible storm coursing around me. I am alone with no one to lean on.

I want to move. To seek shelter from the storm and wait until it passes. I try to get up, but I find myself unable to stand. I have no strength in my legs. I move to all fours attempting to crawl away from the incoming waves, but even that proves impossible.

Lean on Me.

I hear a voice in my head.

Lean on Me. It says again.

My mind drifts to the story of Jesus walking on water. Peter cries out to the Lord asking to join Him on the water. Jesus commanded him to walk on the water, but as the waves got higher Peter began to sink and drown. Jesus pulls him up and asks why he doubted.

Am I doubting His ability to take this burden from me or am I too stubborn to give up my anger? My heart aches as a loud thunder reverberates within me.

I cry out into the darkness. I cry out in fear. I cry out in sorrow. I cry out so that I don't have to feel this heaviness in my heart anymore.

"Help me! Please! I don't want to feel like this anymore," I shout. I don't know how anyone is supposed to hear me over the crashing of the waves and the thunder cracking.

"Please God! Don't leave me! Don't forsake me! Help me to let my anger go!"

In an instant the waves calm, the wind ceases, and the clouds split apart. The sun once covered now shines brightly bringing a sunbeam to my face. I sat back with stunned relief. The heaviness is lifted from my heart.

"I'm sorry," I cry. "I'm so sorry. I didn't realize what this anger was doing to me. Please help me."

I sit in the shallow water, the storm bringing in the tide. I grab a fist full of sand but keep my hand under the water. Even with the now calm waves drifting in, the sand still gets washed away from my hand.

Dana is happy. She is where all of us hope to go someday. That should be enough. So why am I harboring all this anger towards what happened to her? In fact, if I'm hoping to join her then why am I holding onto anger for every person that has ever wronged me throughout my life?

I pick up another fist full of sand and watch as the ocean washes it away again. I breathe in the fresh air and let out all of the burden and anger that I didn't know I was holding on to. I feel lighter now. The rest of the anger that I refused to give up is gone now too. The weight of it is lifted off of my shoulders.

Dana was right, it takes too much energy holding onto hatred and bitterness. I grab one more fist of sand placing the rest of my animosity in it and know that it's God who picks it up and carries it away.

CHAPTER 13

I open my eyes to see Wayne sitting in a chair next to my bed. His arms are crossed at his chest and his head hangs low with soft snores coming out of his mouth. Why is he sitting in a chair next to me? I can see dark circles from under his eyes like he didn't get a good night's sleep.

I clear my throat softly. He opens his eyes in a panic and immediately sits straight up in the chair at full attention. His face meets mine. He moves from the chair to a kneeling position at my bedside.

"Hi, how are you feeling?" he asks, placing a hand on my cheek.

"I'm starting to feel some of the pain, but otherwise I'm okay. What are you doing sleeping in the chair next to me?"

"Do you remember anything from last night?"

I look at him with confusion. I remember building gingerbread houses with the kids and going to bed early before having my dream with Dana. What happened last night that he thinks I should remember? The look on my face gave away my confusion as he answers his own question.

"I guess not. You were crying out in your sleep. Your breathing picked up and you were crying. I couldn't wake you. I couldn't do anything to help you, so I had to call the hospice nurse," Wayne explains.

"I don't remember any of that," I confess, shaking my head. Did Wayne see me crying like I was in my dream? I want to think that that is crazy, but at this point I don't think anything could surprise me.

"You scared me so bad. I woke up to you whimpering like Carmel does when she's sleeping. I couldn't wake you and I got worried. I called the hospice line, and they told me to give you some of that Roxanol and Ativan. Apparently, you don't even need to swallow the pill if it's crushed. Your mouth will just absorb it," he explains further.

I think back to my dream and the moment that I cried out in anguish. I cried out in fear of the storm, but also to rid myself of the hatred and anger that I kept in my heart. That must be what Wayne is talking about. The cry he heard was me crying out in the storm. The medicine or God or maybe even both helped me relax and make the storm pass. Incredible.

"Thank you for calling them and getting me the medicine," I say. I don't want to alarm him by telling him about the dreams I have had recently. I feel as if that is between me and God.

"Of course, Ellie. I would do anything for you." He brushes my forehead with his hand, a habit he hasn't been able to break since I lost my hair. I love the feel of his lips on my forehead as he leans over to kiss me.

I start to stretch out to get up for the day, but I have no energy or even the desire to get out of bed. My muscles feel weak and tight, and I know that I would end up on the floor if I tried to get out of this bed, even with the help from my walker and Wayne. I slept all night and yet I feel as if my time with Dana is like I have been up for twenty-four hours. I am exhausted. My lack of energy overpowers my will to get out of bed and get dressed for the day.

"I know I should get up, but I just can't. Do you think I could just stay in here today?" I plead with Wayne.

"If that's what you want to do. I will bring you whatever you want or need. How about a pain pill to start?"

He shows just a hint of worry.

I nod my head in agreement not wanting my pain level to get out of control. Wayne is back in a few seconds and hands me the small pill and a cup of water. I placed the pill to the back of my throat and took a small sip of water. The first initial sip got the pill down, but the next one had me choking. I am coughing so hard that I think this will defeat the purpose of taking the pain pill.

Wayne is right at my side, rubbing my back and grabbing a tissue off the nightstand at the same time. I take it, but honestly don't know how a tissue is supposed to stop my coughing. After a moment I am able to stop and lay back on my pillow.

"Are you okay?" Wayne asks me.

"Yeah. It just went down the wrong pipe I guess." I nuzzle back under the blankets and close my eyes. It isn't long before I fall back asleep.

I wake up later in the day to my bedroom door being opened. I can hear Katie call out from the hallway. Carmel, once again at my side, doesn't even raise her head to the slight noise coming from the hallway.

"McKenna, what are you doing? Let grandma sleep," Katie scolds in a hush tone.

"Why is grandma sleeping mommy? Is she sick?" The little girl asks innocently.

"Yes baby. Grandma is very sick right now and she needs lots of time to rest."

By the lack of light in the room I would say that it is late afternoon. I look at the clock on my nightstand and see the time is 4:16, almost sunset. I turn my attention to the hallway and see Katie kneeling at her daughter with a soft light coming in. McKenna has her thumb in her mouth with her favorite blankie and stuffed animal tucked under her other arm. She tends to hold them close and suck her thumb when she is nervous or doesn't understand something.

"Maybe I should give her my blankie to make her feel better," McKenna tells her mom as she holds up her blanket.

"That's beautiful baby. I don't think grandma needs your blankie right now though. She just needs some rest, okay?"

I love how my granddaughter is willing to give her most prized possession away to make someone else feel better. I can't stop the words from coming out of my mouth.

"I think a blankie is just what I need," my voice is weak and scratchy, although I am still able to project it enough for them to hear me.

"Grandma!" McKenna yells as she runs to jump on my bed. I weakly turn over so that I can give her a hug.

"Hi baby girl," I say, smiling in her embrace.

"Careful Kenna," I hear Katie say from the doorway. She starts talking to someone from down the hall. "Yeah, she's awake." Pause. "I don't know yet she's hugging McKenna." Pause. "Okay, just give me a minute and I'll let you know."

McKenna pulls back from hugging me and asks, "Grandma, are you feeling better?"

"Much better now that you are here," I tell her.

"Would you like to come play Barbies with me?"

"If you want to bring a few of them in here then I'll play for a little bit, okay? But grandma still feels a little sick so you may just have to tell the stories to me."

"Okay, I'll be right back," McKenna says excitedly. She hops off of my bed and rushes past her mom to collect her Barbies.

"How are you feeling mama?" Katie asks from the doorway.

"Like I've been hit by a truck," I responded honestly. I sit up weakly in preparation for playing Barbies. "Could you turn on the lamp?"

Katie walks in and clicks on the lamp on my nightstand. She sits on my bed next to my legs.

"What else can I do for you mama?"

"Maybe some pain medicine with some hot chocolate, extra marshmallows."

"Do you want something to eat?"

I scrunch my nose and shake my head no. It's funny how I still feel full from the meal I had in my dream with Dana.

"You haven't eaten all day mama, are you sure?" Katie pushes.

"Just the pain pill and hot chocolate please," I say with a pleading look. I don't want to argue about my lack of appetite and needing to eat something just to have the calories. I don't even think I'll be able to drink all the hot chocolate. Right now, it is the only thing that sounds good; anything else may make me nauseated.

McKenna comes back with some Barbies as Katie leaves to fulfill my request. McKenna takes the burden upon herself to entertain me with the stories from her Barbies. I can hear Wayne, Michael, and Katie with their families, even a crying Samantha. I long to be out there with the rest of my family.

Katie returns with my request for a pain pill and a mug of the delicious chocolatey liquid. She gives me a small smile as she places the items on my nightstand and leaves the room.

I place the pill in my mouth and take a sip of my drink. I'm able to get the pill down without difficulty unlike this morning. What seems odd to me is that the sugary drink sounded appetizing when I asked Katie for it. It now tastes like hot liquid mud in my mouth. There is no flavor to it at all.

I think back to the days of quarantine and covid. Wayne and I contracted the virus early on when so many people were getting hospitalized. Thankfully, the virus only took our sense of taste and smell unlike so many others. It wasn't nearly as bad as most people. My current drink reminds me of that, no sweetness, no flavor, just blah.

I'm annoyed and I place my mug back on the nightstand with more force than I meant to. I hate that I can't enjoy even the simplest pleasures like drinking a cup of hot chocolate. I recognize the feeling in my heart now is one of anger. Anger at my cancer and what it is robbing me of.

"Let it go, Ellie."

I hear the words Dana said to me echo through my head, my heart and even my soul.

I breathe in deeply and smile at McKenna dancing her Barbies around on my bed. Yes, I am going to lose a lot, but I have a feeling that I am about to gain so much more. Even the food I ate with grandaddy, and Dana was divine if that is anything to go by.

The little giggles next to me bring me out of my head and I watch McKenna play with her dolls. The sound brings a certain happiness to my heart, and I can't help but appreciate this one-on-one time that I am getting with my eldest granddaughter.

This also comes with an oxymoron of feeling like I am robbing the rest of my family of this time with me. I am not sure how much longer I have before I am no longer able to have those conversations with my kids and husband. I glance from the open bedroom door at the barely audible noises in the nearby room. I long to be out with the rest of my family. Unfortunately, my legs feel weak even just lying in bed and I honestly don't know how I am going to make it out there without significant help.

More time passes as I lose myself in my thoughts before McKenna hears Nathan starting up a new toy with sound. She rushes off the bed to see what Nathan is doing, obviously weary of playing Barbies with me at this point. I am now stuck in my bed all by my lonesome.

Thankfully seeing that McKenna is no longer in the bedroom with me, Wayne walks into the room to check on me.

"Hey sleepyhead," he jokes. He lays down on the bed next to me and props himself up on his elbow looking as casual as ever.

"Hi. Is everyone still here?" I ask.

"Yeah, we're finishing up making dinner if you would like to join us."

I scrunch my nose again at the thought of food.

"No food, but I want to get out of this room. I feel so far away from you all and I want to be a part of everything going on." I have the sinking feeling that I'll fall asleep on everyone. I don't think they will mind. Who would have thought dying could be so exhausting? I don't dare utter those thoughts to Wayne, he has enough on his mind to worry about.

Thinking my recliner was a prison a few weeks ago when everyone else could help set up Christmas decorations doesn't seem so bad now. It's at least better than being secluded in a back bedroom.

"Okay well let's get you out of this bed then," Wayne says, standing up.

"I think we're going to need some help," I say hesitantly.

"Why? What's wrong?"

"I can feel it in my legs. I have no strength in them or energy to walk that far. I don't even think I can manage with my walker at this point."

"Well, we have two options then. Michael, Jason, and I can pick you up and carry you like the queen matriarch of the family you are…"

I roll my eyes at that option, "or?"

"Or I could get the wheelchair from the back of the car and wheel you to your recliner. Though it is going to be a tight fit, I think," Wayne suggests.

"Could we try that option? Knowing my luck one of you will lose your grip on me and we will all be on the floor."

Wayne places a hand over his heart, "you wound me with your words. I'll have you know that I have the strength of ten men and would never drop my queen."

Trying to appease him I add, "It's not you that I don't trust."

He smiles in satisfaction at my response and states, "I'll be right back with the wheelchair and the boys."

At his word, the men spring into action. Within minutes I have a wheelchair at my side, and I am being assisted to stand and pivot to the chair, although not so gracefully. Wayne starts making his way down the narrow hallway.

When making the plans for building the house we decided to go for a narrower hallway to give us extra room in the bedrooms. Looking back now that was a mistake.

While pushing me down the hallway, a wheel got stuck under my robe. Instead of pulling back on the chair and clearing the obstruction, Wayne just pushed harder leaving a long black scratch down the wall from the chair. I put my head in my hands because frankly there is nothing else to do.

I stand to pivot into my recliner and feel as if I just ran a marathon. I am worn out and I didn't even do anything except stand and pivot twice.

Wayne sets the wheelchair aside and plops down in his recliner.

"Well, that sucks," is all he says. I want to agree with him, but the damage is already done and there is nothing more to be said about it.

I look around to see Michael on the couch holding a sleeping Samantha in his arms. I love that his entire face lights up as he looks at her with such love. That little girl already has her daddy wrapped around her little finger. One more time I wish that I could be here to watch her grow up. To watch Michael and Josie learn the ropes of being a parent and help them through the tough things. Tears come to my eyes, but I refuse to let them spill over. I cannot let my family see my sadness and grief. That would ruin the night.

Jason sits next to Michael on the couch watching the football game playing on the screen while the kids play on the ground with some toys. I can hear plates being taken out of the cabinet in the kitchen in anticipation of dinner being ready soon. Over in the empty chair in the corner sits the young man once again.

He looks at me with a smile but doesn't say a word. His smile could light up a room, if anyone else was able to see him aside from me.

"Please talk to me," I beg, not realizing that I said it out loud.

"What would you like me to talk to you about, baby?" Wayne asks. Michael and Jason look at me as well.

"Umm, what's been going on today?" I ask, trying to correct my embarrassment. I feel the heat rise in my cheeks.

"Well, it's been a slow Sunday. Not doing much. We got some more packages today and I've enlisted the help of Katie and Josie to start wrapping some of them," Wayne answers.

"Wayne! You're having our daughters wrap their own gifts? That's cruel," I say in consternation.

"No, of course not! I'm having them wrap the gifts for the grand babies and their husbands. Michael and Jason are wrapping the presents we got for Josie and Katie."

"You're joking right? This is a joke?"

Michael chimes in at that moment, "he's not joking mama. We had to wrap up some gifts today."

I look under the Christmas tree to see a few very poorly wrapped gifts with ribbons that don't match the color of the wrapping paper. I look up at Wayne in horror.

"What? It's better than I would have done, and I wanted to take this burden from you," Wayne says with his hands in the air like 'don't shoot.'

I want to be grateful to the gesture, but it sucks knowing that this is what my girls are going to open on Christmas Day. I guess it's the gift and not how it is wrapped that matters. I still cringe a little.

Josie walks in to announce that dinner is ready while carrying a few more beautifully wrapped presents.

"I'm so sorry that you had to wrap all of those presents along with your own family's," I tell my daughter-in-law.

"Mom, it's fine. What's a few more gifts? Now are we ready to eat?" Josie responds with a shrug of her shoulders.

Everyone starts to get up to make their way into the kitchen. Michael places Samantha in her pumpkin seat still sleeping. I hold my hand out to stop my husband before he can go too far.

He leans over to me so I can ask, "do you think you could make a plate and come back in here to eat it?"

"Are you sure? It's spaghetti," he inquires.

"Yeah, I don't care. I just want to be a part of everything, and I don't think I can make it into the kitchen."

"Sure, I'll put a towel down for McKenna and Nathan. We can let them pretend it's like a picnic."

"That sounds wonderful." He gives me a brief kiss before heading to make a plate.

I am left alone with the young man sitting in the chair. He is once again wearing a green flannel shirt, blue jeans, and boots. I have noticed during his 'visits' that he constantly watches everything intently. He never opens his mouth to utter a single word and all I want to do is ask his name and hear his voice.

"Why won't you talk to me?" I ask in a hush tone so that my family won't hear.

He stands and moves over to look at Samantha sleeping in her pumpkin seat. His smile widens showing off his perfectly white teeth before making his way over to my chair. He kneels bringing his eyes level to mine. He is so close to me that I could reach out and touch him. I want to. I want to see if I can feel his touch. I watch as he moves to grab my hand. Before his hand can reach mine, Michael enters the room with two large towels to place on the floor. I briefly turn my attention to watch Michael. When I look back, I see that the man is gone.

Dinner went smoothly, only Nathan had dropped some spaghetti, but thankfully it was on the towel and not my carpet. Katie and Josie make themselves busy with cleaning dishes after everyone has finished eating. Now I lay back in my recliner ready for bed. I feel as if I have slept twenty hours today and yet I am still so exhausted. I make a mental note to have a conversation with Elisha about this tomorrow.

"Mom, do you want help getting back into bed before we all start to head out?" Michael asks.

I ponder that question for a bit. If they get me back to bed, won't it be more difficult tomorrow to get me out? Plus, there's always the possibility that one of them will put another scratch on my wall.

I finally say, "No, I think I'll stay here for tonight, but I do need some help going to the bathroom."

"Ellie, I can help you with that," Wayne chimes in.

Michael answers back, "Dad, why don't I at least stay while you're getting mom settled. That way if she falls, I can help you get her up off the floor. I'll start packing Josie and Samantha up."

"Do you want us to stay too?" Jason asks.

"Nah, I got it," Michael states with a slap on Jason's back.

Katie and Jason say their goodbyes and head out the door with McKenna and Nathan. Josie grabs the overly large diaper bag and begins to repack everything they brought. I know I am being overly dramatic thinking that she packed an entire Target store in that bag. How much can a newborn really need?

Michael and Wayne help me to the bathroom at the other end of the house where there isn't a hallway to navigate through. It takes me several minutes longer than usual to complete my nightly routine with Wayne's help, but I somehow manage without ending up on the floor. The pain I feel when I sit back in my recliner is amped up to a nine out of ten. I am unable to hide the discomfort on my face.

"Roxanol. Please get the Roxanol," I say, squeezing my eyes shut.

Wayne leaves to get the Roxanol and gives me a dose before handing me a cup of water. It really does taste like crap. Like oil that has been left out for years to spoil. I take a sip of water with hopes to get the taste out of my mouth and I start choking. It seems like the water keeps wanting to go down the wrong pipe.

After my coughing fit, I lean back in my chair with desperation for the Roxanol to kick in. I breathe heavily with a furrowed brow and tension in my arms and legs. Within ten very long minutes I can feel the medicine kick in. I am able to relax back enough that Michael feels comfortable leaving. I love that he makes sure that Wayne and I are good for the night before heading out the door.

I am thankful that my loving husband did not leave my side. He settles me in with my blanket and a pillow from our bed. Only after making sure that I am okay does he complete his usual nightly routine of letting the dogs out one more time and changing to his pj pants. He pulls his favorite blanket out of the hallway closet and his pillow from our bed. He starts placing his pillow and blanket in just the right spot on his chair.

"You're not going to sleep in our bed?" I ask.

"If you're out here sleeping then so am I," he says. "Especially after the night you had last night."

I love this man with all my heart. He is too good to me. He settles into his recliner after kissing me good night. He flips the channel and finds an old sitcom that we have seen one too many times. The volume is turned down low before both of us slip off to another night's slumber.

CHAPTER 14

The next morning, I wake up stiff from sleeping in my recliner. I look over to Wayne's direction to see his chair empty and the blankets are folded neatly on the floor beside his chair. It is Monday morning, and I should be expecting Elisha at any moment.

"Wayne?" I call out.

He pops his head from around the kitchen wall like a cartoon.

"You have summoned me, my lady?"

I laugh at his cuteness and shake my head, "What am I going to do with you?"

"Love me until the world stops spinning."

"Maybe even beyond that," I smile.

He grins back at me and asks, "what can I do for you?"

"Can you help me get dressed before Elisha gets here? Also, I need to use the lady's room."

"How about I wheel you into the bathroom like we did last night, and I'll go pick out some clothes for you."

"That sounds like a plan. Make sure you grab the sexy underwear and my shirt with the plunging V-neck," I tease.

"By sexy underwear do you mean the ones without the poop stains?"

I shake my head again at him and widen my smile, "you're such a butt."

"Yeah, but I'm your butt," he says while getting the wheelchair ready.

I am able to complete a condensed version of my morning routine and get settled back into my chair when Elisha arrives. The problem is that my pain is back up to a nine from all the moving around.

Wayne answers the door to Elisha's knock right when I let out a loud moan from an ache in my stomach. This pain is sharp. It feels as if I have been stabbed by a knife and someone is twisting it. Much like last night I am unable to hide my facial grimacing and guarding of my stomach. Elisha quickly walks past Wayne after he lets her in.

"I'm here. What's going on?" She immediately starts. She kneels by my chair, not bothering to use the chair next to mine like she usually does.

Through clenched teeth I begin to tell her all about the increased pain and the decrease in strength. I want to tell her more, but I don't have that ability at the moment. She turns to Wayne and tells him to give me a dose of the Roxanol as well as the Ativan to aid in my pain management.

She takes out her stethoscope and listens to my heart, lungs, and belly. She starts taking my vitals and jots them down on a piece of paper as Wayne gives me the medication. I grimace at the nasty taste it brings to my mouth. Today Elisha doesn't even bother taking out her computer to chart.

"How much pain medicine have you been taking?" She asks no one in particular.

Wayne and I look at each other with hesitation. If he didn't know then I surely didn't.

Wayne thankfully breaks the silence to answer her, "she has been taking the pills around the clock and she has been needing the Roxanol more often."

Elisha looks at me and asks, "are they working?"

"Not as effective as they used to be even with the Ativan added with my pain pills," I admit.

"Okay, it may be time to increase something. How is your appetite?" She is all business today.

"Non-existent," I reply.

"The Mirtazapine hasn't helped at all?"

"If it has then I haven't noticed a difference," I answer and look at Wayne. He nods his head in agreement.

"I reviewed the call from Saturday night, and I'm glad the medications were able to work effectively that night. Is there anything else that I should be aware of?"

"Actually, yeah, a few things," I say hesitantly. "I have no energy. I'm sleeping over eighty percent of the day and now I don't even have the strength to get up and walk. My walker is useless, and we had to revert to using my wheelchair to get around. Even with just standing and pivoting to get to places takes all my energy. I'm also starting to have trouble swallowing. A couple of times I have choked on water trying to get my pain pills down."

I unload all my frustrations to her, but she just nods her head as if expecting my answer.

Elisha takes a deep breath as she contemplates her next words. "I'm going to step out and call Jeane, the nurse practitioner, to get some updated orders on medications. Once I know the plan from her and the doctor and what they decide to do, then I will come and let you know and do some education with you. Does that sound okay?"

I looked from Wayne to her and back again with concern and worry. "Should we be concerned about something?"

Elisha takes a deep breath and says, "no I'm sorry. It's just been a crazy morning, and I haven't had a chance to stop and breathe. So, I'm a little all over the place." She uses her hand in the air to signify 'all over the place.'

She's talking quickly and stumbling over her words. I feel bad that she hasn't had a chance to catch her breath yet this morning.

I am grateful to my husband as he says, "Well if you need to take a load off then sit back and breathe. We got a chair for you and a bedside table you can use for charting." He gestures to the chair and clears the table to my side.

"That's very sweet of you and honestly I wish I could." She pulls her phone out of her pocket and points to the front door, "I'm just gonna make this quick phone call."

She leaves, walking quickly.

"She doesn't seem like herself today," Wayne states.

I shake my head, "nope, but everyone has their days I guess."

Wayne kisses the top of my head and asks, "how's the pain now?"

"Still at a nine, but I can feel it trying to come down a little." I am thankful that my face is at least relaxed, and I don't look like I'm in as much pain as I actually am. I hate showing that to him because I know he will worry.

Wayne sits back in his recliner, and we wait for Elisha to come back into the room for whatever discussion is needed. I have a feeling that I am showing signs of declining more. I mean choking on water after a tiny sip can't be good, not to mention the fact that I haven't eaten in over twenty-four hours.

I catch my breath at that thought. Has it really been twenty-four hours since I last ate anything? I still don't feel the need or desire to eat at all. If I am being honest with myself, I still feel full from eating the plate of seafood with Dana. That is once again, crazy! That was a dream, not real life. How can a dream make me feel full?

Elisha walks back into our house after hanging up the phone with her nurse practitioner or doctor or whoever it was that she spoke to. She walks over to the chair beside my recliner and sits for the first time.

She takes a deep breath and begins talking, "okay so first things first we are going to increase your Fentanyl patch to the next dosage level. Thankfully, it is due to be changed today so when the new patch arrives from the pharmacy tonight then put the new dose on."

Wayne and I nod our heads in understanding as she continues.

"Next, since the Mirtazapine has not been working for you then it is okay to stop it since you are starting to have difficulty swallowing."

I like that idea, one less pill I have to worry about.

"You are currently taking the highest dose of the oxycodone, and it is not working anymore along with the current dose of the Roxanol. The doctor suggests that you increase the dose of the Roxanol to 0.5 milliliters or 10 milligrams. That should be more effective. Continue to take the pain pills for now, but since you are having trouble swallowing and coughing after drinking water you may have to cut out the pain pills all together soon," Elisha informs.

There's that word again, soon. How soon is soon?

"But if she stops taking the pain pills then how are we going to manage her pain?" Wayne asks.

"Through the Fentanyl patch as well as the Roxanol. Some of my patients are taking the Roxanol every two hours. In extreme circumstances she can have it every hour, but typically we can manage it through our current plan."

I sit back and listen to the conversation being exchanged between my husband and my hospice nurse, soaking up all the information I can.

Wayne continues with his questions trying to understand. "Why would we stop the pain pills? Why can't they be crushed like the Ativan?"

"The Ativan can be crushed, and it will absorb through the mucous membranes of the mouth. Unfortunately, the pain pills don't work like that, and they won't absorb correctly. The little flap that comes down over the trachea to prevent food from going into the lungs is not working properly and if she continues to drink fluid then we risk pneumonia. And that is a different kind of discomfort," Elisha reports.

"So where am I at with everything?" I finally asked her.

She looks back at me with pity in her eyes, she knows exactly what I am asking. She takes a breath and holds it for a moment before speaking.

I feel as if she is needing encouragement so I prompt her, "it's okay, I want you to be as honest as you can. Give it to me straight."

"Today is Monday the 16th. We have nine more days until Christmas. I honestly don't know if you are going to make it. Your body is shutting down quickly and your pain is increasing more. How much did you say that you are sleeping?" She inquires.

I love that my beautiful nurse knows my goal is to have one more Christmas with my family.

"Well yesterday it was pretty much all day. She was probably only awake for a few hours or more. And she can't walk anymore. She slept in her recliner last night because it hurt too much to get back in the wheelchair to go back to bed," Wayne answers for me.

Elisha nods her head as if she is once again expecting his answers and suggests, "Okay what about maybe bringing in a hospital bed? That way you can be more comfortable out here in a bed, but still be a part of family time?"

The suggestion brings on the feeling of nausea. I feel like the bed is the last step. I just know that once I am placed in bed there is no getting out. The thought of lying in bed makes me anxious and overwhelmed. I'm not ready for that. I'm not ready for this. I still have so much I want to say to my kids and grandkids.

And what about Wayne? We have had a lifetime together, more years than most couples get, but he isn't ready to put me six feet in the ground. I'm not ready to leave him yet either.

I don't want to imagine lying in a hospital bed even if that bed is in my own home. I'm not ready.

I shake my head no with tears in my eyes effectively answering Elisha's question. I can feel her empathy as she reaches out to hold my hand.

"Okay, I understand. Just let me know if you change your mind."

I give a short nod. The lump is back in my throat, and I find it difficult to talk about anything else. Thankfully, Elisha wraps up her visit with written instructions on the changes made to my medicine. I'm glad that Katie and Michael will be able to read her notes since neither of them could be here today.

I'm not sure when I fell asleep, but I wake up a little later in the day to Wayne talking on his phone. He is sitting in his recliner speaking with either Katie or Michael. I don't want to interrupt him, so I keep my eyes closed and listen in to the conversation.

"No, she's sleeping right now." Pause. "Elisha said she would start to sleep a lot so no I don't think it's unusual." Pause. "Her pain is getting worse, and she hasn't eaten anything yet today." Pause and then a hitch in his voice. "She said that she may not make it to Christmas." Pause with a sniffle.

177

"Yeah, I think she might like that. Let's do that tonight before the weather comes in." Another pause. "Okay baby. Drive safe getting the kids and we'll see you soon." I heard him end the call and place his phone on the side table.

The T.V. is low with muffled voices in the background. I can hear Wayne stand and take a few short steps to walk over to me before kneeling at my side. He sniffles once more trying to compose himself before placing a hand on my arm and giving me a gentle shake.

"Hey honey?"

"Mmmm," I respond.

"Do you want to try to eat something?"

I really don't feel the urge to eat anything. I would be perfectly content going back to sleep, but I don't want to make him worry any more than he already is.

I open my eyes and say, "a chocolate pudding sounds nice."

He smiles with a small snort, "coming right up. We have some that Katie left for McKenna and Nathan."

I open my eyes fully and sit up in my recliner only feeling a slight increase in my pain level from the movement. I watch as Wayne leaves the room to see grandaddy, Dana and my mystery man sitting on the couch. Grandaddy appears to be the younger version of himself while Dana looks as healthy as ever. My mystery man has never changed. Seeing him always sparks my curiosity about who he is to me. I am hoping that I will find out soon.

"Pudding? Really? That's what you ask for?" Dana says sarcastically. "Very different from the seafood platter you ate with me."

"Or the fried fish with me. And back in my day we didn't have pudding cups. I don't even think it had been invented yet. If so, we would have had to walk up hill for five miles to enjoy a special treat like that," grandaddy teases with a wink in his eye.

"Why does every old person talk about walking up a hill for five miles?" Dana asks while the young gentleman sitting next to her stays silent and just smiles.

"Who are you calling old?" grandaddy asks. At the moment Dana appears older than grandaddy which is making this moment even more hilarious.

"What is going on?" I asked a little loudly.

"We're just checking on you honey buns," Dana states.

At that moment Wayne walks back into the living room and says with confusion, "I'm getting you chocolate pudding. I'm sorry, did you want chocolate ice cream instead? I think we have some of that too."

I shake my head knowing Wayne won't understand me seeing my dead best friend, grandpa, and whoever the other guy is. He will think I have lost all my marbles.

"No, I mean tonight. I thought I heard you say something to Katie about doing something before the weather comes in," I reply, trying not to embarrass myself any more than I already have.

"It's a surprise. I can't tell you. Hopefully, the weather will hold off though. The meteorologist said it might snow tonight."

He hands me the cup of pudding and a spoon before sitting back in his chair.

"Awe, that's nice. You get a surprise. I never got surprises," Dana mock pouts.

"I knew I always liked that young man of hers," grandaddy chimes in.

"Shhh," I let out.

Wayne looks at me, "I didn't say anything."

I feel the heat in my cheeks from embarrassment. I point to the pudding with my spoon.

"So good," I exclaim, trying to redeem myself once again.

I hear Wayne say, 'oh good' while Dana says 'smooth.'

I finished the chocolate pudding which is a shock for me and my lack of appetite when the air around me seems to shift to tense and almost electric. I look over at my three visitors who stare back at me.

Dana's eyes are piercing as she says, "soon."

One word. That one little word that held so much meaning to it. The thought comes to mind from Elisha last week when she said that I would be able to hear, but not respond. I feel as if that moment is coming sooner than I would like. I look up at Dana who nods her head as if she read my mind as clearly as she did in my dream. Grandaddy and the young man also nod their heads at me.

I find myself nodding my head knowing what I need to do. I look over at Wayne who is engrossed in a show playing on the t.v.

I interrupt his mindless watching and ask him, "hey Wayne. Do you think we could call the pastor to come over for a visit? I didn't make it to church yesterday, obviously, and I would really like to talk to him."

"Yeah, I'll call him now." He stands to walk outside to make his phone call. I stop him before he gets too far.

"And can you bring me back pen and paper?"

He stops in his tracks seeming to know why I want the pen and paper. He looks at me and nods but can't bring himself to say any words.

The rest of the afternoon I spend my time writing letters to the grandkids and Josie and Jason. I figure those would be the easy ones to knock out of the way before I get to the more difficult letters of saying goodbye. My special visitors left shortly after Wayne walked out to call our pastor. I'm not sure when they did, I just looked in their direction and all three of them were gone.

Shortly after sunset it was time for my big surprise. Everyone was able to get off work just a little early. The men helped me into Katie's car as it was the easiest for me to get in and out of. The movement from the wheelchair to get in the vehicle was daunting and painful, but after getting settled and taking more of the Roxanol I was ready for whatever my family had in store for me. I am grateful that everyone gave me the extra time needed to get my pain under control before starting up the vehicles to move.

Now I am in Katie's vehicle with all the grandkids and Michael. Wayne, Jason, and Josie are following in the car behind us. We are heading to my surprise, and I am so excited. Anything about getting out of the house is a pleasant surprise.

After about twenty minutes of driving, Katie turns down a road and twinkling lights greet me. Christmas lights. The smile on my face is as bright as the lights themselves.

"Christmas lights?" I asked with enthusiasm. I was scared that this tradition would be skipped this year. I love that Wayne, and the kids thought of this. A tear of happiness glides down my face and I welcome it.

Unfortunately, my cancer wants to ruin this moment with the pain rising in my lower back. I ignore it and try to push it out of my mind. I am hoping that I will be able to have just twenty minutes of looking at the lights. Just twenty minutes, is that too much to ask?

The sounds coming from the back from McKenna and Nathan make my worries disappear and I smile even harder than I was before. Thoughts of my pain jump out of my head. Seeing things from a child's perspective just makes everything better.

The intricate beauty that goes behind making the scenes is fascinating. I love seeing the small light up fish jumping out of the water where a lit up blue pond is. My favorite has always been and will always be the nativity scene with the song Silent Night playing softly in the background. There is something about the peacefulness that calms the soul. I think back to a sermon that I once heard about the nativity scene.

The song plays, 'Silent Night. Holy Night. All is calm. All is bright.' What is not said is the chaos that happened before that Silent Night. Mary and Joseph were shut out of every inn. Her water breaks as she bends over when a stronger contraction begins. Finally, an innkeeper took pity on her and Joseph and led them to a barn next to a mooing cow and baaing sheep. There were no doctors or nurses or even a midwife to help her give birth to our Lord and Savior. It was all on her and Joseph to get through this moment with maybe the help of the innkeeper's wife or servant for towels and water.

After giving birth with no epidural, no pain killers, no help, a screaming child- or what I imagine a screaming baby would do after being born, emerges. A sixteen-year-old Mary nurses her newborn before settling him into a manger for some much-needed sleep. Chaos before peace. Beautiful. Plain and simple.

Katie must have stopped for too long allowing me to admire the nativity scene when we heard honking a few cars back. People are so impatient these days. Can't they just enjoy what they have in front of them at that moment?

On the way home the grandkids thankfully fell asleep. I take that opportunity to talk with Michael and Katie alone.

"I know you guys talked with dad today about Elisha's visit." I start. I don't look back to Michael behind me or to Katie driving the car although I didn't miss her placing both hands on the steering wheel versus the one she had on casually. "Are you okay?" I ask them.

Michael is the first to respond after a long moment, "You asked me to be strong for you and to help give you some laughter. I'm not okay with what is about to happen, but I will be strong for you mama."

An uncomfortable silence falls between us.

Katie swallows hard before saying her peace, "my fears are back of having that last time to talk to you or the last time you open your eyes. I'm scared of the last time you will take a breath. But I know you're in a lot of pain. I can see that, and I will accept the time that I am given with you."

She pulls into our driveway, and I let out a small chuckle at seeing my light up cow on the front lawn mixed with the other Christmas lights. She puts it in park, but no one makes a move to get out of the car.

I take a deep breath, "I know it may be hard, especially with work, but I would like to see more of you guys this week."

"Done," Michael says.

"I'll move some stuff around tomorrow and take the rest of the week off," Katie replies.

I feel relieved knowing that I will get to have some extra time with my loved ones this week.

Michael and Jason help me get out of the car and into the wheelchair as the snow begins to fall. I hold my hand out as a snowflake lands and begins to melt away. I smile at the beautiful thick snowflakes now falling all around us.

"Wanna go for a ride mom?" Michael asks, leaning down into my ear.

"Yes," I say excitedly. I am grateful that I didn't have to ask him to go easy on me. He knew that pushing me too hard could cause instant pain.

He pushes me around the driveway in circles in a dancing like motion when someone decides to add a little music. It's the mother-son song that we danced to at his wedding. I look up behind me and my eyes meet the tear-filled eyes of my son. I laughed when he said he wanted to dance to a song from Disney at his wedding, but 'You'll Be in My Heart' from Tarzan seemed like the perfect song for us.

He pushes me a little longer in a dancing motion before coming around and gathering me into a hug. I want to stand and fully embrace him, but a sitting wheelchair will have to do for now.

"Best dance ever," he whispers in my ear.

I couldn't agree more, although I am having trouble finding the words.

The song ends and I can hear everyone clapping from behind us. As if on cue, the wind picks up, sending a chill down my back.

"Let's get you inside and settled for the night mama," Michael suggests.

I nod my head in agreement. A ping of disappointment settles over me at the realization that I will not get to do this anymore. I will never again be able to dance with my son at a random moment. Or see the Christmas lights with my family. Or enjoy the other little moments too often taken for granted.

I am trying to still be strong. To hold it together for everyone else, me included, but the depression is creeping in ever so slowly with the thought of time and memories that I am going to miss out on with my family.

Even as my boys help me get ready for bed, I know that I will no longer be able to do anything on my own. At least before I had some semblance of being independent. How can a beautiful moment that I just shared with my son turn into a spiral of unending sadness?

The more I go through my nightly routine the more I just want this day to be over with. I request once again that I sleep out in my recliner so that no one has to fuss trying to get me in and out of bed or put another mark on my wall. Another moment of independence stripped away from me.

I take more of the Roxanol and change out my Fentanyl patch to a stronger dose. My eyes close from the exhaustion of the day and before anyone has a chance to say their goodbyes for the night I am out like a light with feelings of defeat.

CHAPTER 15

My eyes open to my alarm clock going off. I reach over and hit the snooze button wondering why in the world I have an alarm clock on. I roll over and try to go back to sleep when my bedroom door bursts open and a young Michael jumps on my bed.

"Mommy! Mommy! Mommy! We watched the news with Daddy this morning and they called off school! We don't have to go! Isn't that awesome?" Michael exclaims, barely taking a breath in between his sentences.

I sit straight up and realize that I am in my bedroom. I look over to my left and see the dresser and mirror sitting there are not the same dresser and mirror I have currently. It is my old one from about twenty-five years ago.

I look in the mirror to see myself once again young, well younger, and with my chestnut hair laying just past my shoulders.

"Mommy, are you okay?" Michael asks, bringing me out of my thoughts.

This must be another dream, or did I just have one of those moments where your life flashes before your eyes, but mine was in the form of a dream. I shake my head in confusion, not sure of what is happening.

"Mommy?"

Oh, yeah Michael asked me a question.

"Yeah, baby. I'm fine. Mommy is just waking up and needs some coffee," I tell him, gathering him up in a big bear hug.

My mind is racing with different thoughts, and I can't seem to piece everything together. I have that feeling, that ESP or whatever, that something big is supposed to happen or is going to happen today, but I just can't put my finger on it.

I make the decision to get up and start my day. Maybe it will come to me as the day goes on.

"Shall we get up and get some breakfast?" I asked Michael. His little face is adorable as it lights up at my question.

"Yes! Daddy made pancakes and scrambled eggs. Can I have hot chocolate with marshmallows?"

"Of course! What other way is there to have breakfast on a snow day?"

We both scramble to our feet and make our way to the kitchen. The smell of freshly brewed coffee, bacon, eggs, and pancakes fill my nose. My stomach growls at the delectable aroma.

I kiss Wayne good morning and grab myself a cup of coffee before making my way to the refrigerator to add my creamer. Katie walks in still wearing her pajamas followed by Samuel.

Samuel.

I stare at him while pouring the creamer into my coffee cup. During my daze, the creamer spills over the side and onto the kitchen floor.

The feel of the cold liquid pulls me out of my trans. I quickly tilt the creamer back right and replace it into the fridge. Wayne bends over at my feet to clean up the mess I just made. He makes quick work of it before standing up to throw the now wet towel onto the counter.

He grabs me by the elbow and asks, "Everything okay?"

I must have a confused look on my face as I watch Samuel take a seat at the kitchen table. He prompts me again, "Ellie? Are you feeling sick? Maybe you should go back to bed."

I shake my head, "No, I'm fine. I think I just had a weird dream last night. Thank you for cooking breakfast."

I kiss him on the cheek and walk over to my spot at the table. I find it funny how everyone has an assigned seat around the table without the label that says, 'this is my seat.' Everyone just seems to know who sits where and no one tries to steal the other person's spot.

Wayne joins us at the table a short time later with a plate full of pancakes and a small plate of butter. We start to hold hands before the meal prayer. My hand grabs Samuel's and I feel an electric spark, like I have missed the feel of his touch for quite some time.

I look over at him and he has his head down in anticipation of the prayer starting. I smile with a tear gleaming to the surface of my eye.

"Ellie, you want to start the prayer?" Wayne asks, looking at me with his head tilted down.

I look around the table and see all three of my children with their heads down waiting for the prayer to start. Michael's legs kick back and forth under the table as he waits impatiently for his food.

"Sorry," I clear my throat, "God is great. God is good. Let us thank Him for our food. By His hands we are fed. We thank You for our daily bread. Amen. God thank you so much for giving us this day, another day on earth to love you and the ability to bless others. Help us keep You in our minds always as we go forth in our day. Amen."

Three little voices and Wayne repeat 'Amen' before everyone starts digging into the breakfast feast.

"So, no school today and the doctor closed the office today with anticipation of the snow. What are we going to do today guys?" I ask, putting a helping of eggs on my plate.

Wayne replies with his usual, "I've got some projects in the shed I was going to do, and I need to do an oil change on the truck. Might run to town to pick up a part."

"That sounds good," I say looking at the kids, "But what about us? What do you want to do?"

Katie replies, "I have a new book from the library that I was hoping to read today."

Samuel and Michael look at each other and both turn to me with a mischievous smile. Samuel's face sports that too adorable dimple to the left side of his cheek. Finally, he asks, "Can we go sledding?"

It is late February and probably the last of the big snows that we will get until next year. I couldn't deny my boys the last enjoyment of winter.

"Wayne, do you think that you can drop us off at the big hill on your way into town?" I ask. My car could get us to the big hill just outside of town, but I never really liked driving in the snow and Wayne's truck is more than capable of making the journey safely.

"Yeah, that shouldn't be a problem. I'll swing back by to pick you up after going into town." He looks at the boys now who are bouncing in their seats with excitement. "I'll take my time at the parts store and then maybe stop at the grocery store to see if they have stuff to make beef stew for dinner. Is two hours long enough for you hooligans to get your sledding out?"

"Yes!" Samuel and Michael exclaim.

Samuel turns to Michael and says, "I bet you're big enough to ride on my sled and I can use Katie's since she's not going. We can ride down the biggest hill and throw snowballs at each other."

"Yeah, and we can dodge them like their missiles like Captain America," Michael replies.

I smile at the exchange that continues between my sons. A forever best friend is what I hoped Samuel would find in his younger brother and it seems like my prayers were answered.

I begin to clean up breakfast after everyone is finished and has gone their separate ways. I placed the leftover bacon in the refrigerator to use in the beef stew tonight. I take out a box of Jiffy corn muffin mix from the cabinet and put it on the counter to go with our meal. Although I could cook the muffins from scratch, doing so would prevent me from spending quality time by the fireside with my family.

After ensuring that my kitchen is once again spotless, I set out to grab the things needed for our sledding adventures. I brew a pot of coffee and place it into a thermos to stay warm. I fill another thermos for the boys with hot chocolate. I added the marshmallows knowing that they would dissolve by the time they got to enjoy them, but it would add an extra flavor of love.

I walk into Katie's room and plop myself down onto her bed. She is sitting with her back against the wall and a book in her hand. She doesn't look up from her book, only a small smile creeps across her face letting me know I got her attention.

"Are you sure you don't want to go sledding with us baby girl?" I ask.

She places a bookmark in her book and sets it down. She lets out a sigh before saying, "mom sledding is for babies and I'm not a baby anymore. I have better adventures to read about in my books where I can stay safe, warm, and comfortable."

"Well, I can't argue with that logic. But can I entice you with a steaming cup of hot chocolate with marshmallows?"

"Is it okay if I just stay here and read my book and drink my hot chocolate?" she asks in an almost begging tone.

"Of course it is. I left you a cup on the kitchen counter," I replied.

I kiss the top of her head as she picks up her book to begin where she left off. I slide off her bed and make my way out of her room and down the hall to Samuel and Michael's.

We have the extra bedroom for Michael to be able to have his own room, but too often Wayne and I would walk into Samuel's room to see one sleeping on the floor and the other in the bed. After a while Wayne just decided to build the boys bunk beds and move Michael in completely. I can still remember the smile on their faces when we opened the door to show them their new beds.

I hear a thud as I reach their bedroom door, effectively pulling me out of my thoughts. I open their door to see chaos. They seem to have pulled every piece of clothing out of their drawers and closet and are rushing to put the warm clothes on.

Wayne is a man who loves to have his tools clean and put away in their certain drawers when they are finished being used. I am the same way with my house. I cannot stand a dirty house or an unorganized one. It gives me anxiety and hives to think about all the dust and dirt that can live on surfaces.

I try, not so successfully, to hide the anger building up inside of me. Samuel sees me standing in his open bedroom door and freezes.

"Sorry, mama. We were trying to find our clothes for the snow, and we got a little carried away," he says, ashamed.

I take a deep breath. This is supposed to be a fun day. One where lasting memories can be made, I feel it. I will myself not to raise my voice or get angry.

The boys stand still waiting for my response. I hate that they're already expecting me to get angry at them.

I take one more deep breath before telling them, "I'm going to get ready cause your father is going to want to leave soon. When we get back from the hill you both need to clean this up before we sit down for dinner. Deal?"

"Yes, ma'am," Samuel and Michael say in unison.

I turn to walk to my bedroom to put on my warm clothes determined to let the chaos of that room go. Something still feels strange and off about this day, like I should be remembering something. The hair on the back of my neck is standing straight up.

I sit down on my bed and try to remember what it is that I should know about today and I am coming up blank. After a few moments of blankly staring at the wall and nothing coming to mind, I shrug my shoulders. It will come to me eventually if it is really that important. I push the feeling aside to put on some warm clothes for sledding.

I give Katie one more kiss before heading out to the truck. Wayne thankfully has it warming up as I reach it with both thermoses in hand. I climb into the passenger seat and put my seatbelt on. Samuel and Michael are bouncing in their seats with smiles so wide that their faces may hurt later. Wayne starts backing out of the driveway and toward our adventure.

"Are you guys going to be warm enough?" my loving husband asks.

"Yes, I got my coffee and hot chocolate. The sun is shining, it's only thirty-two degrees and thankfully there is no wind. A perfect day for sledding," I reply.

"Okay, but there's no shelter if you get too cold," he protests a little.

"Dad that just means we have to play a little harder to warm up," Samuel chimes in.

"You're right buddy," Wayne says looking at him in the rearview mirror. "You boys mind your mama now, you hear?"

"Yes sir," Michael and Samuel reply.

Wayne and I look at each other for a moment and smile. It only takes us an extra ten minutes to reach the sledding hill on the outside of town. That of course is not what it is called, but locals have been coming to this spot for as long as I can remember. The property is privately owned, but the owner of it is a gentle old farmer who has never minded the sledding activities that go on during the winter. If you cleaned up after yourself, he didn't mind that people used it for sledding.

We climb out of the truck and grab the sleds from the bed. I give Wayne a quick kiss goodbye before the boys and I make the trek up the hill. Thankfully, some other kids and parents had the same idea that Samuel and Michael did. I can see a trail carved out in the snow making it easier for us to climb. When we get to the top, I see Wayne's truck off in the distance making his way to town.

"This hill is higher than I remember," I say to no one in particular. My breathing is labored and heavy in the frosty winter air.

Samuel giggles, "mama you say that every year when we come here."

"Well maybe Old Man Turner adds dirt to it each summer to make it bigger," I say, playfully pulling his hat down over his face.

Samuel laughs as he pulls his hat off and fixes his hair before putting it back on.

"Come on Samuel! Let's go," Michael squeals out. He's already sitting on the sled impatiently waiting to go down the hill.

Samuel quickly jumps on his sled and the two slide down with giggles echoing in the air. I watch as my two boys complete the same run repeatedly. The smile never falls from my face or theirs.

The winter weather puts a chill in the air and the hair stands up on the back of my neck once more. I look up to the sky. The clearest light blue with not a single cloud in sight. The sun shines brightly on my face, a nice contrast to the chill up my spine. I gaze out to the rolling hills of bare trees and fresh snow. A picture-perfect moment.

My thoughts are interrupted with a snowball to the face. I shake my head trying to figure out if that snowball was intentional or an accident. I look over to see Samuel smiling at me with another snowball in hand.

"Oh, it's on," I laugh as I try to form a snowball.

Samuel, Michael, and I spent the next several minutes making snowballs and throwing them at each other. My lungs needed a break from all the unconditioned exercise I'm currently getting. I strategically placed myself in front of a sled waiting to go downhill.

Samuel throws his snowball perfectly to hit me in the chest. I dramatically fall back onto the sled, clutching my heart, as it begins to slide down the hill.

The sled stops at the bottom of the hill, and I look up to see my boys clapping at my acting scene.

I roll off the sled and try to stand but end up slipping on ice. I realize that the snow has started compacting together from all the kids and parents sliding down. A sheet of ice has started to form, and the sleds are drifting further down the way. It takes me several tries and a crawl before I'm able to make it back to the hill.

The little reprieve from sliding down the hill was fun. Now I look up to its daunting size that I'll have to climb, I know this is going to make me winded. I reach the top huffing and puffing from the cold air. I always found it interesting that it feels like I am getting enough air, I can feel it going in and out of my lungs, but it doesn't seem like enough. Or I am just getting too old to do this stuff.

I sit down and pull out my thermos of coffee in hopes that the warm liquid will also warm my insides. Samuel and Michael join me in drinking their hot chocolate. Samuel leans on me on one side and Michael leans on me on the other. We all look out into the distance in silence.

I looked down the hill and noticed a large snowman with a little snowman family had been built. I see the largest snowman has a green scarf that looks oddly familiar. I look at Samuel and notice his green scarf is no longer around his neck.

"That snowman family is adorable. That green scarf will definitely keep the big one warm," I say with a mischievous grin.

Samuel hesitates before saying, "they ran out of scarves and that little girl started to cry. I just wanted to make her happy, so I gave her mine."

I smile down at my son. "You have one of the biggest hearts of anyone I know. I'm so proud of you for giving to someone else in need."

"Thank you for bringing us today mama," Samuel says.

"Yeah, thanks mommy," Michael agrees.

I put my coffee down and placed my hands awkwardly over their ears in an attempt to hug them. "My favorite memories are the ones I get to make with you guys," I say.

Off in the distance I see Wayne's truck pulling down the road. I am relieved to get out of the cold, but disappointed that the fun is ending. I pick up the lids to the thermoses and screw them on.

I sigh, "There's your father's truck. You guys get to go down one last time and meet your dad at the bottom."

Samuel stands up and starts moving to his sled. He gets himself situated and turns to me, "And mama we will get our room cleaned up first thing when we get home."

I smile at him as he pushes off the top of the hill.

"Come on mommy, ride down with me," Michael says.

I sit behind Michael and place the thermoses in between us. The hair on the back of my neck is standing up, more so than before. This time it comes with a new panic feeling that reaches my chest. It feels like someone is squeezing my heart. I look around to see where the danger is coming from.

I push off the top of the hill and my eyes follow the hill downward to Samuel in front of us. He's at the bottom, but his sled continues to push forward.

He moves past the point where I stopped earlier and onto the patch of ice. The ice glides him further and faster than he was before.

The reality of it happened so quickly, but I am watching it in the slowest motion possible. Samuel is giggling on his sled as he hits the ice. A car is coming down the road with Wayne's blue truck shortly behind it. The sound of brakes and a screeching car. I want to scream out, but no sounds or words escape my mouth.

I place my hands over Michael's face so that he doesn't see what inevitably is about to happen next. I close my eyes as well when I hear a loud thud.

Our sled comes to a stop, and I jump up quickly. I kneel over to Michael and place my hands on the sides of his face so that he only looks at me.

"Baby, stay right here. Close your eyes and sing a song in your head, okay? Don't open your eyes until daddy or I come to get you. Do you understand?"

Michael is crying with giant crocodile tears, knowing what just happened to his older brother. "Okay mommy. Is Sammy going to be okay?"

"I don't know, baby. Mommy is going to go find out," I couldn't lie to my youngest, he's too smart and would see right through it.

Michael thankfully does as he is asked. He closes his eyes, placing his little mittened hands over them and starts singing Jesus Loves Me.

I turn to the direction of Samuel and the car. I can see Wayne out of the corner of my eye with the truck in park. He's going to the same place as I am. To our son.

With each step my chest gets a little tighter, the air gets a little harder to breathe and the world around me closes in a little more.

The lady driving the vehicle is out in front looking down and not moving. She must sense that I am there, and she moves to the side. I steal a quick glance at her direction. Her face is pale, a hand covers her mouth and the tears filling her eyes are about to spill at any moment.

I look back to see my son lifeless. His eyes are open and staring up at the sky. His chest was not moving. Wayne reaches him about the same time I do. He places two fingers on his neck to feel a pulse.

He bursts into tears and falls into me with the realization that our son is gone.

CHAPTER 16

A crowd now forms around the tragic scene unfolding in front of me. I wail into Wayne's arms at the loss of our son. The squeezing in my chest does not let up as Wayne pulls me tighter against him. I yell no in a voice that doesn't seem like my own.

Wayne rocks me back and forth. At one point he yells out all his anguish into the world. He finishes and then is right back to rocking me, holding me strongly in his arms. He's slightly turned away from Samuel's body, not wanting to see it again. I, on the other hand, cannot stop looking into my son's eyes.

How could this have happened? How could such a beautiful day end so wrong? My hope for lasting memories is now tainted with the sound of the thud that will replay in my ears and the sight of Samuel's chest no longer rising.

This isn't happening. This is all a bad dream. A horrific nightmare that I will wake up from soon. I need to touch him myself. I need to lay my hands on his body and maybe I can shake him awake.

I'm in denial. I know I am, but I can't stop from going to my son.

I begin to crawl out of Wayne's arms around me. My hands and knees touch the coldness of the ice on the road, and it sends a shiver down my spine. Wayne reluctantly lets me go, knowing that I need to see for myself that our son has left us.

I reach Samuel. My Samuel. My loving little boy who will never grow up and become a firefighter as many little boys dream of. He will never fall in love and get married. He will never know the joy of having a son as wonderful as him.

Through my tears I can see that he has not moved and has not taken a breath. I reach for his small hand and hold it in mine.

My sobs begin again. I hear the world around me. People are coming closer to take a look at what happened. Sirens echoing in the distance. A small child a few yards away sitting on his sled singing Jesus Loves Me.

I close my eyes to drown out the noise, to will myself anywhere but the place that will forever hold a black mark in my heart. Ever so slowly the noises start to fade. The mumblings of the people surrounding us turn muffled and the sirens closing in now seem more distant.

My eyes shut tighter. Almost there. Just drown it out a little more. As if on cue everything goes silent. I don't even feel the cold any longer under my knees. All I feel is the lifeless little hand in mine.

Suddenly I feel a warm larger hand begin to cover mine. I open my eyes and look up to see everything has fallen away around me. Wayne is no longer at my back. Michael is not seen in the distance sitting on his sled. The people around us are gone. I glance down to see that even Samuel's body is no longer lying on the cold hard ground.

My eyes move to look at the hand that now touches mine. It's warm. Goosebumps cover me with the feel of his touch.

My gaze floats up to the man I've been seeing at home for the past few weeks.

Once again, he's wearing a green flannel shirt, blue jeans, and boots. His hair is dark and a little longer on the top with a five o'clock shadow on his face.

He looks at me with a beautiful smile that shows off a dimple to the left cheek. His smile meets his eyes as he says, "Hi mama."

I hear him, clear as day, but my mind is not able to comprehend what is unfolding in front of me. This handsome, grown man just called me mama.

My heart fills with knowledge that the person standing before me is Samuel. My Samuel is all grown up. My hand, not being held by his, reaches up to touch his face. I feel the tiny hairs covering his cheek as I look into his eyes. The eyes look much like mine.

It is him and my heart swells with joy.

Much like the moment with grandaddy, I rush to embrace him in a hug. My hug turns into a tackle and we both land on the ground. My tears turn into soft giggles. His smile is even brighter now, if that is possible. He helps me to a standing position and gives me a proper hug.

"Thank you! Thank you for coming to see me! I had hoped that I would be able to see you when grandaddy told me I would be getting visitors," I say through happy tears. I wipe a tear away as it falls past my cheek.

It's crazy to think about how my son is now taller than me. Standing close to six foot four and a man when I lost him as a boy. I see him, feel him, and can now hear him yet my mind is still whirling at the realization that I'm here. I drift back to thinking about what just happened. It wasn't a dream. I was reliving the moment that I lost my boy.

Why? It's not like I could forget it. So why did I have to relive that fateful day?

The happy tears turn back into tears of despair.

"I'm sorry baby. I'm so sorry," I cry out.

Samuel continues to hold me in a hug as I bury my face in his chest. I feel him trying to comfort me as he rubs my back. I shake my head. I should be the one comforting him, not the other way around.

"Sorry for what mama?" he asks.

I take a step out of his arms and look up at him. "For not being able to save you."

There's so much more that I want to tell him sorry for. For those moments when I lost my temper and my patience with him as he was growing up. For not taking more time to spend with him and Michael and Katie. For not being able to give him a lifetime of memories. All these thoughts swirled around in my brain.

"Mama, you were and are the best mom I could have ever asked for. You gave me everything that I needed and could've hoped for. You showed me love and how to love others. I don't remember those times that you lost your temper or had a little less patience. I remember the storybooks you used to read to me and the coloring at the kitchen table. I remember you packing picnics for us during the summertime by the pond while we fished. I remember the good. And you couldn't have saved me from this. It was my time to go," he says, the last part nonchalantly.

I shouldn't be surprised that Samuel was able to know everything that I was thinking about. I still find it perplexing. That will take some getting used to.

"I just hate that you missed out on all those moments with the family and with Michael. He became a little lost without you. You didn't get to do so much that life has to offer. I knew there was ice at the bottom of the hill. We should have moved further away from that part. I should have done something instead of watching it unfold in front of my eyes," I state. My mind is going in multiple different directions, and it is making it harder to concentrate.

He grabs both of my hands in his and kisses the back of them. He looks me in the eyes, willing me to calm down.

"Remember what you taught me when I was upset?" he asks.

I shake my head no, my mind still firing in this direction and that. Is this what an ADHD person feels like? Or is this anxiety?

He calmly says, "take a breath."

I do.

"Good. Now another."

I take another deep breath and feel myself relaxing. My mind is coming back into my control, and I am able to calm it down.

"Come sit down on the curb with me."

He takes my hand and guides me over to the curb. I look around to see the still beautiful landscape of snow-covered hills. I see my breath in the air, but I don't feel the cold. There is no chill in the wind. I feel quite comfortable despite it being a winter's day with snow and ice on the ground.

I sat next to my son. Oddly enough I don't feel the cold from the snow as I sit. It feels like everything is frozen in time and there is no cold or wet, just the perfect temperature and perfect setting. Samuel sits with his knees bent and his arms resting on them. He sighs and begins to speak.

"I didn't miss out on anything mama. I got to be a part of every birthday, every celebration, every milestone. I was there at Katie and Jason's wedding. I was there at Michael and Josie's. I got to see my nieces and nephew and have watched them grow up. Well maybe not Samantha yet, she's only a few days old," he chuckles at the small joke.

I stared at him in disbelief of his words. I heard him, but understanding is another concept altogether.

"I also watched you cry yourself to sleep for months after I died. Anytime there was a moment of happiness you felt guilty because I wasn't there to enjoy it with you," he pauses. "But, mama, there's no reason for any of that. I know you were sad and you're sad now about all the things you think you are going to miss out on. I can tell you that you're not."

We sit in silence for a moment as his words try to penetrate my mind. My thoughts drift to the saying that is used all too often, *everything happens for a reason*. I get it, I really do, but that doesn't mean I have to like it. It doesn't take away from the nights I cried myself to sleep or the birthdays that came and went that I didn't get to celebrate with my son. I may not miss out on future events with my family, but they will miss my presence. I also know that they will feel the same way I felt knowing Samuel wasn't there in person to enjoy family time.

I lean into Samuel's side. He puts an arm around my shoulder and rests his cheek on my head. The simple gesture gives me comfort.

"I've missed you, Sammy."

"I've missed you too, mama."

"I know God has something so much more planned for me, but it hurts. This hurts, all of it and I want the hurt to stop. I miss them and I haven't even left them yet. I don't know which death is worse, the sudden never getting to say good-bye death or the long agonizing one," I begin to cry. I ponder my question and that just makes the pain increase. I feel the pain of losing my son way too soon and the pain knowing that I will be leaving the others too soon as well.

My head falls to my chest, my legs bent to allow my arms to rest. I feel defeated, my heart feels heavy, and I am in desperate need of peace. Samuel rubs my back to offer solace.

"I feel like I have let go of the anger that I was holding onto, but this sadness will not leave. I know I have been sad for a while. Since the day you died honestly, and this pain won't leave. I think about the pain that you must have felt that day and it eats me up."

"Mama, I never felt the pain from the car. I remember being alive and then somehow more alive, but I was never in pain, and I am so grateful for that."

I can't stop the words from coming out, "what happened after you died?"

"Every journey is a little different, just like every person is a little different. But, for me, I was sliding on the sled when I heard a thump. After the thump I felt myself being pulled up into a pair of arms. I looked up to see a beautiful angel carrying me and flying away from my body. I didn't feel scared or worried, just a sense of peace. My angel told me that someone wanted to talk to me. We flew up past the clouds into the most amazing meadow with the softest green grass," he glances up at the sky as he recalls the memory.

I look up to the sky with him and every so slowly I start to feel my sorrow turn into joy. I began feeling a little excited with anticipation for him to continue.

"I met Jesus, mama," he looks at me with his wonderful smile. There is a sense of tranquility in the air, and it calms me as he moves forward with his story. "We talked about many things. It was incredible and I constantly felt His peace and love. He asked me if there was something that I wanted to do on earth that I didn't get to. I said yes."

I furrowed my brow, "what is it that you wanted to do?"

"I told Him that I wanted to visit the lions that Daniel did when he was thrown in the lion's den. And then I told him that I wanted to see the whale that Jonah spent three days in," Samuel says.

I smile at the memory that Samuel's favorite stories from the bible were of Jonah and the whale and the lions that didn't eat Daniel. I always loved the enthusiasm that Samuel felt when talking about Jesus or reading his stories from his children's bible. It made me feel like I did something right as a mom.

"So did Jesus help you see the lions?" I ask.

"Oh, yes. While we were talking in the meadow, seven lions came out of the tree line and towards us. There was a male lion with the biggest mane of orange, brown, and tan. Mama, it was incredible. The sight of this lion was better than any movie, picture, or trip to the zoo. Behind it came four female lions followed by two cubs. I looked at Jesus in disbelief, but He nodded his head and told me that I could play with them. I ran right up to the male lion and gave him a hug around his mane."

"You weren't scared?"

"There's nothing to be scared of in heaven mama. Plus, Jesus was right there. It's not like He was going to let the lion eat me or something."

I roll my eyes, "okay, good point. And then what happened?"

"So, the lions and I played for what seemed like hours. The mane of the male lion was soft. Many times, I found myself nuzzling his neck. We playfully wrestled and I got to scratch their bellies, which they really enjoyed. When I was finished playing with the lions Jesus took my hand and led me to a cliff with a vast ocean below it. It sparkled in the sunlight like a thousand tiny diamonds. It was the brightest blue; I don't think I've ever seen a color that could match its brilliance. He told me that the whale was waiting to meet me. I looked out and saw a whale breaking the surface and spouting water into the air. Next thing I know I am in the water and swimming next to the whale that swallowed Jonah," Samuel says with excitement in his voice. "I thought I had to hold my breath under water, but I didn't need to. It was like I turned into a fish or something and I got to swim with the whale. It was so incredible, and I knew that it was going to be one of the first things I wanted to tell you whenever I saw you again."

My heart swells at the knowledge that my son was okay. That he lived even though he died. He starts telling me more about the other adventures that he took starting with seeing grandaddy and Dana. He explains that he would get to meet many other kids who had passed away too and make everlasting friendships.

"So, you see mama I was fine. It hurt me to see you, Mikey, dad, and everyone suffering because I wasn't there anymore, but I went to 'a happier place' as they say," he uses finger quotes around the cliche saying.

I smiled and looked up at Samuel. The sun is shining directly behind his head giving off an ironic halo of light.

Of course, reading my thoughts Samuel gestures around his head and says, "like my halo?"

I giggle and give him a little nudge with my shoulder.

"It gives me peace knowing that you didn't suffer and that you had the most incredible adventures that people could only dream about," I trail off.

"But" he motions for me to continue.

"I just can't stop thinking about your father and the rest of the family. Your dad even yelled at me one morning and said that I wasn't allowed to die," I shudder at the memory.

"I remember. I was there for that," Samuel states. "But come walk with me for a moment."

He gets up and holds out his hand for me. I take it and stand with ease. We walk over to the tree line, our steps making a crunching sound in the snow. The snow has a beautiful, brilliant light about it. Calming and soothing, like nothing else in the world matters and time can stand still.

We reach the area where the bare trees meet the open snow plains. Samuel points to the ground and says, "watch."

I look to see an area of snow melt away impossibly fast. In its place grows soft green grass and a few wildflowers. I marvel at the small flower with light purple petals and yellow center. Beautiful, simple and complex, but perfect just the same. I look at Samuel in bewilderment.

He smiles at me and states, "Your sorrow can feel like the weight of the world is on your shoulders. Like time slows to a stop and everything and everyone is passing you by. If you let it, it can swallow you up like an avalanche that won't let go. But trusting in God will melt it all away. In its place will be the growth of something new and wonderful."

More snow is melting away going beyond a few trees. I look up at the tree to see it blooming with fresh leaves of all vibrant greens. I smile and turn to Samuel at the miracle performed before my eyes.

"Don't just let the anger go mama. Let the sadness go too because there's no room for that where you're going. You told Michael and Katie that it's okay to be sad for a while, but not to let it consume you. Don't let it consume you. Have the peace and knowledge that God will take care of it all. Blessed are those who mourn, for they will be comforted. He will watch over our family and guide them. He will wipe away every tear and be there just like He always has."

I nod my head at his words. How could I have forgotten the words I had spoken to Michael and Katie? I believed in them then so why shouldn't I now? I close my eyes and try to breathe in the tranquility surrounding me and breathe out all of my sadness and sorrow. My yoga breaths are coming in handy once again. My initial response is to start crying out for the loss of what could be when that feeling of peace begins to overwhelm me.

Months ago, I accepted my diagnosis of cancer and the battle that I had to begin. Weeks ago, I accepted my fate of starting hospice and trying to get my pain under control.

However, I never accepted my destiny to die. Death has always been that scary concept, the big elephant in the room that no one wanted to touch with a ten-foot pole.

I start to think about death as not the end of my life, but the birth and beginning of a new one. One where I will be reunited with my friends and family. I will gain a life that no longer holds any pain, anger, sadness, or despair. I have a new beginning waiting for me and I no longer feel sad because of it. I feel excited. I take this moment to mourn the loss of my future memories that I will no longer get to have with my family. With one more deep breath, I let it go.

Yes, I am leaving my family and that sucks. However, I know that God will watch over them just as He did for me when Samuel passed. Knowing that Samuel got to be a part of our family memories also puts a peace in my heart that I will be able to be a part of Wayne, Katie, and Michael's after I'm gone.

I open my eyes to see that every bit of the snow has melted away. A beautiful meadow of wildflowers bloom as the sun shines down. Samuel chuckles at my astonishment. A butterfly flutters by my face and flies off to the next flower. Birds chirp happy songs in the trees above. Everything about this place is wonderfully made and I have no words to truly express my feelings of happiness and contentment.

Samuel embraces me in a hug, "you're almost there mama."

He lets me go and begins to walk away without another word. My hand still reaches out, hoping to feel his touch for just a moment longer. When his hand leaves mine, he disappears from my sight.

I sit down on the grass and smile to myself. I got to talk to my son again. I got to hold him in my arms. I look up to the sky and whisper a 'thank you' to God. I close my eyes and feel myself falling back into the reality of my life.

CHAPTER 17

My mind awakens before my eyes open. I am in that weird state of hearing everything around me before fully waking up for the day. The pain in my stomach is roaring up to become intolerable. I'm frozen in fear that if I move it will immediately jump to a ten. There is not much that I can do except to continue to lay quietly in my recliner with my eyes closed. Unfortunately, the stiffness in my neck and arms starts to become uncomfortable and ache to be moved.

I hear the crackle from the fireplace and the low mumblings of the T.V. I can feel the air shift as someone walks into the living room. Whoever it is, is trying to be quiet in hopes of not waking me, little do they know that I am already awake. I feel a hand on my forehead, maybe checking to see if I have a fever? The hand is big and calloused. Wayne. I smile at the feel of his touch. I can't wait to tell him about seeing our son.

"Good morning sleepyhead," he says with a small chuckle clearly seeing the grin on my face, "or should I say good afternoon?"

My eyes open at those words. I look out the window and to my surprise I see a beautiful shining sun high in the sky illuminating the fallen snow. It is bright and I almost need sunglasses to look. The air is peaceful and serene that only fresh fallen snow can bring.

With my eyes now open, my body fully succumbs to the rising pain. I grimace and guard my belly.

"How bad is the pain, Ellie?" Wayne asks in a calm, but demanding tone.

"Bad," is all I can manage to say. I grip my belly tighter and scrunch my face harder. I'm not sure why, it's not like doing that will make the pain hurt any less. Thoughts of wanting to tell Wayne about Samuel escape my mind. I must remember to tell him later.

"I'll be right back with the Roxanol."

Less than a minute later my attentive husband is at my side and giving me the much-needed pain medication. I taste the oil as it reaches my tongue and muster up the ability not to gag. Although I detest the taste, I am thankful for the relief it will provide.

"I crushed the Ativan tablet and put it in the Roxanol to help as well. The on-call nurse last night suggested to start giving you both whenever you needed the pain medicine," he reports.

I look at him with confusion.

"Why did you call?" My mouth is dry and my voice sounds like I have been smoking cigarettes.

"You were crying out a lot again. I didn't know if you were having pain or if it was anxiety. I had to give you multiple doses before you were able to calm down."

I look up at him to see the worry clear in his eyes and even a hint of fear for me. His beautiful eyes that have been passed down to our children, have seen so much. Behind the worry I can also see his love and devotion. What I treasure most is that he has never looked at me with pity, well aside from that one time when I asked him to end my pain.

He continues, "they were going to send a nurse, but I was worried about how they would get here. We got a couple more inches than what they were originally expecting and as you know we are the last to get plowed. So, I called the on-call nurse about every hour for a few hours until we were able to get you to settle down. Elisha has already called this morning and said that she might not be able to make it out here, but she would visit tomorrow morning when the roads are safer."

I nod my head at his words. The pain just continues to get worse as the days go on. I can feel my body shutting down the weaker I become, and I just know in my heart that I am riddled with cancer.

I just have to make it to Christmas Day. I want one more Christmas with my family. Please God don't take me until then, I pray silently.

I close my eyes to continue my pleading with God that He doesn't take me sooner than that. I can hear Wayne settle back into his chair and reach for the remote. I listen to him yawning with a loud sigh and moan at the end. He must not have gotten a lot of sleep last night watching over me. He is my guardian angel in human form.

"Katie and Michael said they can start taking turns spending the night here. I got off the phone with them this morning," he says before another big yawn.

I want to argue with him that Katie has two little ones to look after and Michael just had a baby and needs to be there to help Josie, but I just don't have the energy.

"When will they be here?" I manage to ask. At this point I think it might be futile to argue and clearly Wayne could use the extra help taking care of me. My heart breaks. I know vows say, 'in sickness and in health,' although when you're standing up there and saying the words in front of God and everyone, you don't really think about the 'in sickness' part until it becomes a reality.

"Katie is coming tonight. She'll sleep in her old room and Jason will bring over the kids tomorrow. She was able to get everything switched around at the store so she can have the next week off. That manager she hired is really stepping up. Michael asked if he, Josie, and Samantha could come to stay with us for a few days as well. He doesn't want to leave Josie overnight by herself with the baby."

I turn my head quickly to look at Wayne, "what did you tell them?"

"I said we have plenty of room and if that's what he wants to do in order to be there for Josie and Sammy, but also spend time with you then he is welcome to come over."

I sigh in relief knowing that I will get to spend more time with my kids before I leave them. That thought shifts from the calmness of knowing there is a plan in place to tension building in the air. I know there is the unspeakable topic of my ultimate demise, it hangs in the air like a thick fog by the riverside. Wayne seems to always be dancing around the topic, but never fully embracing it or saying it. I know this will be hard on him. On all of them really, but there's nothing more that I can do except hold on until Christmas. I can muddle through the pain and nausea until then. I can do that for them.

I feel myself slipping back to sleep. Exhaustion is pulling at me which is ridiculous as I barely woke up to say a few words. Nonetheless, sleep is calling my name and now I welcome it. Remembering to tell Wayne about seeing our son slips away as blackness covers my vision.

The days go by in a haze. I wake for short periods of time. It is never long enough to have an extended conversation with my loved ones, just enough to know that they are there for me and know what day it is. Sometimes it is the stimulation they give me that awakens me from my Sleeping Beauty slumber, other times it is the pain.

A few days ago, I needed extra help going to the bathroom. Getting up was a chore and caused extreme discomfort. To add salt on a wound, I wasn't able to empty my bladder completely, so I kept going to the bathroom almost every hour. I hated that Wayne, Michael and Jason had to take turns getting me up. By the end of the day all of us were exhausted.

Thankfully, Elisha started making extra visits and calling on the days that she doesn't come to see how I am. This is a weekend that she is on call, and I could not be more grateful. She decided to make an extra visit today.

It is the Sunday before Christmas. I am almost there. Just keep holding on, I repeat this silently to myself.

Shortly after she arrives, Wayne begins to explain in great detail our struggles of going to the bathroom and that the pain and exhaustion from it is causing not only me but our entire family. She nods her head while looking at me out of the corner of her eyes as if she is expecting this. I close my eyes. I am not interested in being a part of this conversation. I am content with whatever decision is made.

"The mind is no longer talking to the rest of the body, and a lot of times people will start to retain urine. She's not emptying her bladder completely, so she constantly feels like she has to go to the bathroom. I would honestly recommend placing a foley catheter in to drain her bladder for her," Elisha suggests.

Michael is sitting on the couch holding a sleeping Samantha. He voices his concerns. "Wouldn't that cause an infection? I know in the hospitals they are always trying to get those things out."

"There's always a risk for infection. The benefits of having a foley at this point outweigh not having one. Every time she has to get up to use the bathroom it is causing her more pain and discomfort. She will start having the urge to go more frequently and at the same time she is becoming weaker, so we risk falling and hurting ourselves. If we place the foley catheter we risk infection, but I will teach you how to thoroughly clean it which will reduce the risk. I will also be able to see what her kidney function is doing," she explains.

"What do you mean see what her kidney function is doing? Like sending the urine off to the lab or something?" Wayne asks.

"No, I can see what her urine looks like and the darker and more concentrated it gets it means the kidneys are shutting down. When that happens, patients tend to start sleeping more."

"She's already sleeping a lot," Katie chimes in.

"Yeah, is this from the medications?" Michael adds.

Once again to Elisha's credit she doesn't get offended or snippy at the questions. I remain sitting in my recliner listening at the exchange. I am leaning more towards placing the foley catheter, anything to have less moments of pain are a plus in my eyes. I have needed more of the Roxanol lately and it has also become almost hazardous to swallow any sort of pills or drink fluids. A few bites of pudding or applesauce is all I can tolerate at one time.

"To answer that question the answer is yes and no. No, the pain medication is not directly involved with causing someone to sleep. Remember with hospice we don't sedate or do anything to speed up the process. We just make it comfortable. Right now, the cancer is using up all of your mom's energy, so she doesn't have the ability to stay awake for long. She is not really eating or drinking anything to give her more energy. If she tried to eat or drink more, it would cause more pain and discomfort. When she is awake it is because she is being stimulated by the pain, anxiety or by you conversing with her. When she needs the pain medications and remember you can see that through her nonverbal cues like increased respirations or facial grimacing, give her the medicine. Roxanol and Ativan will take that stimulation away and she will be able to relax. When the body relaxes then she will likely fall back asleep. However, if she is awake and talking to you and she has no pain then it is perfectly fine to let her enjoy those moments with you."

I know that I have my eyes closed, I have no energy to keep them open. However, it still feels weird knowing that my family is talking about me without adding me into the conversation. I want to shout, "hello! I'm right here and listening to you! Talk to me, not about me!" I remain silent though.

Elisha has one thing right; the cancer is taking up all my energy, I have nothing left to contribute aside from sitting down and listening to all that is going on around me.

My family became understanding of the education that is provided to them when Elisha finally turned her attention to me. She places her hand on my arm and gently shakes me. I open my eyes to see everyone's attention placed on me.

"What?" I asked in consternation. In the back of the room, I see Samuel smiling down at himself like he heard my thoughts once again.

"I was just telling your family about placing a foley catheter. It would drain your bladder for you and then you wouldn't have the pain of getting up. Is that something that you would like to do?" Elisha asks.

I can't bear the thought of my boys taking me to the bathroom one more time. The decision seems like an easy one to make.

"Yes, please. Place the catheter."

She nods her head. She turns to Wayne and states that a catheter kit is in her car, and she will be right back.

The catheter is placed with no fuss, and I immediately feel the relief of my bladder being emptied. The fluid being drained is the darkest urine I think I have ever seen. My hospice nurse explains that my kidneys are starting to shut down which is why I am sleeping more. She continues some education with

Wayne and Katie on how to clean the foley to prevent me from getting an infection.

Elisha begins packing her stuff up to leave with the promise to call the next day. I reach out with a shaky hand and place it on her arm to stop her. She looks at me with concern.

"I think it is time to order that hospital bed," I say with no hesitation.

Wayne knows how I have felt about having a hospital bed in my home. We discussed it when I was still at the hospital.

"Ellie, are you sure that's what you want?"

I can hear the tinge of despair in his voice, but I know my time is coming. I have three days left until Christmas Day and this recliner is becoming increasingly uncomfortable. At least with a bed I can lie flat or on my side.

I look at Wayne and answer, "yes."

I can see the tears fill his eyes with the knowledge that I won't be leaving that bed. He will never see me walk or sit in a wheelchair. I will never see any other walls than the four that currently occupy my sight. I will be stuck in that bed until my death. I have come to terms with that, and I am ready for it. As each day comes, I keep telling myself to hold on just a little longer.

Wayne nods his head in acknowledgment to my request and Elisha leaves us to order up the bed. It doesn't take long for the bed to be delivered. Thankfully, the boys were able to move furniture out of the way so that the bed would fit right where my recliner sat.

Last night I did not have any dreams, and I felt a twinge of disappointment. I want to not only see more of grandaddy, Dana and Samuel, I want to talk to them without looking like I lost my marbles. I want more of that sense of peace and love, not the pain and rising anxiety. There are now moments of having trouble breathing to add to my discomfort.

Now I sit here in my living room in my hospital bed with less than two days until Christmas. My house has never sounded more cheerful, and it brings a warmness to my heart. I still feel the elephant in the room, heck Dana, grandaddy, and Samuel are always standing in the back of the room as a constant reminder for me. However, today is a good day. Today I feel like I have a lot of energy to enjoy myself with my kids and grandkids.

Even with my newfound energy, I still have this nagging feeling in the back of my mind telling me that this is the last day I will get to have. If that is so, then I intend to soak up every moment that I can.

Katie and Josie have taken it upon themselves to manage the kitchen and get the cookies and other goodies ready for Christmas. I love hearing them tinker around in the kitchen putting together the ingredients for the snacks.

I'm left in the hospital bed in the living room. I smile at the sight of McKenna and Nathan playing on the carpet near my bed. I'm still able to look out the window and watch the birds play at the bird feeders, I love seeing them play.

Today three Cardinals jump and hop around while occasionally eating the seeds. It didn't go unnoticed that the birds seem to be around more when grandaddy, Dana, and Samuel are not.

Wayne, Jason, and Michael occupy themselves with 'manly' things in the garage or the beloved work shed. They take turns popping their heads in to see if there is anything that the ladies need. Everyone smiles because we all know they're just checking to see when the cookies are done. I'm amused at how Josie and Katie secretly place the finished cookies in the microwave or other containers so that the boys don't get to them. The snickers coming from the kitchen after the men leave disappointed is quite comical.

I turn to stare out the window at the three cardinals at play. They hop from place to place on the ground pecking at the seeds to find the perfect one to snack on. Their colors are a vibrant red. It is a stark contrast to the little bit of white snow that hasn't quite melted away yet.

I hear Katie enter the room and tell the grandkids that it is time for lunch. They leave the room with a cheerful glee of food. I hear her turn the volume down and start walking over to me, to ask if I want something to eat. I know I am going to disappoint her when I say no, so, I keep my eyes on the playful little birds.

Before Katie reaches my bed, I break the silence.

"They are such beautiful creatures, aren't they? They don't have a care in the world. They don't have to worry about whether they did enough to make it to Heaven. They wake up each day to find food and other birds to play with. Maybe they will make a nest and find another bird to love, raise some baby birds, but the worries always seem to rest with us."

Katie reaches me and sits down in the chair next to my bed. She places her hand and mine.

"Is that what you're over here thinking about so hard? Mama, you are the kindest person I know. The gates of heaven will be wide open for you to enter."

"You say that with such confidence," I reply, turning and looking at her for the first time.

"Trust in Jesus. Isn't that what you always say?"

I place my hand on her face, memorizing it.

"I do trust in Him. He has never lost faith in me and any sin that I committed in my lifetime, and trust me there are many, they are all washed away with His blood. I know this in my heart, but I always have the worry that I will reach Him and say, 'Look at all the good I did in your name' and He will turn away from me and tell me to depart from Him. That He never knew me."

Katie's face breaks into a smile. I am confused at what I said that was so amusing when she says, "well then don't say that to Jesus."

My face breaks into a smile and I let out a small chuckle.

Katie continues, "humble yourself before Him and the rest will take care of itself. Stop overthinking it mama. Talk to Him like you would an old friend. Like you always do."

I take a deep breath and let it out, "it looks like my job is done. You're reminding me about stuff with God now. Remember to be that person for your kids and even Samantha as she gets older."

Katie solemnly nods her head and looks down, "I will mama."

At that moment we hear the men walk in from the back door looking for food once again. Michael pops his head in from the kitchen to ask if Katie or I needed anything. I take that opportunity to speak with my son and have that alone time.

"I just need you Mikey," I tell him.

Katie kisses my hand and stands from her chair. She walks past Michael and turns her head back to me before leaving the room. The look she gives me is one of love and sorrow. It is as if she knows that is the last time that we will have a one-on-one conversation. There is so much more that I want to tell her, so many things left unsaid. I wish there was more time.

Michael comes to sit at the spot that Katie just vacated. As if rehearsed, he too picks up my hand and kisses the back of it.

"Hi mama," he says.

I smile at him, "Hi Mikey."

"I miss you calling me Mikey."

I tilt my head, "I thought you always hated it. You once told me that it was a child's name, and you were a grown man."

His eyes begin to fill with tears, "and what I wouldn't give to have you call me Mikey a thousand more times."

Everyone seems to know that this will be the last conversation with them. The elephant in the room is blowing his trumpet although no one still wants to say the words.

Samantha can be heard letting out a fussy cry from the kitchen. Michael turns his attention briefly towards the kitchen to see if Josie needs anything.

"It must be feeding time," Michael says, making conversation.

"Let her make mistakes, okay?"

He turns his attention back to me with furrowed brows.

"She's a baby mom. What are you talking about?"

"I'm talking about when she gets older, and she wants to try a new sport or new fashion trend or even date a boy. Give her that grace to know that you're always there to help her but allow her to make the mistake. She will never learn otherwise. After Samuel died you were incredibly careful, and it took a while for you to learn from mistakes 'cause you tried so hard not to make them. She's going to fail and that's okay. She has an amazing dad to help her pick up the pieces when she does."

"Yeah, you're right. I think that's why it took so long for me to grow up. I don't think you would have liked me when I first joined the Navy."

"Yes, I would have, I love you. Always have and always will. Remember back when you were still in the Navy, and you would call me."

Michael seems more confused now, "yeah, where are you going with this?"

"I always ended the phone call with 'if you need anything I am just a phone call away.' I wanted to make sure you knew that no matter what you do, did, or whatever, I would always be there for you."

He sniffles and looks down.

"I know mama, I remember. I knew I could call you or dad for anything. Some things I was just embarrassed about," Michael states.

"Well give Samantha that same knowledge that you will always be there for her no matter what. Allow her to make mistakes, within reason of course," I smile.

"I will mama. At least I will try."

"And I may not be able to answer you directly, but I will still be a phone call away. And by phone call I mean a prayer away."

Michael smiles back at me. He stands up and bends over my bend to wrap me in a hug.

"I love you," he whispers in my ear.

"I love you too, Mikey."

He pulls back and wipes the few tears that managed to escape with the back of his hand.

"Are you hungry? I could make you a ham sandwich," he suggests.

"Actually, a ham sandwich sounds amazing, but only if it comes with a fried egg on toast with mayo."

Michael chuckles, "coming right up mama."

I smile to myself as he leaves the room. Ironically, Wayne steps in behind him. I guess I'm getting all my big talks out of the way now.

Instead of taking his usual spot in his recliner, he sits on the side of my bed. He smiles at me. I'm not sure how to even start or what to say to him.

"I…." I trail off. That gosh darn frog is back in my throat making it difficult to form words.

He grabs both of my hands in his. I love the feel of his touch. His calloused hands and fingers the size of sausage links. I know one thing is still true in my heart; I will miss the feel of his hand in mine.

"It's okay, Ellie. We don't have to say anything. We have been together for over forty years. I know what's in your heart cause it's in mine too."

I nod at his words with tear filled eyes. I want so much more than this. This is a gift that God is blessing me with, the ability to say goodbye. I love that I am able to have this, but I don't even know how to say goodbye. There's just no good way of saying it.

I hope that Wayne is right and that he feels everything that I want to say to him in his heart. I just can't bear the words coming out of my mouth. This will have to be enough. For all of them.

Michael returns a short while later with my ham sandwich. It's the best sandwich I could have ever hoped for. Somehow, I know that it will be the last thing I eat, and it was divine.

A short time later, of course my pain increased significantly causing me to take more pain medicine. The cancer is willing itself to be at the forefront of my mind so that I can't enjoy my last conscious moments with my family. I welcome the pain medicine and make every effort to push it out of my mind as I attempt to smile and laugh with my family.

We end the day with everyone gathering in the living room with blankets and pillows. The Christmas tree gives off a soft glow as the fireplace and T.V. illuminates the rest of the room. A Christmas movie plays softly on the screen with no audience to marvel at its cinematic scenes. Everyone seems to have drifted off to a land of dreams where sugar plum fairies dance in their heads.

Michael is snoring with his mouth wide open. He is sitting up on the couch with Josie's head in his lap. Samantha sleeps soundly in the pack-n-play beside them. Katie and Jason lay on the blown-up mattress in the middle of the living room snuggled under a quilt from the spare bedroom. I look over to see that Wayne has his eyes closed with Nathan tucked in close to his side in his recliner while McKenna snuggles deep next to me in my bed.

This is peace. I take a slow deep breath to ensure that I do not wake McKenna. I could not have asked for more than this. To be surrounded by my favorite people is all I ever wanted.

I look up to the T.V. to see what part of White Christmas is on when I notice someone standing to the right of the entertainment center. I glance over to see not just one person, but three. Grandaddy, Dana and Samuel. They all smile at me and walk over closer to my bed carefully stepping over my sleeping guests.

I suddenly wonder what would happen if Dana or Samuel accidentally tripped over Michael's stretched out legs.

Samuel smiles as I finish my thoughts and states, "he wouldn't even feel it mama and where's the fun in that?"

I let out a silent chuckle, keeping in mind that McKenna is still sleeping in my arms. Grandaddy, Dana and Samuel make it to my bed and stand around me. Dana reaches out her hand and I gladly take it. I can almost feel her touch. It feels like I am grasping at water. I can feel it around my fingers, but I can never fully grab ahold of it and squeeze it.

I suddenly feel my strength give way to me. It slips away and I have no more left to give. Today was my last day. My last day to enjoy the beauty that life has to offer. I am grateful that it was such a joyful day, and I was able to hold my pain at bay. A blessing that did not go unnoticed, at least by me.

I use one more small surge of energy to lift my head off my pillow and look at my loved ones gathered in this room. I have so many things to wish for them, to tell them, but only three words come to mind.

I love you.

No one looks up. No one can hear the words as I do not have the strength to utter them aloud. With a tear in my eye, I lay my head back down on my pillow. Grandaddy, Dana, and Samuel smile down at me as Dana continues to hold my hand. I flutter my eyes closed for the last time.

CHAPTER 18

I awaken in a weird state. It's as if my body has been jolted awake by some sort of electric shock. I open my eyes and find myself standing at the foot of the hospital bed. I look to the bed to see myself lying still with McKenna curled into my arms. My breaths are even and shallow.

This cannot be right. How can I be there and here at the same time? This does not make any sense. I pick my hands up to inspect them. Yes, these are my hands, but they are different somehow. They do not carry the wrinkles that the passing years have caused. I place my hand on my stomach where the grotesque cancer seems to have settled and made a home. I do not feel the bloating of the cancer. My stomach is flat. With a smile I bring my hands up to my head. Hair.

I look back to the woman lying in the bed with my granddaughter in her arms. That is the person that I remember, the person that I have become. That sickly, old cancer patient with too thin cheeks and a scarf around her head from lack of hair. Defining wrinkles cover her hands and a belly protrudes out. If that woman was younger, it would perhaps bring joy at the possibility of a new life growing inside her. The truth is much darker than that as it is full of a succubus meaning to take me from my family.

I look away in disgust. I hate that that is how my family sees me. I pray that they remember the strong vibrant woman I once was and not the fragile one I have become.

I hear my grandfather clock chime, ringing to the sound of midnight coming upon us and it is December 24th. One more day.

I look around to see that Samantha has stirred from the noise, waking up Josie in the process. She must have that new mother's instinct to wake with every little sound the baby makes. She sits up and looks around the room before standing up and quietly walking over to Samantha's pack-n-play. Sensing that her baby girl is about to wake up fully, Josie picks up her daughter and takes her into the other room before her wails wake anyone else up.

I call out to Josie to see if she needs any help. She does not hear me.

I walk down the hallway with only the light from the back bedroom to guide my way. I can hear Samantha is fully awake now as she screams from the bright light being turned on. I stop at the doorway to ask once again if she needs help.

Josie is carefully trying to cradle Samantha with one arm while trying to get her strap down to breastfeed with the other. Michael comes down the hall and around me to assist his wife. No one makes any acknowledgement that I am there.

"Michael, I can help. What do you need?" I ask. I am beginning to get frustrated. I know new parents don't want to feel as if they are a burden on others, but it's always good to have a little extra help, especially in the middle of the night.

I start having a sinking feeling that they can't hear me or even see me. I wave my hands in front of their faces like I have seen in one too many bad movies about dead people. Neither Michael nor Josie makes any indication of seeing my ridiculous movements. I walk back to the living room to my hospital bed. On the way I pass by the mirror that hangs on the wall by the bathroom. I see the younger version of myself with shoulder length chestnut brown hair. My complexion is perfect, even make-up could not make me look as beautiful as I do now. I no longer have dark circles under my eyes and the hazel color around my pupils seems to be brighter. If I had to guess I would say I look like a better version of my early thirties. I am wearing a beautiful white cotton dress with eyelets in the hem at the bottom and around the sleeves. This is not something I would typically wear, especially since I always tend to be too pale for the color, but somehow, I pull off the dress. My feet remain bare with perfectly manicured toes.

I reach the hospital bed and look down at the sad old woman in my place. Her breaths match mine. I can still feel the pain in my belly from the cancer, although it doesn't seem to be as sharp as it once was. My curiosity is now getting the better of me. Previously I would have dreams, and I would be a younger version of myself, however, never have I looked at my old body and seen the happenings of everything around me.

I search the room for grandaddy, Dana, or Samuel and find nothing and no one. The room is just as I had left it prior to closing my eyes, well aside from Michael and Josie now being in the back bedroom with Samantha.

I'm about to throw myself into a panic, a panic that I see my old body responding to, when I hear a bird chirping and a light shining to my left. I turn to look to the side of me and see that the exterior wall of my house is now gone. I no longer see a barrier between the inside of my house and the outside. What puzzles me even more is the sunshine and warmth of a summer's day that I can now feel.

Is this real?

I reach my hand out beyond the point of where my exterior wall should be. I feel the warmth of the air on my fingertips.

Cautiously I take a step over the imaginary line that should be a wall. My bare feet touch the softest green grass. The sensation is what I imagine stepping on a cloud would be like. I take another step further and smile up at the sunlight as it warms my face. Those moments of peace I felt during my dreams now overwhelm me. I look back from where I came and feel guilty for enjoying this without my family. Wayne and the others continue to sleep in the darkened room, not bothered at all at the light that only I can see.

I hate that Wayne is not sitting by my side. There is just something about having your better half with you that can make even the most enjoyable moments better with just their presence. Since I can't have him with me at this moment I plan to sit and enjoy the warmth of the sun. I pray that Samuel or someone else will eventually come to sit with me soon.

As I make my way to the center of the green pasture, I think about how much I hate being alone. The feeling of going through this alone makes it worse. I find the center and sit with my legs stretched out in front of me. My hands brush the top of the grass, and a feather-like sensation grazes my palm.

This is where the sun is at its brightest, as if it is shining a spotlight on this exact spot. I close my eyes and recall my life since getting my diagnosis. I have never truly been alone. Wayne was there with me when I was diagnosed and then again when I signed consents to start hospice. My kids remained by my side throughout the last couple of weeks. I also got to have grandaddy, Dana and Samuel with me to help me on my journey. It's as if God Himself is telling me that I have never been alone. If I haven't been alone throughout all of that, then why am I thinking that I will have to go through this alone as well?

I take a deep breath and calm my nerves. With my eyes still closed I can focus more on the sounds around me. The crickets play a happy tune as multiple different birds chirp in their own language. I feel the flutters of something on my face and open my eyes to a Monarch butterfly flitting past me. A soft breeze flows through the air and tall grass at the edge of the meadow sways to its power. Beyond the tall grass stands a few sparse trees with a gentle creek lining the meadow. I can hear the water flowing past the rocks on the bank of the creek. All my worries dissipate and become nothing more than a bad thought.

I have felt this peace before in the recent dreams I have had. This, however, seems, I don't know, more. More pure. More intimate. Just more than something that can simply be described as peace. It feels as if nothing bad can happen here and any worry that may be conjugated will disappear in an instant, like mine just did.

I continue to sit in the middle of the meadow looking out at everything around me. Some movement to my right catches my attention. It's my home with most of my family still sleeping inside.

It seems odd that the exterior wall is gone, and I can look inside without actually being in there. It reminds me of a dollhouse I once had as a little girl. I could see all the rooms of the house and place my dolls where I wanted them in each room.

I shake my head bringing my thoughts to what originally caught my attention. Michael and Josie are coming out of the back bedroom and bringing a sleeping Samantha back to the pack-n-play. Josie gently lays her down in a clean swaddle. Michael walks over to my hospital bed and looks down on me.

Even from this distance I can tell his face is worried. I can almost feel his anxiety start to creep up. He gently picks McKenna up from my side and places her onto the couch, covering her up with a blanket. He is lucky that McKenna is such a heavy sleeper. He walks back over to me and stands at the side of my bed staring at me.

"What's wrong?" Josie asks, coming to his side.

"I don't know. Maybe I'm just being paranoid."

Josie places a hand on his shoulder and says, "you're not paranoid. What's got you looking at mom like that?"

He takes a breath and is about to ask his question, then hesitates. Finally, he stutters out, "does… does mom's breathing look different to you?"

At his question Katie is throwing back the quilt and moving to my bedside. Now all three of them are staring down at me and watching my breathing. It makes me feel as if I am a circus monkey and the audience is watching with anticipation for me to perform my next trick.

I take a deep breath in and let it out. I feel the fresh air going into my lungs. Is my body doing something different with my breathing?

"She's breathing kind of shallow," Katie reports. "Is she waking up at all?"

Michael places a hand on my shoulder and gives me a gentle shake while saying, "mom. Hey mom."

Nothing.

I feel the shaking and the pain that it brings. I see that my body doesn't respond.

"Mama, wake up," he says with a little firmer shake.

Nothing. I want to tell him to stop shaking me. I can feel the pain from the movement, although it's dull, I still feel it.

The quiet commotion is enough to wake Wayne from his slumber. He rubs his tired eyes and starts making his way out of the chair while trying not to wake Nathan.

"What's going on?" I can feel his anxiety increase as well as he gets down on his knees by my bed. He grabs my hand, and I can barely feel his touch. It feels like the connection between us is being severed.

"I can't get mom to wake up," Michael says urgently in a quiet voice.

Wayne strokes my forehead in a loving way and looks at me with sadness in his eyes. For a moment no one says anything. They all just watch me as I lay there with shallow breaths.

He takes a deep breath before saying, "well she has had a long day. Maybe she is just exhausted from being awake all day yesterday. Let's give her until morning and if she doesn't wake by ten then I'll call Elisha."

Everyone nods their heads in agreement with the plan. I watch as Michael and Katie go back to their resting places while Wayne takes the chair beside me.

I love my husband for not wanting to leave my side. Once again it feels as if God is telling me that He has never left my side either. Wayne has been so strong throughout all of this. Although I think back to that disastrous Friday morning after Thanksgiving when he practically screamed at me that he's not ready to let me go.

"I said yes to hospice, but I'm telling you no to dying." I remember him saying.

How could I do this in front of him? How can I let him watch me take my last breath? It will ruin him. It will ruin all of them.

My heart fills with joy that my last moments will be surrounded by family, but at the same time how can I protect them from the torture I know it will cause watching me take my last breath?

I can feel my breath quicken and my body copies the anxiety that I am currently feeling.

I watch Wayne being attentive towards me. He is counting my rapid breaths. He gets up and walks calmly to the kitchen. He returns a moment later with a syringe of medicine. It barely registers the slip of the syringe past my lips. The once disgusting oil of medicine hits my tongue and to my surprise I don't taste it.

My husband sits back in the chair by my bed and resumes holding my hand. I wish I could feel the callousness of his hands. It's one of the things about him that I love so much. His hands made the quiet statement that he works hard in all that he does. He worked hard on our marriage, in raising our children, he works hard at being there for everyone around him.

His hands to anybody else would not mean a single thing. To them they are just a working man's hands. To me they are the hands that held me on cold nights. They built us a house and home. They are the strong hands that have kept me from falling apart many times this last year and over our lifetime together.

I wish that I could be there to speak to him. To tell him everything that I hold dear in my heart. Did I tell him that I loved him enough? Did I show him how much he meant to me? Was I a good enough wife? These questions I reflect on as I remember the words that Elisha spoke to me some time ago. "Hear but not respond." There is no more that I can do, my time is up on saying so many lost words.

I send a silent prayer that Wayne knows my profound love and affection for him. I pray that he feels all of the missed things said between us in his heart.

I continue to bask in the sunlight reminiscing about my life with Wayne. I lean back on my hands and tilt my face towards the heavens as I close my eyes. The birds chirping and the still running waters over the rocky creek bring a pleasant sound to my ears. Anytime I feel anxiety or worry creep up it is as if this place refuses to allow me to sulk in it.

As I relax further with the warmth of the sun on my face I feel a sudden presence on my right side. Just before I can open my eyes a figure walks up to me blocking out the sun's glow. I open my eyes to see a beautiful young woman.

At first the brightness behind her makes it difficult to make out exactly who she is, the halo of light around her consumes my focus. Soon my eyes adjust, and I can see her clearly. She looks much like I do with some of her own unique characteristics. She has fuller lips and blondish brown hair, but her eyes, nose and high cheekbones match mine.

Mama.

I leap up from my sitting position, forgetting all that is happening in my home, and throw myself into her open arms. Her laughter fills the air as she squeezes me in a tight hug. I melt into her arms. I loved being able to see grandaddy, Dana, and even my son, but there is something about a mother's presence that makes all the worries of the world slink far away.

A mother's love is not something that can truly be explained. It is not just love and compassion for your children; it is deep devotion, sacrifice and pain. It is many days of being completely selfless, patient and forgiving even when others forsake it.

At the same time, you can never genuinely appreciate your own mother until you become one yourself. At that point, you will start to see the sacrifices she made for you as a child. You will see the joy she had when you had joy, the heartbreak she felt as you went through difficult times, and the passion she has at being your biggest fan.

A mother's love is the evidence of God's love for us, although it is only a sliver of God's guiding hand in our lives. Running into your mother's arms is like coming home after a long trip or a distressing day. It immediately brings peace, warmth, and happiness.

I pulled back from my mama to look into her eyes. She has tears welling up as well.

"I've missed you," I say, wiping away the tears with the back of my hand.

"I've missed you too, my Ellie," mama says.

We both smile and giggle nervously not knowing where to go from here. I want to continue to stare at my mama and memorize her facial features once again. I thought I knew my mama's face, thought I had her burned into my memory. Unfortunately, over time things become askew and the memory is never as good as the real thing.

My mama holds my hand as we sit down. I find it odd that I am beginning to feel her hand more than I can feel Wayne's calloused one.

"It's because you have a foot in this world and a foot in the previous one," mama states with a smile.

Oh, right. She can probably read my mind here as well.

She looks down at our clasped hands smiling, "yes, I can."

"How come I can't hear your thoughts then?" I ask.

"Because you haven't made the decision to come over fully and leave your earthly body behind. You're still full of worry."

I nod my head at her observation, "How can I not be? My mind feels like it is going in multiple different directions. I worry and then feel peace and then I worry again and then feel peace. It's a vicious cycle. I just want to know what is going to happen to Wayne and Michael and Katie? How are they going to get through this?" I take a deep breath and continue, "I understand that I had anger in my heart. The sadness of not seeing my family was growing and starting to consume me. Dana and Samuel helped me with that. My heart feels lighter, and I have become accepting of everything."

Mama interrupts me, "Ellie, you haven't become accepting of it because you are still full of worry. Why can you not let God take control of this part? Put it in His hands."

Nothing like your mama to put you in your place. My heart feels heavy with burden again, like all the progress I have made has gone out the window. I'm disappointed at feeling the anxiety and pain twist in my heart again.

My mind drifts to Michael's fit in the work shed, Katie's tear-filled eyes at the kitchen sink and Wayne yelling at me telling me that I am not allowed to die.

"I see," mama says, nodding in sympathy with my thoughts. "Let's see what God can do for you today. As you told Katie, lean more on Him."

There's nothing I can do but agree. The more I think about it the more I feel this burden, like someone has placed a chain around my heart and weighed it down with weights.

I need something to help release me. Permission maybe? Knowing that my family will be okay without me. I'm not sure.

I push it to the back of my mind, although I can still feel its nagging weight. My mama is here, and I plan to be present with her. Everything else can wait.

We sit back down on the blanket of soft grass and relish the quiet presence of each other. Looking into her eyes I remember those beautiful moments of her helping me with my homework at the kitchen table, teaching me how to ride a bike, and shopping with me for a dress for prom. The pain of losing her was almost unbearable.

I lost my mama so quickly. In the blink of an eye, she was gone. I spoke with her before she went to bed on the evening she passed away. I woke up the next day to find my world had turned upside down.

I begin to wonder how my mama was able to leave me so easily. I'm currently struggling with knowing that I'll never talk to my husband or kids again. Maybe it's because I am dying of cancer, agonizingly slow, while she passed away suddenly in her sleep. Heart attack.

I am suddenly curious, and the words pop out of my mouth as if I don't have a filter, "mama, how were you able to leave me so easily."

She looks at me with shock and a hint of disappointment.

"Ellie, I didn't mean to leave you. You were about to get married to a good man and the love of your life. I would have given anything to physically be there to walk you down the aisle."

She pauses.

"But…" I encourage her.

"I thought it was a dream," she says shrugging her shoulders, "I was walking in a meadow much like this one and I saw mama and daddy. I couldn't help myself; I ran into their arms. I felt peace, like a peace I could have never imagined before. And then in an instant I was in His arms."

"Who?" I ask.

One word. One simple word is all she said, and behind that word came so much feeling and meaning.

"God's."

A silence falls over us as we both take in the past. I guess I cannot blame her for leaving. If this feeling of peace is even half the peace that I will feel in His presence, then I would have gone running into His arms too. I wish I could get rid of this feeling of worry, this struggle that continues to plague me.

I look back towards my home and see that the evening has gone away. Light fills the living room, and no one is sleeping anymore. The time span of being with my mama seems to have sped up the time where my physical body currently resides.

Mama and I watch for a moment as my family goes about their day. Katie and Josie make themselves busy by cleaning up the living room and making breakfast for the children while Jason entertains them. I can see Wayne still sitting in the chair next to my bed. He rubs his eyes from exhaustion as Michael comes to his side.

"Dad, how about I take over for a while. You should get some sleep," Michael whispers in his ear.

"I'll just go make some coffee and call Elisha."

"It's not ten yet," Michael states.

"No, but it'll come quick enough, and I don't think Ellie is going to wake up."

I watch as he leaves the chair for Michael to sit. He ambulates with a defeated man's walk to the kitchen. He pours himself a cup of coffee before heading to our bedroom to change his clothes.

Our bedroom. I guess it's now going to just be his bedroom. Another ache hits me. Letting go is the worst challenge I have had to face. I would take the worst of the cancer's pain to this feeling of my heart breaking. The cancer's pain has become a dull distant memory. To be honest I don't really feel it anymore. This pain, these shards of glass ripping at my heart, is almost unbearable.

I feel my mama's hand at my back, rubbing and trying to soothe me.

"I'm so sorry. I wish I could take this from you. I remember you felt this pain at your wedding too and it broke my heart as well."

"You were at my wedding?" I say in shock.

"Of course I was. I helped you plan it for months. I wasn't about to miss it."

I smile at the thought of my mama being there on my wedding day.

"I remember when you put on your wedding dress and clipped your veil into your hair. You were so stunning that it took my breath away." Mama places her hand on my cheek as she recollects the memory. "You stood at the window looking out at the continual rain that dripped down from the sky. Tears came to your eyes wishing that I were there to comfort you and telling you that rain is lucky on a wedding day. Do you remember what happened next?"

Smiling, a little laugh escapes me as I say, "I asked God for comfort and to give me a sign that you were there with me. Within a few minutes the sprinkles of rain stopped, and the sun peeked through the clouds. I saw a rainbow in the distance, and I knew that everything was going to be okay. I could feel you there with me."

"When it was time to walk down the aisle you could have walked in the middle, but you moved slightly to the left-hand side. I walked down with you and gave you away to a man that I knew was going to love you and cherish you the way I had always hoped someone would. I took a seat in the empty chair that you left for me. Grandaddy sat in the space you left for him as well. We watched you get married. We watched your first dance with joy from the sidelines. At the end of the night when all the guests were gone, you played the Judds 'Mama He's Crazy.' It was the perfect choice. You wanted me to know that Wayne was the right man for you, and he is. You danced to it out on the dance floor alone with the lights dimmed. You were remembering me and grandaddy while you were dancing. We were dancing with you too."

"You were?" I choked out.

"Yes, so you see, you're always there to support your family in all walks of life just as God is there for them. Sometimes feeling the presence of a loved one who has passed is through the presence of God."

I look down and start picking at a blade of grass. I'm not sure how to respond to that. Is that what I need to let go of my worry? Is it as simple as putting my faith in God that I will get to look in on my loved ones from time to time?

"It is that simple Ellie. Where is your faith?"

"I have faith, mama," the words ring true in my heart. "I have faith in God and trust in Him. After hearing stories from you and grandaddy and even Samuel, I know that I will get to look in on Wayne and the kids every now and then. It's just…" I hesitate. "It's just that I want to make sure that they will be okay now. That my leaving them will not cripple them in any way."

"You want permission that it's okay to go."

I tilt my head to the side and contemplate her words. The truth of them hit home and I realize that that is exactly what I want. I want to know that Michael, who was so against me starting hospice, will be okay. Katie, who was so lost in her thoughts that she forgot to enjoy the present, won't fall back into that unhealthy habit. And my loving husband, who refused to allow me to pass away, won't fall to pieces at seeing my death.

I want to continue to protect my family in any way that I'm able to. Maybe that means spending one more Christmas with them. Maybe that means waiting for their okay before I go. I'm not sure yet.

In the midst of talking with mama and struggling with my thoughts, I didn't realize that Elisha had shown up to the house. I hear her begin talking to my family. I turn my focus to my home and my loved ones inside.

"Her blood pressure and oxygen are low. As you know, she is not waking up. I believe she has transitioned, and she is in the active stages of dying."

Her words hit Wayne, Michael, and Katie. I see Katie place a hand over her mouth as if that would keep her tears at bay. Michael and Wayne sit in stunned silence. The room is quiet for a moment before Elisha continues. Thankfully, Jason took the kids into a spare bedroom to go down for a nap.

"I would like to encourage you to continue to talk to her, reminisce and share memories. When you are ready, give her permission that it is okay to go. I know that it is the hardest thing to do, but that might be what she is needing to hear."

I smile at the intuition this nurse has. She is right in all aspects. I just wish that I could speak to my family again. I want them to be able to hear my voice just one more time.

Michael speaks up, "how do you know that she can hear us?"

"From experience with almost every patient. I had one patient where the family surrounded her bedside, and they started talking about who gets what."

"That's disgusting," Katie interrupts.

Elisha continues, "I agree fully. Anyway, the patient heard this and somehow was able to sit straight up in the bed and kicked her entire family out. She called her lawyer and changed her will that all of her possessions would be sold off and given to charity. After paying for an emergency notary, she laid back down and passed away."

"Wow, that's incredible," Michael states.

"Yes, it is. And I can give you many more examples just like that and that is how I know that patients can hear everything going on around them."

She pauses a moment allowing her words to sink in before adding, "patients also know who is in the room and when they are alone. I'm not entirely sure how they know, but they do. I've had patients wait until they are completely alone, or they have waited until all of their family members are present around their bed before passing."

"You must have seen it all," Wayne blurts out.

Elisha takes a moment to think about his words before responding, "I've been doing hospice for seven years now and every time I think I have seen it all something else comes along to blow my mind. Each moment is a blessing and although it is difficult at times, I thoroughly enjoy what I do."

"We're glad that you are here to help us through this," Katie says behind tears of sadness.

"I'm on call tomorrow, so if you need anything then just call the hotline."

Elisha begins to pack her things and make her way towards the front door. Michael stops her with a question before she can leave.

"What do we do about the pain medication?"

Elisha stops and turns back. She looks at Wayne, addressing him as head of the family.

"She can have the medications every two hours as she needs them. Now I have had families where they give the medicine regularly every two hours and some just when the patient needs them. If you feel that she needs the medicine, then I recommend you give it. If she needs it more than every two hours then call the hotline, and we can take it from there."

Wayne nods his head in agreement at her words. He remains silent. I can tell that he has that 'frog in his throat' again.

I take comfort in the fact that my mama is at my side, I'm not sure I can get through this part without her. I clench her hand and look around to any place but my home. I can't bear to see the look in their eyes and knowing that my days are literally numbered. Possibly even hours. Supposedly that exact detail is up to me and God if grandaddy is correct.

I leave my post of watching the ongoings of my home and turn to face the sparsely wooded area with a creek. I walk towards it with my mama at my side. I reach a large oak tree and peer around the rough bark of its trunk. Around it the sound of the creek gets louder. I see the crystal-clear waters that flow by. The rocks below hold steadfast to their grip on the bottom, refusing to let up and let go.

It feels as if it is God's love for me, steadfast and unwavering.

I reach the creek and bend down to clean my hands. I feel an unyielding need to clean my hands. I look over to a frog who hops in the water at my sudden presence. Mama stops at the edge of the bank and leans against the big oak tree. She watches me carefully.

I dip my hands into the water half expecting it to be freezing cold. The water is the exact temperature I imagine it needs to be to be comfortable. As I clean my hands I begin to feel the burden of my heart lift more and more. The words 'healing waters' come to mind.

"It happens like that. The water is helping wash you clean. It not only cleans your hands, but it cleans your soul," mama says calmly from the tree.

The feeling of my clean hands doesn't seem to be enough anymore. I want every part of me to be clean. I want my mind, my heart, and my soul to be clean for God. Without a second thought I plunge into the water, not caring that my dress will be soaked.

I wade myself into the deepest part of the creek. It doesn't come remarkably high, the water hits just below my hips. I look over to mama who gives me an encouraging nod of her head. I sit down in the water, plug my nose, and take a deep breath.

I lay back in the water and feel it as it rushes over my head. I rest under water for a moment as I drift down the streams just a few feet.

Sitting straight up in the water, I burst into tears. These are not tears of sadness, loss or even anger, but tears of joy. Joy that I get to come home soon. Tears of joy that I might be worthy of the promises of Christ.

I feel most of the burden lift from my heart. I wish I could leave all of it behind. I know that God will take care of not only me, but my entire family as well. Remembering those moments in my life when I felt the presence of grandaddy, Dana, Samuel, and my mama, I smile. It was a song here, grandaddy's favorite bird chirping, or the feel of the wind as I thought of a loved one. They were always there, never abandoning me. Just as God has not abandoned me. More and more He is showing me that not once has He ever left my side. Through all my trials of this life God has made Himself known. It is whether or not I was actually paying attention to it that makes the difference.

I can still feel some of the weight of the chains around my heart, keeping me in this place. I know that it is getting permission from my family that I am needing to have this feeling lift. That burden unfortunately has not left my heart, much to my disappointment.

I stand and start making my way back to mama who waits for me on the bank. The smile on her face brings a smile to my own. Looking down to watch my footing I see a large rainbow trout swim past my feet. I grin at the thought that grandaddy would have loved to catch a trophy fish like that.

I reach mama and she holds out a hand to help me up the bank. Standing at the top I huff out a breath. I place my hands on my hips and look around. Much to my surprise my clothes are completely dry.

"Cleansing isn't it," mama states.

I chuckle, "yes, it is. In more ways than one."

We walk to the middle of the meadow again and I look out at the beauty surrounding me. The wildflowers that grow beneath the trees sway in the wind as the bees' buzz into the center of it to obtain some of its pollen. The leaves give a soft rustling as the wind lifts to the tall branches.

Over to my right stands my home with my loved ones inside. I can feel the worry that fills the room. Time has once again sped up. This is one thing that I don't think I'll be able to get used to. I look into the house and see that the lights are all on and the fireplace is lit up. Everyone is back in their respected places of sleep as they were the night before. The presents from Santa are placed specially under the tree with the cookies partially eaten and milk drained from the glass by the fireplace. I hear my grandfather clock chime. Midnight.

It is Christmas Day. I made it.

Mama takes both of my hands in hers and smiles. She tilts her head up to the sun with closed eyes and smiles even more brightly. Her smile could match the brilliance of the sun in this moment.

"Ellie?"

"Mmm?" I focus my attention solely on her.

"It's Christmas Day. Your goal of making it to Christmas has happened. And He is ready for you, waiting with open arms. Are you ready to go?"

CHAPTER 19

Sucking in a breath of air, my knees buckle, and I give in to the weight of my body. My breath is labored and heavy. I cannot fathom the reality that I have found myself in. I sit with my knees bent. Wrapping them in a tight hug, I place my head on my knees and cry.

Mama bends down beside me and places a comforting hand to my back. Her touch helps soothe me enough to think straight. I slow my breaths down and breathe in through pursed lips.

He is ready for me. God is ready.

It hits me that the goal of my entire life has been to get to heaven, to spend eternity with my Heavenly Father. Sure, I had other goals in between; marrying the man I love, becoming a mother and raising God-fearing children, and having a happy life. Those goals and aspirations I have hit, the ones I didn't are a distant memory and have been forgotten over the years. The ultimate goal has always been to make it home, to heaven.

This goal, this gift, is within my reach and yet I am hesitating.

Tears continue to fill my eyes as I look up to my mama.

"I'm not ready yet. I haven't said good-bye. I can't leave them without saying good-bye." My voice cracks on the last word.

"What did grandaddy tell you?"

My tears ceased at once at remembering grandaddy's words. "That if I need a little more time then I can ask that of God."

Mama continues to rub my back as she smiles, "exactly. Keep in mind though that when God says your time is up, then it is up. His plan is perfect. You can't mess with His plan."

I am not sure why, but the memory of Monica in Friends dramatically telling Chandler that he can't help her make Christmas candies because he doesn't know the system pops into my head.

Mama bursts into laughter at the scene that just played out in my head.

"Yeah, that is a good way of putting it."

I smile and stand up feeling a little lighter. Dusting my dress off I look at mama.

"I need a little more time. I want to do this properly and say my good-byes even though I know they won't hear me."

Mama links her arm in with mine as we leave the meadow and head towards my house.

"Let's enjoy Christmas with your family then," she says.

We walk arm in arm back to my house and cross the invisible line acting as a barrier between the inside of my house and the peaceful meadow with still waters. Through the light of the room, I can tell that sunrise is approaching.

"This whole time working differently is really taking me for a loop. I feel like the clock just struck midnight and now it's already time for the day to start."

"Like I said previously, God's timing is perfect," mama interjects my thoughts.

Looking out at my family sprawled out on the floor, I start to appreciate the meaning of family and everything that it entails. In the world passing by it's easy to get lost in the midst of a crowd. Family, whether it is by blood or the family you choose, can see you for who you are. They accept and appreciate you, flaws, and all. That feeling of love is immeasurable. To truly be the person you are through moments of disagreements and tragedy and struggle can make or break this life. I realize that going through the motions of day-to-day activities, I have lost that connection. I missed the point.

Life is not about completing tasks, or making the highest salary, getting the best of whatever is being sold, or anything that society considers necessary. It is moments.

You will have many moments throughout your life. Some are small and insignificant while others are large and can be life altering. Each moment in time defines who you are as a person. When you get to the end of your moments you want to know whether those moments mattered, whether you made a difference. At least that's where my mind is at.

Throughout my life I wonder if I have made a difference. Did I show enough love and kindness and goodness? Did I matter in this world of almost eight billion?

As the saying goes, to the world I am just one person, but to that one person I am the world. I can see that as I walk through my home and see a blown-up mattress in the middle of the living room floor with a sleeping Jason, Nathan, and McKenna. Michael is resting in the chair by my hospital bed while Josie and baby Samantha occupy Wayne's recliner.

I can smell the aroma of freshly brewed coffee and bacon being fried. Wayne and Katie are hard at work in the kitchen making breakfast for everyone.

Mama and I take a seat at the island and watch my husband and daughter bustle around cooking this and that.

"Do you want to start on the eggs, and I can start getting the kids up?" Katie asks.

"In a moment, the bacon still needs a few more minutes," Wayne replies.

Katie appears to be keeping herself busy with wiping down the counters. She doesn't realize that Wayne has turned his attention from the bacon to face her.

"Katie."

She doesn't hear. Katie continues her crusade in cleaning the kitchen. I turn to mama with hurt. This will break her. Mama gives me a tight smile at hearing my thoughts.

"Baby girl, stop for a moment." Wayne grabs her by her upper arms and turns her to face him.

For a long while both of them stand there and stare at each other. Katie is the first to sever the silence as she breaks down. Wayne embraces her into a hug as she bursts into tears.

"It's going to happen today, isn't it?"

"I don't know, baby."

"I don't think I can do this."

"Yes, you can. You have all of us here to help you. We are going to have a good day. We are going to open presents with mom, spend time with her, and make these moments happy for her. I think we can do that for mom."

"I just want to hear her voice one more time."

"Well, I got that."

Wayne pulls back from hugging Katie and pulls out his phone. Both Katie and I look at it with a puzzled expression on our faces.

"After a visit, Elisha suggested that I record Ellie's voice. So, one night when you guys were over here, I recorded her talking to McKenna."

I wish I could hug him. I wish that I could tell him how much I love him for being so thoughtful of that. Katie is smiling from ear to ear with anticipation of hearing my voice. Before Wayne can press play on his phone, she places a hand on his.

"Hold on," she says. "Hey Michael, come here."

I can hear Michael get up from his seat by my bed and make his way into the kitchen. He walks into the room with a yawn.

"What's up?" He asks.

"Dad recorded mom's voice."

"Play it," Michael says with excitement. He's now awake and at full attention staring at the phone in Wayne's hand.

Wayne hits play on his phone and holds it out for everyone to listen. The room goes silent aside from the sizzling bacon on the stove.

"Well, that sounds like a fun day Kenna," I hear myself talk through the phone.

"Grandma, do you think you can read me a bedtime story before we have to go home?"

"Do you have a story in mind, or do you want me to read a book?"

I remember this night well. It was right after I stopped eating solid foods and right before I started declining rather quickly. I held McKenna in my arms. I knew that Katie and Jason were starting to pack things up to get ready to leave, but I just wanted to hold my granddaughter for a little while longer.

"Hmmm. Can you make up a story about a pirate and a mermaid?" McKenna is heard asking me.

"A pirate and a mermaid?" I exclaimed.

"Yeah! We watched The Little Mermaid like a bazillion times, and I need a new mermaid story."

For the next few minutes, I heard the recording of my voice talk about mermaid adventures and escaping from pirates. The sound of my voice on Wayne's phone makes me cringe, like nails on a chalkboard. It makes it worth it when I see the faces of Michael and Katie, tears of joy and not sadness.

"Like I said, you married a good one," mama states, pushing her shoulder into mine.

"I definitely did," I nod my head. I can't seem to tear my eyes away from my husband. Even on my literal death bed, he continues to surprise me.

For a time, all three stood and looked at the phone well after the recording ended. The smell of burnt bacon begins to fill the room.

"Crap," Wayne exclaims, shoving his phone back in his pocket and turning his attention to the breakfast he's burning. "Well, I hope you like crispy bacon."

Michael and Katie laugh. I can't help but chuckle as well. This was a perfect memory, one that I am glad I got to witness even though I am technically not there.

"You will get to have many moments like this. From time to time, you get to look in on your family and the joy that they have will fill your heart."

I smile, but the words of acknowledgement get caught in my throat.

Soon the kitchen is busy with little feet and questions about opening presents.

"Mommy! Santa came! He drank all the milk," Nathan says excitedly to his mom.

Katie rubs his short hair back and grins at her son. "He did? That's so awesome buddy."

"Yeah, Santa knew that we were staying at grandma and grandpa's house."

Her eyes get big that only talking to a child can do.

"That is crazy buddy. After breakfast we will have to open some presents, huh."

"Can we open them now?" McKenna asks. Her hands are clasped in front of her in a prayer motion. She gives her best puppy-dog eyes in hopes that it will get her what she wants.

"Grandpa just finished cooking the eggs for breakfast. Let's eat first and then we will dive into the presents."

"Yes ma'am," both children say in disappointment.

"Let's go have breakfast with mom in the living room," Wayne says.

"But grandpa, grandma is still sleeping," Nathan reports.

"It's okay buddy, just don't spill your plate and get food on the carpet. That will wake grandma up for sure," Wayne says teasingly.

"Dad, are you sure you want to eat in the living room?" Michael asks.

"Yeah. I want to spend as much time with her as possible. Also, it's been a few hours since she got the medicine. Can you crush the Ativan and mix it with the morphine? The syringe by the sink is clean."

Michael does as he is asked and gets my medication ready. I want to cringe at the thought of the kids spilling bacon grease onto my carpet, but I guess making these memories is more important than a little grease.

Mama and I follow everyone in the living room. Jason finishes putting the last blanket in the spare bedroom when Michael walks in with my meds. I watch from the corner as Michael slips the syringe in my mouth and pushes the plunger in. He grabs my hand and gives it a tight squeeze. Looking down at my own hand, not the old lady's hand he is currently holding, and I feel almost nothing. The small tingle of a sensation, but not the feeling of someone else's hand in mine.

After breakfast is eaten and the crispy bacon consumed, everyone sits around the Christmas tree and fireplace waiting for presents. Wayne begins to sort out all the presents to each person. I love seeing the excitement on everyone's faces. It's a tradition in the family to watch each person open one present at a time so that the enjoyment of Christmas can last, and the anticipation of the next present can build.

With everyone over at our house Christmas morning, the presents around the tree are piled very high. The living room appears more like a hoarder's house than the cleanly kept home it usually is. Only a small pathway to the kitchen for refreshments can be seen around the boxes of presents. Ribbons and bows are thrown all over the floor as gifts are opened. Today could be such a sad day as I know that my time is limited to hours, but I am so thankful that even with my passing hanging in the air, my family can still have something to smile about.

Mama and I smile and reminisce in the corner about our past Christmases together as everyone continues to open their gifts. At this moment I feel content and happy. Although my face shows a grimace from pain occasionally, I am thankful that I only feel the dull ache from it. I think the distraction of watching my family helps as well as knowing that with each passing minute I'm closer to going to my forever home. I just need to find the right time to say goodbye.

A few hours pass before the gifts are all opened, and the trash is picked up. Nathan and McKenna are about to start opening their new toys when Wayne stands in the middle of the room and says there are a few more gifts to be handed out.

Standing up against the wall, I'm as confused as everyone else. What gift is Wayne talking about? They opened all the gifts that we had picked out for them. Michael and Katie looked back under the tree to see if a present had been missed. I watch my husband leave the room and head back towards our bedroom.

Wayne returns a brief moment later with three small bags and two large ones. He places a small bag by McKenna, Nathan, and Samantha. He places a large bag in front of Katie and Jason and then Michael and Josie. In the bag is an envelope sticking out.

I sucked in a breath. I know exactly what this is, but she said it wouldn't be ready until after Christmas.

"You can all open them at the same time," Wayne announces.

McKenna and Nathan pull out a scented teddy bear made from one of my favorite shirts while the letter addressed to them falls to the floor. Josie helps take out Samantha's bear and places her letter on her lap. Jason takes their letters and sets them aside while Katie pulls out a large quilt the same time Michael does.

The teddy bears and quilts are better than I had imagined them. McKenna hugs her bear tightly while Nathan makes his roar.

"These…." Katie starts. She rubs the fabric of the stretched-out quilt.

"These are her shirts," Michael finishes.

There is not a dry eye in the room as even Nathan and McKenna realize that their teddy bears are made from grandma's shirts.

Wayne speaks as everyone continues to admire their new gift, "she had them made special for each of you. The seamstress wasn't going to be able to get the quilts done in time, but after hearing Ellie's story she called in some help. I got to pick them up yesterday."

"And the letter?" Michael asks.

"She wrote them herself after she found out that you weren't going to get the bears and quilts for Christmas."

The room goes silent for a long moment. I look over at mama with a stunned look on my face.

"You married the perfect man," she says with a smile.

A truer statement could not have been said.

"Yes, I did mama."

"Do you want to go read your letter?" Katie asks McKenna.

She nods her head and before I know it everyone is in a separate part of the house reading their letters in private.

"Did you not get a letter dad?" Michael asks.

He shakes his head no, "I told her that I didn't need a letter to know how much she loved me."

In truth, Wayne saw how exhausted I was becoming and told me not to worry about my letter to him. We talked all night that evening, although it still doesn't seem to be enough. I guess that's a part of life, always wanting more.

I leave my spot on the wall and follow Katie, Jason, McKenna, and Nathan to the spare bedroom. Mama follows closely behind me. Katie reads McKenna's letter aloud to her while Jason reads Nathan's to him. There is laughter and tears as both children hold tight to their new teddy bears. They soon finish and McKenna and Nathan are off to play with their new toys, leaving Katie and Jason to read their letters. Katie begins reading hers silently while Jason reads his.

"What did you tell Jason?" mama asks.

I look at her with amusement, "What? You mean you don't have X-Ray vision and can read the letter from over here?"

She gently pushes my shoulder at my teasing, "no, you butthead. I'm not omniscient."

I smile, "to Jason I said that I barely remember a time when he wasn't a part of our lives. He is the son-in-law that I prayed for, and I am so thankful that Katie has been able to lean on him in times of need."

"And Katie?"

I look over to my daughter, the woman who first made me a mother. I remember holding that beauty in my arms and thinking, Lord, I hope I don't screw her up.

A smile slowly forms on my face, "I told her that I am so proud of the woman she has become. That it may be a cliche saying, I stand firm on the truth of those words. It has been one of the greatest joys of my life watching her grow and take on the world. She has been everything I could have hoped for and more. And when I lost you, mama, I felt like I lost a piece of myself. Having Katie I felt like I found it again. I told her to think back on our trips we took together and encouraged her to make them with McKenna. You'll never regret taking that time out to spend with your daughter."

We stand for a moment longer before leaving them to finish their letters in silence. I find Michael and Josie with a sleeping Samantha in the kitchen. Michael has his quilt over his lap as he reads his letter in silence. Josie reads her letter as she rocks Samantha in her arms.

"What about Josie?"

Chuckling, I say, "well to Josie, I thanked her for being able to put up with Michael."

Mama looks at me with confusion.

"Listen, I love my son so much, but sometimes he can be a lot to handle. How does he put it? 'Get a hair up his ass.' He will do something crazy or buy a new truck or car or boat or get a dog on a whim. I knew it was going to take a special woman to be able to put up with Michael and his antics and she's it. She grounds him in a way that he needs."

"I get it. It's the same way that Wayne grounds you and pushes you to be the best version of yourself."

"Yeah, it is," I grin.

As I look at Josie in admiration for marrying my son, I hear Michael chuckle from next to her.

"Now what did you write in his letter that is so funny."

I pier over his shoulder at the part that made him laugh.

Smiling, I reply, "he's at the part where I recalled him hitting a baseball when he was younger. He hit the ball so hard, and I wasn't paying attention that it hit me on the leg and left a bruise for a few days. That's the point in time when I realized that we could not play baseball in the house anymore."

Mama throws back her head in laughter. She places a hand on her chest in hopes that it will help catch her breath.

"How old was he?" she asks between breaths.

"He was three!" I exclaim and start laughing with her.

We catch our breath, and the laughter dies down when I notice a stray tear coming from his eye.

"I wrote that he is the greatest gift to our family. His laughter and quick wit help make everything seem not as dim. I told him that he's going to make the most incredible father to baby Samantha and any other babies that may come into his life. The fact that he's scared about screwing up shows that he's going to be a great dad. He will worry and rethink his parenting skills and ask questions to his dad. That's what makes a good parent."

I feel mama place a hand on my back. Turning to her I see the love in her eyes and the agreement with my words.

"You gave them a really great gift Ellie."

"Thanks mama. I'm so glad that I get to have these last moments with them. I'm also thankful that I don't feel the pain anymore."

We move from the kitchen into the living room where Wayne sits by my bedside. I find it fitting that the dogs are right by his side. Carmel has gently positioned herself on the bed and is curled in a ball by my feet. Moose is sitting at Wayne's feet with his big head in his master's lap.

I watch him close his eyes and take a deep breath, allowing himself to simply be in this moment. The crackling of the fireplace is overheard with the distant mutterings of the children in the back room playing with their new toys. It feels as if time has ceased all together. He opens his eyes and watches every breath my body takes as if it's a gift itself.

The light shifts in the silence of the room. The setting sun casts a golden light on the opposite wall of the living room. I turn my attention to the imaginary barrier between my home and the beautiful meadow with chirping birds. The sun still shines just as bright as it did when I first entered.

"There's no night. No darkness or shadows. Only light. But Ellie, your day is coming to an end," mama reports.

I nod my head and look back to my husband. This moment of silence has spoken louder than words ever could, but I still want to hear the words that it is okay. That he will be okay.

Shortly after sending that silent prayer of acceptance, Wayne grabs my hand and takes a deep breath. He brings my delicate hand to his lips and kisses the back of it.

"The only thing I wanted in my life was to love you. From the moment that I saw you in that science class, I knew that you were going to change my life forever. I don't know how to do this without you, Ellie, but that will be my burden to bear. I can't keep being selfish with you. I want you to know that it's okay. You don't have to keep holding on to all of this pain and suffering. If you want to go, then it's okay to go. Please don't hold on for me or the kids, I will make sure that they are okay. If you see Jesus, just take his hand, and go. It's okay."

His words send a release of pressure off of my heart. I clench my chest and feel a burden lifting and disappearing like the ash from a fire rising into the air. I want to hug him, but I know he won't feel my touch.

"Thank you," I tell him, knowing that he won't hear my words, but praying he feels them somehow.

I didn't realize that during his talk with me that Katie had walked into the room. Her soft sobs startles Wayne and he drops my hand to the bed.

He gets up from the chair next to my bed, annoying Moose in the process. The lazy dog moves to lay in his dog bed by the end of the couch. Carmel remains by my side.

Wayne takes a few steps over to Katie and embraces her in a hug. He rubs her back and says soothing words to her that I am unable to hear. After a moment, he pulls back and holds her at arm's length.

"It's your turn, baby girl. We can do this for mama."

Katie nods her head and wipes the tears away with the back of her hand. She walks over to my bed and takes the spot where Wayne was sitting. Grabbing my hand like her daddy, Katie begins talking to me while Wayne walks away to give her privacy. I continue to stand by my hospital bed with my mama at my side, giving me strength.

"Hey mama," she starts crying. I can't help the tears that flow out of my eyes as well. Minutes pass before she can continue.

"I am sitting here and trying to find the right words to express what's in my heart. I am coming to realize that no words can truly capture my love and gratitude for you. I don't want to say goodbye because saying those words feels impossible right now. You have always guided me through life with your wisdom and unwavering love. You taught me so much more than words could convey. Your hugs were my fortress, your laughter my melody to life. Through every triumph and every stumble, you were there as my steady rock and now I'm losing you. I told you once that you are the one person I can't be selfish with, but I find myself being selfish because I don't want you to go." She takes a deep breath before continuing, "You gave us the gift of another Christmas so now I must give you the gift of giving you permission to go be with Jesus and Samuel and everyone else waiting for you."

She pauses one last time, trying to get control of her emotions, "Until we meet again, I will continue to hold your love as a light that guides me and a warmth that comforts me. Thank you, mama, for everything. It's okay to go. I will make sure dad is okay and watch over Michael as well. Go be my guardian angel and watch over us."

Her words lift another piece of the chain from my heart. I feel lighter with more peace, although one more link to the chain is keeping me grounded. I long to let it go, but that is something that only Michael will be able to help me with.

Nighttime has come upon us as the light in the room fades into darkness. The only light illuminating is from the fireplace and twinkling lights from the Christmas tree. Everyone seemed to be in the kitchen eating when a little voice called out to a quietly crying Katie.

"Mommy, why are you sad?" Nathan asks. Katie jumps slightly at the sound of her son's voice. She gently places my hand back over my chest and places her son in her lap.

"Because grandma is going to be with the angels and Jesus, buddy. Mommy is just sad that she's leaving"

Nathan's eyes get big. "But mommy, we can go visit her. We can. We can take snacks and go see her."

Katie smiles at the innocence of her child and hugs him tightly.

"One day buddy. One day we will get to see her again."

Like only a small child can, Nathan changes the subject abruptly, "mommy, daddy says I have to eat some green beans before I can go back to playing with my toys. And I don't like green beans."

Nathan crosses his arms over his chest and pouts.

"Well, if daddy says you gotta eat green beans then you gotta eat green beans. Would you like to dip them in Ranch?"

"Only if you come with me mommy."

Nathan gets down off Katie's lap and grabs her by the hand to pull her towards the kitchen.

"That sounds disgusting," mama says leaning over to me.

I shrug my shoulders, "sometimes it's the only thing that gets these kids to eat. Smother vegetables in Ranch or Ketchup.

We move to sit on the couch as my family eats in the kitchen. Looking over to the hospital bed I see the frail old lady filled with cancer. Her breaths seem more shallow the deeper breaths that I take. The anxiety of this world seems to have moved on. It's as if it can't touch me anymore. For that I am so grateful.

"I'm almost ready mama."

"I know. Take your time Ellie."

The excitement of Christmas is wearing on everyone. It didn't take long after dinner to have the blow-up mattress and pillows and blankets back out in the living room. Wayne kisses my forehead before settling in his recliner. Josie holds Samantha in her arms while Katie, Jason and the kids occupy the mattress on the floor. Michael sits in the chair next to my bed.

Mama and I are back standing in the corner watching everything happening in the room. Michael hasn't said anything since he's been sitting by my bed, which gave me hope that I would finally receive his approval to pass.

We are two Christmas movies into the silence of the room when Michael finally breaks his silence. He first looks around the room to see that everyone has fallen asleep. He grabs my hand, much like Wayne and Katie, and begins to whisper to me. To anyone else in the room they would need a megaphone, but to me, I can hear every word as if he is talking normally.

"You don't have to fight anymore mama. It's okay to let go. I love you so much and I know that somehow you will be with me to guide me through this life. I don't know how, but I feel it in my heart. Thank you for being my mama and giving me everything. Now it's time to give you back to Sammy. Give him a big hug from his little brother. I love you mama. You can stop fighting."

His words and permission are short and bittersweet, but it's all I needed to feel that final weight lift off my heart. I feel free and profound peace.

I look around the room at my family and think about the incredible memories that we share. Some are good, great even, and some are not so good, but all of them are ours. My life cannot be summed up in one moment with one person, but many. All the trials and heartaches, beauty, and love had made me the person that I am today. I wouldn't change one thing because the end result may be different than where I am standing at this moment.

I wish I could tell each of them thank you for everything, not just giving me their permission to move forward with this next chapter in my life, but for their love and the ability to be their mom, grandma, and wife.

My grandfather clock strikes midnight. I look to see that everyone has fallen asleep. Michael is softly snoring in the chair next to my bed while everyone else is cuddled with a blanket and pillow. Even Carmel and Moose are asleep in their doggy beds.

"Are you ready to go?" Mama asks, clenching my hand.

I take a deep breath and nod with a small tear in my eye.

A rush of air that only mama and I can feel blows through my living room. I look towards the other end of the room and in walks a larger-than-life person. No, not a person. An angel. This angel walks with a confident step, knowing that she will not trip on any of the toys or blankets scattered across the room.

My angel wears a soft golden tunic held together by rope tied around the waist. Brown hair cascades down like a flowing waterfall to her mid back. Not a hair is out of place. The shoes strapped on look like gladiator shoes with the toughest leather holding it together.

In an instant, my angel slowly brought her wings out from around her. I marvel at their beauty. The brilliant white shows a contrast to the golden brown that outlines each feather. Like her hair, each feather is perfectly in place.

My angel reaches me as I admire everything about her.

"I will see you soon, Ellie," mama says as she starts to walk away from me. She crosses the invisible line that leads into the green pastures and calming waters.

After passing through that barrier, the exterior wall of my house comes into view. I turn to my angel and nod my head once. She gently walks around and hugs me from behind.

Somehow this incredibly beautiful angel fits in the small area that I'm standing in.

I wanted to ask her to wait one more minute, but I didn't need to speak the words. She felt it in my heart.

I look at my loved ones sleeping around the room. If I could have imagined my death it would be like this. Surrounded by the ones I love and knowing that my passing will not cripple them.

Goodbye has always seemed to be final, too ending. Goodbye is what probably should be said in a moment like this, but I can't bring myself to say the words. Because it's not goodbye, it's not final. I will see you again with that cryptic word, soon,

So, for now, I look to my sleeping family and say, "thank you."

I look over to my clock and see 12:06 on December 26th. With one powerful push off the floor, my angel lifts me into the air, and I find myself watching my home disappear like a dot on a map. This tunnel of rainbow light surrounds me, and I am not afraid. This is exhilarating.

I understand what Samuel meant when he said that he never felt the pain of death. He felt alive and then more alive.

We reach a meadow, much like the one I was in with mama. I turn to thank my angel, but she is gone. I look around to see where I'm at. In the distance I see grandaddy, Dana, Samuel, mama and so many others running towards me. Behind them stands a kingdom with walls that stretch as far as the eye can see. Each building glistens with the light that is coming from within.

Before I can take a step towards my loved ones, I see a beautiful bright light to my left. I have to cover my eyes for a brief moment. When they finally adjust I see a man walking towards me. His presence brings the feeling of immense peace. He is average height with olive tone skin and piercing green eyes. I know that I have never met this man before, but in my heart I feel as if I truly know him. He spreads his arms out and embraces me in a hug with more love than I have ever felt before.

I melt in His arms. Throughout my life I have never felt more accepted than I do now. I want to cry with happiness and overwhelming love. I let the tears flow.

He whispers in my ear, "You made it. Welcome home."

ACKNOWLEDGES

Have you ever had a moment growing up where your parent asked you to do something, but you didn't or kept forgetting because you were so engrossed with an activity or a game? Upon the third time of asking you to complete a task they may pop you upside the head to get your attention. That is how I feel with writing this book. I had this idea about eight years ago, but never wrote anything down. About four years ago I wrote the first chapter, but then I stopped. Finally, about a year and a half ago, I felt the Holy Spirit 'pop' me upside the head telling me to write this book. Each time I wanted to stop, or I let life get in the way of writing, the Holy Spirit would shake me to start writing it again. It's like I kept hearing God's voice to write this story to bring people back to Him.

That is my hope. That whoever reads this story, it solidifies your faith in God that He's got this. You don't necessarily have to like it as you're walking your path, but He does ask that you trust Him. So, thank you God for sending me the Holy Spirit. Thank you for helping me navigate through this book and getting it published for the world to read.

Thank you to my loving husband for always being there for me. A lot of this story is our story. As it says in this book, my biggest regret is not seeing what I had in front of me and wasting five years of not being with you. I love you with all that I am. Thank you for believing in me.

Thank you so much to my mama and my grandma. Both have been a guiding hand in my walk with God. My grandma is that stronghold for our family, always guiding us to Christ. Her faith makes me want to have a better and closer relationship with God. My mama has always been my biggest fan and advocate. Thank you for reading the first draft and correcting things I missed. Also, for helping me keep the timeline straight. I love you so much mama!

To my Solace Hospice ladies. Thank you so much for taking a chance on me and helping start my journey in hospice care. Thank you for the opportunities, experience, and support. Lauren, Julie, Macy, Gina, Amy, Kayla, Sam NP, Kelly, Katie, Ellen, Colleen, Tammi, Pam, Banu, Brenda, Sarah, and Dr Cox. I appreciate everything you have done for me.

To my Evelyn's House family, especially Abby who was my first reader and would help give me suggestions. Jasmine who let me bounce ideas from and gave me encouragement. Dawn for her constant support with giggles. Lindsay, Michele, Katie, Mary, Beth, Chevonne, Aliyah, Kelly, Sara, Chris, Steve. Denise who also helped me with ideas for parts of the book. To Dan the Man for your sarcasm and humor, it just makes the day better. To my fearless leaders, Ann, Natalie, Tiffaney, and Shannon, thank you for guiding me further into helping our patients and being a better nurse. Jeane, my NP, for helping me with the education dialogue and helping me see things from a different perspective. Dr White, Dr Holthaus, and Dr Bakanas for letting me learn from you and showing me how to approach situations differently. Your wealth of knowledge helps me be a better nurse and gives our patients and families better comfort. Thank you to all my peeps at Evelyn's House for allowing me to bug you non-stop with this book.

Finally, to the reader. Thank you for putting your faith in me with A Pathway to Goodbye. I hope that this gave you some insight into hospice as well as what to expect. Whether you have lost a loved one, are currently losing a loved one, or you yourself are going through the process of dying, I hope this book gave you some comfort. One of my favorite memories of working at Evelyn's House was a patient who had a full conversation with God. She told God that she wasn't ready to let go and asked if she could have a few more days. Her daughter and I stood at the foot of the bed, shocked by the patient's words. She was able to get a few more days with her family by her side before passing peacefully. There are many more examples that I could give, but all of them solidifies my faith in God and in Heaven. May God bless you and keep you.